Placing his foot back in the saddle, he mounted. Looking down at her, he felt his insides tighten.

"Why don't you just say it?"

She chewed her lip. Please, he prayed, don't let her cry.

"Say what?"

"That I'm a despicable son of a bitch for springing Beth on you the way I did."

The words hung between them like a pall. It was the first time the idea had been said aloud, not thought, but openly conceded.

Summoning a smile, she whispered, "I don't think that at all. Beth will make you a good wife. I want nothing but happiness for you."

Pain touched his eyes briefly.

"Adam."

"Yes."

"I did love you."

Their eyes met in the moonlight. "I loved you, too, Vonnie."

"Have a happy life," she whispered.

Nodding, he reined the horse and rode off....

By Lori Copeland
Published by Fawcett Books:

PROMISE ME TODAY
PROMISE ME TOMORROW
PROMISE ME FOREVER
SOMEONE TO LOVE
BRIDAL LACE AND BUCKSKIN

BRIDAL LACE AND BUCKSKIN

Lori Copeland

FAWCETT GOLD MEDAL • NEW YORK

A Fawcett Gold Medal Book
Published by Ballantine Books
Copyright © 1996 by Lori Copeland

Library of Congress Catalog Card Number: 95-96237

ISBN 0-449-22546-1

Manufactured in the United States of America

First Edition: April 1996

10 9 8 7 6 5 4 3 2 1

Prologue

1865
Nevada

A beleaguered set of riders topped a small rise. Shoulders rounded and heads bobbing with fatigue, the weary band rode slowly toward home.

Heat rose from the rutted surface in shimmering mirages as the horses' heavy hooves left puffs of dry dust in the air. The backs and underarms of the men's uniforms showed dark sweat pouring from bodies so thin, bones showed through their pale skin.

The soldiers were young; mere boys, actually. War had aged them far beyond their years, stripped their faces of innocence, toughened their hearts and attitudes. Fatigue and bitterness marked their features now, and their eyes darted warily to every bush and ditch.

Could it possibly have been only three short years since they had ridden away from their families, filled with idealism, confident of victory?

"Let the Yanks come!" they'd shouted. The South would give them what for and send them packing, tails tucked in shame.

"Don't cry, Mother, I'll be back before the wash dries on the line!"

With fear in their hearts and prayers on their lips, mothers watched their sons ride into battle.

Fathers stood by, grim-faced, throats working against painful knots that choked the very life from their own hearts. A man didn't cry, but he hurt. Hurt real bad.

Reaching the crossroad, the soldiers separated to head for their homes. Three would ride south, the others, north.

Removing his hat, the oldest, El Johnson, spoke first, his voice dry and void of emotion. Tired.

"Guess this is where we split up."

The men nodded briefly to one another before reining their horses in opposite directions. They rode only a few yards before El turned back to call over his shoulder.

"No need to let this ruin our lives. War is war. A man shouldn't be judged for doing what he's called to do."

The men's minds were unwillingly forced to relive the past few hours. There wasn't a one who would swear they intended it to happen. Coming up on that family—

Nerves frayed, tempers short. The war was over, but apparently the family hadn't heard the news.

Each rider searched his conscience for some explanation, a straw to grasp to alleviate his own guilt. Had he believed his life to be at stake? Was that why it happened?

There was no way of knowing now whether the family meant them harm. But if the farmer hadn't pulled his rifle—if El hadn't panicked and fired first—

If.

If.

It all happened so fast. One minute they were warily eyeing each other, the next, violence erupted.

Brutal, unflinching violence.

Shots rang out. Screams filled the air.

Why? God, why?

Heat had wrapped the men like a hot, wet blanket, stifling and oppressive, the air permeated with the stench of sweat and blood. Time had seemed to stand still, as they were transported to what surely must be a taste of Hell.

Afterward, the men stared transfixed at the lifeless bodies slumped on the blood-soaked ground, horrified by their own unexpected brutality. The old man, his wife, two sons, and a daughter stared sightlessly up at them.

No matter how many times they witnessed death, it made them sick to their stomachs. How did such injustice happen?

Not a man there could say. They were not bent on vengeance. They were going home.

Home!

The war was over—there wasn't supposed to be any more death in the name of glory.

The tangible smell of death had hung thick in the air. Someone finally spoke, his voice a harsh whisper. "Let's get out of here."

The men stood paralyzed, hats in hand, tears rolling from the corners of eyes as they viewed the carnage. One began to recite the Lord's Prayer in hushed tones.

The youngest suddenly bolted toward the bushes to be
sick. Another suddenly sobbed openly.

Finally, someone spoke, though none were certain to
whom the voice belonged. "We can't just leave them
here—we have to bury them."

They looked at the young girl, maybe three, four
years old, a rag doll clutched tightly to the front of her
blood-soaked dress.

"That wouldn't change anything. Let's just get out of
here—"

"Somebody's got to bury them. It's not fittin' to
leave them here like this."

A couple of the soldiers quietly moved toward their
horses for shovels.

As the sound of steel bit into earth, El slipped over to
search the wagon for valuables.

The others stayed back, trying now to distance themselves.

Jumping down from the wagon a while later, El
grinned, holding up a black velvet pouch for one of the
boys to inspect. "Look at this."

The soldier eyed the sack warily. His filthy uniform
was ragged, his shoes worn through at the soles and
toes. "What is it?"

"Jewels. Priceless jewels." El lowered his voice so
the others wouldn't hear. "Rubies, sapphires,
diamonds—there's a king's ransom here."

The boy turned away. "Put it back—we can't take
it—it's not ours."

"Are you crazy? And leave it for someone else?" El's
eyes darted anxiously to the men digging the graves,
then back to the young soldier. Thrusting the bag into
the boy's clenched fist, he growled, "Look, I'm not

proud of what happened either, but it happened. Keep your mouth shut—I'm going to search the bodies."

The young soldier watched with revulsion as El rolled the farmer's lifeless form onto its back and searched the coveralls. Removing a gold pocket watch, he slipped it into his own coat.

Turning away, the boy fought a wave of sickness.

When he looked up again, one of the others was walking toward him. The weary soldier stopped short to lean on his shovel, his eyes fastened on the velvet bag. His gaze hardened. Disgust showed in his strained features.

The young boy swallowed, his Adam's apple bobbling up and down nervously. He wanted to shout that it wasn't his pouch, that El forced it on him, but his horror at what he had seen stilled his tongue, and words failed him. Loathing burned hot in the other man's eyes as he spun on his heel and walked off.

As the last spadeful of dirt covered the graves, the silent accuser averted his gaze. A muscle worked tightly in his jaw, and condemnation burned brightly in his eyes.

The group stood motionless, staring at the five fresh graves. Numb, they finally turned and walked back to the horses.

As El passed the young soldier, he grabbed the pouch, emptied most of the contents, then thrust it back at him.

Staring at the sack, the young boy swallowed. "What's this?"

"Your part of the booty. Keep your mouth shut."

The boy whispered, "I don't want it."

El said angrily, "Don't be a fool. You've got a family to think of."

Swinging into his saddle, he motioned the small party to move out.

The young soldier stared at the pouch, bile rising to his throat. Spiraling out of the saddle, he stumbled to the bushes and lost the little bit of food they'd scavenged that day.

This day will burn forever in his memory. . . .

Chapter 1

Rural Noğales, Arizona Territory
1898

In the Year of Our Lord 1898, several notable events occurred: The United States declared war on Spain over Cuba; Americans destroyed the Spanish fleet at Manila.

Ernest Hemingway, American writer, was born, as was U.S. boxer James Joseph (Gene) Tunney, who would later upset Jack Dempsey for the 1926 world heavyweight boxing championship.

The War of the Worlds by H. G. Wells and George Bernard Shaw's *Caesar and Cleopatra* were making a splash in literature and theater.

In the exciting fields of science and technology, Pierre and Marie Curie discovered radium and polonium, and German count Ferdinand von Zeppelin built his first airship.

But the most memorable event in Vonnie Taylor's life took place in rural Nogales, Arizona, that year when

Adam Baldwin unexpectedly announced his engagement to Beth Baylor.

"I do declare, he has the best-looking behind in Pima County." Hildy Mae Addison's eyes were riveted on the gorgeous sight as she tossed her head back and quickly drained her punch cup.

"Hildy Mae!" Mora Dawson laid a hand across her mouth to harness her astonishment. "You should be ashamed of yourself!"

"For what? He does." The young woman's eyes focused on the delightful object longingly. "It's positively divine."

"To-die-for divine," Carolyn Henderson concluded.

Vonnie Taylor edged forward, eyeing the tray of cherry tarts, attempting a show of enthusiasm she didn't feel. "My, doesn't the pastry look wonderful?"

Mora sighed. "I wonder if Beth knows how lucky she is."

"She knows. And even if she didn't, she'd say she did."

Giggles broke out. Beth was known to go to any lengths to keep peace. At times she could be insanely agreeable.

"Ladies," Vonnie cautioned. "Beth is a lovely person."

They all readily concurred that Beth *was* the nicest person anyone could hope to meet. And the *luckiest*. When the eldest Baldwin son announced his engagement to Beth Baylor, the town's eligible female population groaned with envy.

Vonnie casually bit into the flaky crust, feigning indifference to the conversation although her insides churned like a waterwheel. *And now, the nicest person*

*in Pima County would marry the best-looking fanny in
Pima County.*

How utterly ideal.

The girls nodded as Janie Bennett and her fiancé,
Edward Lassitor, strolled by.

"Evening, Jane, Edward."

"Evening, Hildy." Jane exchanged friendly smiles
with the others. "Mora, Carolyn, Vonnie."

Simultaneous pleasantries prevailed.

"Janie's so nice," Carolyn said as the couple walked
on. "I can scarcely wait to see her gown ... Vonnie,
you can't keep us in suspense any longer. What's it
like?"

"Ah, but you'll *have* to wait until the wedding."
Vonnie tried for a teasing tone, doing her best not to allow her feelings to show.

Beth might be the nicest girl in the county, but few
wouldn't agree that Vonnie Taylor was the prettiest.
Coal-black hair, amethyst-colored eyes, dimples men
found adorable.

"You're not serious! You're honestly going to make
us wait until the wedding?" Mora and Carolyn
chorused.

Hildy's generous lips formed a pout. "You're cruel!"

Her words held no malice, but belied real appreciation for their friend's talent. Vonnie Taylor wasn't just
pretty fluff; brides came from as far away as the West
Coast to purchase one of her exquisite gowns. At the
tender young age of twelve, she had shown an astonishing ability with needle and thread. By fifteen, anyone who saw her work marveled that she was gifted.
She could craft a simple piece of lace into a work of
art.

"I'll bet the gown's frighteningly expensive," Mora guessed.

Carolyn sniffed disdainfully. "Edward can afford it."

"Edward won't be paying for it. Tool Bennett is paying for everything," Mora confided.

"Who said?"

"I overheard Mrs. Bennett telling Martha Gibbings at the fall church social last week. The wedding is costing a fortune, but Tool won't hear of anything less than the very best for his only daughter."

"Oh dear Lord." Hildy's voice dipped to a reverent whisper. "Look at the way those trousers hug that caboose." To Vonnie's consternation, Adam Baldwin's behind was once again the focus of attention.

"Not only does he have the best-looking backside, he's so good-looking, he makes my teeth ache," Hildy whimpered. Wearing dark gray trousers, frock coat, and burgundy vest, Adam Baldwin was devastatingly charming.

Vonnie picked up a silver tray of *bizcotela* and brightly offered it around. "Cookies, anyone?"

"I've heard he's also quite the gentleman," Carolyn confided, thoughtfully selecting a sweet. "Beth said he hung *wash* for her when she was stricken with the monthlies last week."

"He *didn't!*"

"He did! Beth said so herself—" Carolyn leaned closer. "But she swore me to absolute secrecy, so don't breathe a *word* of it to anyone."

Three heads nodded and three pair of covetous eyes returned to the tightly sculptured buttocks of Adam Baldwin, the good-looking rancher, deep in conversation with Territorial Governor C. Meyer Zubick.

"I tell you, son," the governor was blustering. "It's

foolish for the county seat to be 135 miles away—clear over in Tucson. Something has to be done about it!"

In the middle of the governor's sentence, Adam turned to glance quizzically in the direction of the women.

"Personally," Hildy murmured, "I'd take any one of the Baldwin brothers."

"To where?"

"Who cares?" Mora and Carolyn said in unison, laughing at their little joke.

The four men bore such a striking resemblance, it was impossible to say who was the most attractive. They each were endowed with dark-brown, wavy hair, those irresistible Baldwin sky-blue eyes, and skin tanned deeply by the hot Arizona sun.

Adam, Andrew, Joey, Pat. The brothers were the crème de la crème of Pima County. Raw, virile manhood easily at home in buckskin or expensive Boston tweed.

"Why, Carolyn, what would James say if he heard you drooling over the Baldwin brothers?" Hildy chided.

Carolyn's cheeks pinked as she daintily lifted her cup to her mouth. "James and I are just friends."

"Sure, you are." Vonnie finally entered the good-natured kidding, revived by the change in subject.

Hildy suddenly froze, her mouth formed around a cookie. "Oh my gosh. He's walking this way."

Every eye focused on Adam Baldwin effortlessly weaving his way across the crowded room. His gaze lightly swept Vonnie as he approached the four women. "Ladies?"

Carolyn blushed. "Hello."

"Is something wrong?"

"Oh, my goodness, no," Hildy assured him, realizing he referred to their staring.

"No?" He smiled, revealing even, white teeth beneath a dark tan. "Then I trust you're having a good time?"

"Oh, wonderful," Hildy said.

"Everything's so nice," Carolyn murmured.

"The food's delicious," Mora assured him.

"I'm glad you're enjoying yourself." His eyes returned to Vonnie. Offering his left arm, he smiled. "Vonnie? Would you do me the honor?"

Vonnie shivered as Adam's eyes moved over her with easy familiarity. "Of course, Adam."

Mora, Hildy, and Carolyn watched with envy as Adam escorted their friend onto the dance floor.

P. K. Baldwin glanced up from his conversation with the governor, his thick brows showing disapproval of his son's choice of dance partner.

Gathering the hem of her gown in her hand, Vonnie met Adam's eyes in silent challenge. They gracefully fell into step with the music. Eyes the color of a Montana sky gazed into hers. Indeed, Adam Baldwin could make a woman's head spin.

"You look lovely tonight."

"Thank you. We were just commenting that Beth is positively radiant."

His eyes flicked briefly to his fiancée, who was dancing with Carolyn's father, the honorable Judge Clive Henderson. "Yes, Beth is a beautiful woman."

His voice set off the same familiar rush of heat deep inside Vonnie. The resonant baritone always left her feeling slightly giddy. Seven years had failed to change anything.

"You're very fortunate."

"Yes, so I'm told."

The woodsy spice of his cologne circled her as his hand rested lightly at her waist, gliding her effortlessly around the floor. The pressure of his fingers resting freely against hers made warm eddies move up her spine. Waltzing beneath crystal chandeliers where dappled prisms of light swirled among the smiling couples, she felt like Cinderella.

Discreetly drawing her closer, Adam whispered softly against her ear. "Why are you here?"

"You need to ask?"

Faking a blissful smile, Vonnie gripped the hem of her gown tightly, almost flying over the floor in his light embrace. Her dress of yellow silk trimmed with black lace ruffles whispered delicately against the coarse fabric of his dark-gray trousers.

His voice held a slight edge now. "Do you plan to make a scene?"

She peered up at him, her eyes wide as if the mere thought of making a scene was shocking. "Me? Heavens no. Why would I make a scene?"

"Call it a strong hunch," he answered, tight-lipped.

"I wouldn't miss this for the world. Rural Nogales is a close-knit community. If any member of the church failed to show up at an event of this magnitude, the neighbors would talk."

"Hell, Vonnie."

"Damn, Adam."

"Watch your language."

The tempo changed, and the dancing couples fell into slower step.

"Mother seems to be enjoying herself." They danced by the punch table, smiling pleasantly. "She's eaten at least six petit fours." Vonnie's gaze focused on the fragile-looking woman sitting just inside the verandah doorway. Cammy Taylor, a quiet, unassuming woman, sipped punch, pretending polite interest in Vera Clark's endless chatter. Vera appeared to take Cammy's nodding courtesy for rapt attention, but Vonnie knew better. Her mother wasn't interested in Vera's gout. She was here tonight to see how the other half lived.

"I notice Teague isn't worried about proprieties." Adam's warm breath fanned her ear, and for a giddy moment the room seemed to tilt.

"Father?" She laughed. "A team of wild horses couldn't have brought him here tonight."

Coolness shadowed Adam's eyes.

She tilted a violet glance up at him and clarified, though it wasn't necessary. "I believe his exact words were, 'I'd sooner be in a room of rattlers.' "

Chiseled lips parted to reveal a row of perfectly matched teeth as the lethal thrust was graciously accepted. He leveled his gaze. "You'll be sure to give Teague my best."

"He'll be thrilled, I'm sure."

Lifting a dark brow, Adam seemed to be waiting for the other shoe to drop. When she didn't immediately respond, he said quietly, "There's bound to be more you have to say."

"Oh, yes, there is. Thank you . . . and you can go to hell, Adam Baldwin."

Pulling out of his arms, she quickly walked off the dance floor. Ignoring the shocked expressions on her friends' faces, Vonnie swept by them and disappeared onto the verandah.

Caught by surprise, Adam tried to cover the awkward moment by casually threading his way through the crowd.

Acknowledging the various greetings, he followed

close on Vonnie's heels, pulling the double doors behind him for privacy.

"All right," he accused. "Say what you came here to say."

"You really want to hear it?"

"Vonnie, *don't* make a scene," he warned.

Whirling, her eyes locked with his in a spirited duel. "Over you? Don't make me laugh."

"What are you really doing here tonight?"

Her brow lifted with mockery. "Who would have a better reason to be here?"

"You're going to be difficult about this, aren't you?" Stepping back, he struck a match, his hands trembling as he cupped it against the light breeze. The tip of the cheroot glowed as he lit it. Tossing the match away, he impatiently drew on the cigar. "Hell."

"My sentiment exactly."

After a while, Adam penetrated her thoughts. "I hope we can handle this in a civil manner."

Vonnie wrapped her arms around herself and moved to a low wall covered by scarlet bougainvillea. "I'm not sure I can be civil, Adam."

Propping a boot on the flowered garden ledge, Adam drew in a mouthful of smoke, then let it drift into the night. Finally his gaze traveled back to her. "You're looking good."

Moving another step away, she gazed at the brilliant sky. The stars looked so close, she was sure that she could reach up and touch them. She could remember only one other night when they'd been so bright.

"You don't have to say that."

He looked away impatiently. "I wasn't saying it because I thought I had to say it."

"Then, thank you." Her voice was even more unsteady than she'd feared.

The silence stretched interminably between them. His cheroot must have lost its taste, she thought with a small degree of satisfaction when he impatiently tossed it away. She watched its red arc against the darkness.

"Damn it, Vonnie!" he burst out. Grasping her by the shoulders, he shook her gently. "What did you expect?"

What did she expect? Resentment flooded her. What did she expect? Tears burned her eyes and she blinked, making her gaze meet his.

Turning away, he said, "Stop looking at me that way."

She closed her eyes to keep from seeing him at all.

His voice held quiet desperation now. "I don't know what you expected—" He struggled for the right words. "You didn't think it would go on forever like this, did you?"

"I don't know what I thought, but I didn't expect you to ask Beth to marry you." Her voice sounded small, hurt.

For the briefest of moments she thought she saw regret in his eyes. But then it was gone. She steeled herself against the feelings roiling inside. "Congratulations. With Baylor's land and your family's vast holdings, the Baldwins will own a sizable chunk of Pima County."

"I'm not marrying Beth for her land."

"Then why are you marrying her?" Vonnie held her breath as she waited for the answer. *If you say you love her, I'll die.*

"I want to get on with my life."

She averted her eyes. "Do you love her?"

Please, say that you're not doing this out of love, her

heart pleaded. *I'll accept that you marry her, but I can't bear it if you love her.*

This time he was the one who looked away. "What does love have to do with it?"

"Are you saying you're not in love with her?"

His voice turned harsh again. "I'm marrying Beth, understand?"

Oh, she understood. She understood only too well. He was just like his father: headstrong and brash. Drawing the tulle-and-lace scarf closer over her shoulders, she shivered. Though the air was mild, she suddenly felt cold. Hadn't she known it would come to this? Hadn't she told herself a million times it would end this way?

"I assume you want my cooperation?"

His gaze avoided hers. "Yes."

Closing her eyes, she vowed she wouldn't cry. She couldn't give him that satisfaction. But tears were already spilling from the corners of her eyes.

"When?"

"As soon as possible. I'll speak to Clive and ask him to dispose of the matter as quickly and discreetly as possible."

Vonnie swallowed against the painful knot forming in her throat. "Does Beth know?"

"No," he said quietly, his gaze flicking anxiously toward the closed door. "No," he repeated, "and I see no reason to tell her."

She turned away.

"There's no point in her knowing."

"I'd want to know," she argued, turning to face him.

"Well, you're not Beth."

"No," she said, turning away, praying she wouldn't cry. Not now. "I'm not Beth. Silly me, I'm only your wife."

Stepping off the verandah, she disappeared into the darkness before she made a bigger fool of herself than she already had.

Chapter 2

It was impetuous ... Daring ... Stupid, they'd decided in the dawn of reality.

Propping his booted foot against the windowsill, Adam tipped his chair back and focused on the rain pattering against the study window. God, they had been so young. Young and crazy.

Striking a match, he lit a cheroot and blew a stream of smoke toward the ceiling, his mind still on the summer of '91. What a mix they'd been. Innocence combined with the foolish cup of youth.

It had started with puppy love that had steadily blossomed from the time Adam had first seen pretty little Vonnie Taylor at the First Freewill Baptist Church's annual Fourth of July picnic.

Add seven years, a hot summer night, and a full moon, and you had trouble. He'd grown from a barefoot show-off into a hot-blooded seventeen-year-old buck. Vonnie had sprouted from an impish cherub into an unusually buxom fifteen-year-old, who, with the glance of an eye, could make his blood race through his veins.

Stir in raging hormones and the spice of being forbidden even to talk to one another, and you had an explosive batch of trouble.

In those days neither one of them understood the bitter feud that raged between the two families. They knew there was bad blood between P. K. Baldwin and Teague Taylor, but at nine and seven, they didn't attempt to understand the origin of the dispute. Whatever was bothering P. K. and Teague happened long before Adam and Vonnie were born.

As Adam was piling potato salad on his plate that hot July afternoon, Vonnie had sidled up beside him, dressed in a lavender calico dress and matching bonnet. She'd sipped a cup of cool lemonade, tilted a look up at him, and told him his future. "I am going to marry you someday, Adam Baldwin. We're going to be lovers."

He'd just about dumped his plate of food in Flossy Norman's lap.

"You don't even know what 'lovers' means," he accused as a red blush crawled up his neck. He didn't either—exactly.

Tilting her chin haughtily, she glared at him in challenge. "Do too."

From that moment on, Vonnie Taylor hadn't been far from his thoughts.

Adam slid further down in the chair, a smile forming at the corners of his mouth as he recalled the sassy little wench she'd been. They'd been too naïve, and too involved in insulting one another, to care that P. K. Baldwin had forbidden his boys to associate with the Taylor girl. Consequently, the Baldwin brothers went out of their way to plague her. And she returned it tit for tat.

Every Sunday Adam and Andrew stared a hole through Vonnie Taylor the whole time they sat across the aisle from her in the First Freewill Baptist Church.

The diminutive black-haired charmer stared right back—singling out the eldest, Adam, to unleash her flirtations upon. He'd poke out his tongue, cross his eyes, push up his nose in preposterous faces in hopes of making her laugh out loud. But she'd look right back at him over her hymn book and never crack a smile. Though he'd do his darnedest to stare her down, she wouldn't budge an inch.

As the years passed, the Sunday morning glances grew less hostile. Liquid, clear-blue eyes searched sleepy lavender ones with mild curiosity. Shy Sunday-morning smiles replaced silly faces, and his efforts to attract her attention grew more bold.

Bringing pieces of bacon from home, he'd created tiny little sandwiches out of the Lord's supper and shared them with his brothers.

He tied Beth Baylor's braids to the church pew.

He silently, but no less earnestly, rolled his eyes while emphatically mouthing Ilda Freeman's soprano solos along with her.

At fourteen, he responded to the preacher's request for hymn suggestions by shooting his hand into the air and waving it for attention. He'd requested that they sing "Gladly, the Cross-eyed Bear."

Embarrassed by his theatrics, Vonnie refused to meet his gaze as the congregation dutifully turned to page thirty-six in their hymnals and sang "Gladly, the Cross I Bear" to a slow, dragging beat.

Adolescence evolved into early teens. Young, lithe bodies filled out—his narrow shoulders broadened, legs lengthened, muscles grew hard, and the peach fuzz on his jaw became a real beard that had to be shaved every day; her oval face matured into a puzzle of tilted lavender eyes, pert nose, and narrow chin. Her quick, thin body softened and rounded into a tantalizing shape that made him itch to touch it. The silent attraction between the oldest Baldwin boy and the Taylor girl flourished.

By his seventeenth birthday he'd developed a full-blown case of lust for Vonnie Taylor. That was the summer they'd started sneaking away to Liken's pond. Things were starting to get out of hand. They both knew they were courting danger, but that made their clandestine meetings even more alluring.

The pond, one of the few that survived the hot summers, was tucked behind scraggly creosote bushes that lined the bank. A few yards out, yuccas pointed their white flowers toward the clear blue sky, their green spiny leaves contrasting with the sandy soil. Piñon and fir trees crept close to shade the banks after noon. Joshua trees mingled with ash, oak, and juniper. The saguaro cactus marked the desert. But where Adam and Vonnie sought privacy, the leaves of the sycamore shaded them in the summer, and floated its leaves like boats on the water in the fall. It was a special place, a place of magic.

"Adam Baldwin! Stop!"
Vonnie choked as he dived beneath the water and grabbed her foot, dragging her under with him.
As they surfaced, she was spitting mad. "You're hor-

rible!" she accused, gasping for air and splashing him at the same time.

Grinning, he yanked her under again.

This time they broke the surface together, locked in a fierce embrace. They traded long, hot kisses, their legs tangling in the warm water as their hands explored one another.

Cattails stood in clusters around the rim of the pond. On the bank, wild morning glories bloomed among the creeper vines. In the distance the San Cayetano mountain range silhouetted the flawless skyline.

"Mmm . . . you taste good, Adam Baldwin," she whispered, abandoning her pretense of being irritated with him.

She giggled when his hand slipped inside her pantaloons to caress her bare bottom and pull her close to him.

"You feel even better."

It was Saturday. Chores were done. A shimmering sun beat down on the scorched earth. The fragrance of grass baking in the heat floated on the air. The water was delicious against their heated skin.

The pond was a good two miles from George Liken's house. Only an occasional, wandering Hereford intruded upon their privacy.

Treading water, they faced one another, arms looped over shoulders, legs touching, savoring the stolen moments. If P. K. or Teague ever got wind of the secret meetings, there would be hell to pay.

Squirming closer, she seductively ran her tongue along his bottom lip, rubbing her nose against his.

"What did you tell your father?"

"Told him I'd be with Tate Morgan shoeing a horse. He'll say I was if anyone asks. What about you?"

"Doing needlepoint with the new neighbor, Nettie Donaldson."

"Mmm . . ."

He caught her mouth, his tongue slipping easily inside. Young bodies strained together, but wet clothing hindered progress. His long, slim fingers fumbled to loosen the knotted ribbon at the neck of her camisole as the kiss grew more demanding. Giving up, he compromised by cupping her breast inside the soft cotton garment.

"God, Vonnie," he breathed, breaking away suddenly. "I can't take much more of this."

"I know," she groaned. For weeks they'd had the same argument. Kisses were no longer enough. They wanted more. Needed more.

"There's no reason we can't," he pleaded, his voice thready with passion. "I'm crazy about you."

She rested her head against his shoulder. "I know," her voice cracked. "I feel the same about you . . . but it wouldn't be right."

"It is right," he argued. "I love you. That makes it right." His lips nibbled kisses along her jaw, reaching her shell-like ear. "I'll be careful . . . I won't hurt you . . . please, Vonnie. It'll be good . . . I promise—"

"Adam," she whispered desperately, her eyes closed tight, her fingers curving into his shoulders.

"Don't you want me as much as I want you?"

"Yes. You know I do." Her fingers rested against his taut jaw. "We . . . we just can't."

Grabbing her hand away from his face, he pressed it to the front of his trousers. "I can," he promised, his eyes begging to prove himself.

Her eyes were sleepy with desire. "Adam . . ."

His mouth stopped her plea. Clinging helplessly to him, she returned his passionate kiss.

Even now, years later, Adam could smell the sweetness of her skin, still feel the silken curtain of her hair floating in the water.

"Am I interrupting, son?"

Adam brought the chair legs to the floor with a thump, sat up straight, and forced himself to focus on his father, who stood framed in the doorway. Still a commanding figure, at fifty-two, his snow-white hair was the only external evidence that the years were passing. But Adam knew that his father's health had not been good the last few years.

"No, come in, Dad."

P. K. entered the study carrying a snifter of brandy. He caught Adam's glance at the glass and shrugged. "Rain has my knee acting up."

Sinking into the oversize leather wingback chair, he stretched his legs out in front of him, balancing the brandy on his thigh.

"Nice party last night."

Laying a stack of papers aside, Adam reached for the grain report he'd been reading earlier.

"Yes, Alma knows how to give a party."

"Umhum," P. K. mused. "Don't know what we'd do without Alma. Fine woman. Beth have a good time?"

"Seemed to."

"Now there's a woman you can be proud of, son. Beth's a fine choice for a wife. Comes from good stock. None finer than Leighton and Gillian Baylor. Guess you'll be starting a family right away?"

"Beth and I haven't discussed children."

"Haven't discussed kids?" P. K. chuckled. "Am I getting that old?"

Adam focused on the grain report. "What's age got to do with it?"

"Oh, I don't know. Two young people in love—I'd have thought the subject might have come up. Thought maybe new ways had changed the idea of not discussing it until after the marriage—but apparently it hasn't." P. K. sipped his brandy and studied Adam through the glass. "You're going to have kids, aren't you? None of us is getting any younger, you know—"

"Actually, Dad, I haven't thought about it." Children were the last thing on his mind. He had the wedding to get through first.

"I wouldn't put it off too long," P. K. advised. "Time passes quickly."

"I know, Dad. You want grandchildren."

"Damn right I do, and I'm not apologizing for it. Should have a houseful by now."

Alma bustled in, carrying a tray with cups and a silver pot of fresh coffee. The Hispanic wonder was more than a housekeeper; she was a vital part of the Baldwin family. She had single-handedly raised Andrew, Pat, and Joey after Ceilia Baldwin's death when Adam was ten.

"I thought you gentlemen might want coffee."

"None for me, thanks," P. K. said as Alma set the tray on the corner of the desk.

"Perhaps you would like one of the nice cinnamon rolls I just took out of the oven, *sí*?"

Adam smiled. "Just coffee, Alma."

She patted his lean cheek maternally. "You should eat. You will need all your strength to make many *niños* for your father, *no?*" Picking up the silver pot, she smiled at P. K. "*Señor* Baldwin?"

P. K. toasted her with his brandy snifter. "I'm drinking my pain tonic."

She shifted an irritated look at him before shuffling out on slippered feet.

As the door closed behind her, P. K. pushed to his feet and stepped to the window. Tugging the curtain aside, he watched the rain roll off the roof of the hacienda and splash onto the rock verandah.

Adam's head bent over another report, but he didn't see it. He heard the rain drumming on the roof, but his mind had already returned to that hot summer day seven years earlier.

"Adam, this is crazy!" Vonnie laughed as they raced through the small grove of trees, hand in hand. The sky was in the midst of another spectacular sunset.

Flinging his arms wide, Adam let out a joyous whoop, making her laugh harder. She tried to clamp her hand over his mouth, but their feet tangled and they toppled to the ground, laughing. Between short, raspy kisses, they hugged each other so tightly they thought their ribs would crack.

He could hardly believe it yet. He'd finally convinced her to marry him!

Rolling beneath her, he looked deeply into her eyes. "I love you, Vonnie Taylor."

He could see in her eyes that she believed him, to the very depths of her soul.

"You know we're going to be in trouble when they find out."

"Trouble" was putting it mildly. His father would

horsewhip him. "Who cares? They can tie me to the stake and burn me alive," he vowed. "We're going to do it."

"But how do we even know the judge will travel this road—"

His mouth covered her, stifling her protests and stealing her breath.

"I overheard the men talking at the feed store, yesterday," he whispered. "They said a judge from Prescott was coming through here. All we have to do is look, Vonnie. We'll find him."

"But it's late . . ."

"Come on." He pulled her to her feet.

It was nearly dark when a dust-covered Jenny Lind buggy, with patched roof and floral curtains for privacy, came down the road. Vonnie and Adam studied it and the lanky driver from the shadows.

"Do you think it's him?" Vonnie whispered.

"It's got to be."

The tall, thin man in the dusty black-frock coat and stovepipe hat gingerly stepped down from the buggy and gathered some pieces of wood. In a few minutes he had a campfire going and a skillet on the fire, into which he forked thick slices of bacon.

Adam and Vonnie approached the campsite hesitantly. "Judge?"

Startled, the man frowned up at them suspiciously.

"What do you want?"

Drawing a deep breath, Adam cleared his throat. "Sorry to interrupt your supper, sir, but me and my lady here . . . we want to get married."

Straightening, the man studied Vonnie. "Married?"

"Yes, sir."

Adam was holding her hand so tightly, she protested with a soft whimper.

The old man's pale eyes swept Vonnie, lingering on her mature breasts.

"Your folks know about this?"

"Yes, sir!" Adam lied.

The man's eyes narrowed on him.

"You are the judge, aren't you? We heard you were coming."

The man nodded slowly, his gaze drifting back to Vonnie.

"You can marry us?"

"If you got a dollar for the license—"

"I got a dollar," Adam said, digging into his pocket and producing a silver coin.

The coin Adam dropped into the judge's narrow hand disappeared into the pocket of the shiny suit jacket.

"Got a ring?"

"No, sir," Adam said.

"You sure you want to do this, young lady?"

"I'm sure," Vonnie said.

Adam put his arm around her, and he drew her closer to his side. She felt safe.

The judge dusted his coat and straightened it, then settled his hat more firmly on his head, tugging it down low on his forehead. They could barely see his eyes now.

"Do you love this . . . woman?"

"I do," Adam said.

"You'll take care of her come hell or high water?"

"I will."

"No matter what happens, you'll stay with her?"

"I will," he vowed.

"Young lady, do you love this man?"

"I do," she whispered.

"You'll take care of him come hell or—"

"I will."

"No matter what happens, you'll stay with him?"

"I will."

"Then I pronounce you man and wife. Kiss your pretty bride."

Adam's arm tightened around her as his lips brushed hers hotly. *"I love you,"* he whispered against her mouth.

"I love you, too."

The judge bent to turn his bacon before it burned. *"Where you heading now, young people?"* His gaze returned to Vonnie. *"Goin' to have a honeymoon?"*

"We're staying with friends tonight," Adam said.

"Not going to Nogales?"

"No."

"Planning on walking, are you?"

"We got horses, by the trees."

"Uh-huh. Well, my blessin's to you both."

"Thanks, judge. Thanks a lot."

An hour later Adam and Vonnie reached the boarding house that sat at the edge of a crossroads. The crossroads had a store, a church, a one-room school, a stable, three bars, and little else.

The aged lady who answered their knock was a bit put out that they arrived so late. They had to shout to make her understand they wanted a room only for the night.

"You want what? Supper's over!"

"We don't need supper. We need a place to stay," Adam shouted. *"A room."*

"A broom! What do you want with a broom?"

"A place to sleep," Vonnie offered, pantomiming
sleeping by tilting her head and folding her hands
against her cheek.

"We just got married," Adam said.

She frowned. "Buried!"

"Married!" He showed her the wedding license.

Finally, the old woman understood, directing them to
a tiny but cozy room at the top of the two-story clap-
board structure. They raced up the stairs. Slamming the
door, they fell across the bed laughing.

"What a story to tell our children," Vonnie gasped.

Adam rolled on top of her, threading his fingers into
her hair. Undoing the shiny mass, he let it fall to her
shoulders. "We'll have lots of things to tell our chil-
dren," he murmured, his lips working their way from
her mouth along her jaw to her ear. "And I'm going to
thoroughly enjoy making them."

"Have you spoken to Beth about the building plans?"
P. K.'s voice once again broke into Adam's thoughts.

Getting up, he moved to the file cabinet. "No, but I'll
get around to it."

"Get around to it? Son, it takes time to build a house.
We'll need to get the men on it as soon as possible.
You'll want to move your bride in shortly after the hon-
eymoon, won't you?"

"I'll talk to Beth, Dad."

P. K. had raised his sons with an iron hand; no give,
no take. His way or no way. The land, Adam knew,
had been a hard taskmaster. Building a ranch the size
of Cabeza Del Lobo—Wolf's Head—out of the desert
had been grueling, demanding more than most men
could give. Many had folded up and left, selling out to
the highest bidder, often P. K. But his father had stuck

it out, made his mark on the land. He'd done it without the support of a wife, while raising four sons with
only the help of a housekeeper. Adam respected him
for that. They'd butted heads over a lot of things, but
how to run the ranch wasn't one of them. P. K.'s in-
stincts about cattle and horses were still unquestion-
able.

The Baldwin ranch was a sumptuous establishment
with patios and flowering gardens surrounding spacious
adobe buildings. P. K. Baldwin owned four *sitios* of
land, 73,240 acres, but he controlled more than a million acres surrounding Nogales, Arizona. At the peak of
his prosperity, the ranch supported 50,000 Hereford-
graded cattle, 15,000 horses, and 6,000 mules. Some
thirty Mexican and Opata Indian families lived on the
ranch, harvesting hay, vegetables, and fruit, in addition
to overseeing the livestock. The Baldwin water supply
was plentiful; five springs, creeks that flowed in the
spring and fall, and an underground river easily tapped
by wells.

Forty acres situated to the south of the main hacienda
were reserved for Adam and his wife. Pat, Joey, and
Andrew had been allotted similar passes of land with
adjoining property lines.

P. K. had made sure that when his sons married, they
had ample room to raise his grandchildren.

Letting the curtain drop back into place, P. K. returned to the chair. "Noticed you danced with the Taylor girl last night."

"Mmm," Adam responded absently.

"Was that necessary?"

Filing a folder away, Adam closed the drawer. "Only
being polite, Dad."

P. K. grunted. "Noticed her useless father didn't bother to show up."

"Did you really expect him to?"

"I expect nothing out of Teague Taylor." P. K. took a swig of brandy. "The no-good son of a bitch."

The dispute between the two families had gone on for so long, Adam had long forgotten what had started it. Whatever had sparked his father's ire, the resentment still ran deep after all these years.

"Better leave that woman alone. She'll get you in trouble," P. K. muttered.

Adam glanced up. "Who?"

"The Taylor girl."

"Her name's Vonnie, and she's hardly a girl anymore."

"Vonnie," P. K. repeated. "I don't care what her name is, you leave her alone." He was muttering again. "I've seen her type. Sashaying around—turning men's heads with those strange-looking eyes—you leave her alone. And you tell Andrew, Pat, and Joey to do the same. There isn't a Taylor worth their salt."

Adam couldn't remember how many times they'd had this conversation. It was getting old. "Why tell me? I'm engaged, remember?"

"Engaged or not, you keep your eyes to yourself." P. K. frowned. "There was a time I worried about you and the Taylor girl."

Adam looked up.

"Don't think I didn't see the way you two looked at each other when you were younger. I'm not blind. Many a Sunday I considered throwing a bucket of water on you to cool you off. You were just lucky Alma convinced me that it was childish attraction. For a time, I was starting to wonder."

Adam bent low over the desk. "I didn't look at Vonnie Taylor any certain way."

"The hell you didn't. I'll tell you now what I told you then. You stay away from the Taylors. All of them."

"Personally, I think you overreact when it comes to the Taylors."

"You don't know a thing about it. The Taylors are trash!"

"How can you say that? Next to Cabeza Del Lobo, the Flying Feather is the most prosperous ranch in the county."

"The Flying Feather, my ass. Teague wouldn't have a damn thing if he hadn't won that pair of ostriches in a poker game fifteen years ago."

"Maybe, but he took a pair of birds and built them into a sound business."

P. K. scoffed again. "He wouldn't be worth a plug nickel if he'd *lost* that poker hand. Until Teague won those birds he was dirt-poor. The community felt sorry for Cammy Taylor, having a baby girl to raise and Teague out gambling away every cent he earned. If it hadn't been for neighbors' charity, Teague's family would have gone hungry many a day."

Now, the Taylors were second in the community only to the Baldwins, a bitter pill for P. K. to swallow.

Adam pushed to his feet, his voice bordering on impatience. "Exactly what happened between you and Teague Taylor that's made you such bitter enemies?"

P. K.'s features darkened. "It's between me and Teague."

"That's unfair, isn't it? You demand I stay away from

the Taylors, yet you've never given me a reason why."

"You don't need a reason why. You just stay away from them."

Turning from the window, he downed the last of his brandy. The subject was closed.

"You won't forget to talk to Beth about the house plans?"

"I'll speak to her tonight."

"Good. I'll tell Manny to start on your furniture. I thought cherry would be nice. Nice, big pieces—maybe done up in Aztec fabric in reds, blues, and yellows. What'd you think? Something colorful?"

Adam felt the familiar surge of resentment. P. K. controlled his son's life down to the furniture he would sit on.

"Beth and I haven't set a date, Dad."

He brushed the minor detail aside. "It'll take a while to get the furniture built. No use waiting until the last minute. What do you think? Aztec fabric?"

Adam shrugged. "Talk to Beth."

Moving back to the window, P. K. gazed out. Adam could see the pride glistening in his eyes. Cabeza Del Lobo had been built by sweat and hard work. No one had ever given P. K. Baldwin anything. He had taken ten acres and carved out an empire.

Teague Taylor had won two birds and lucked out.

Adam studied his father from beneath lowered lashes. He stood at the window, his lean body more bent than Adam remembered, shifting with his weight on one leg to rest the one that ached. He suddenly found himself wondering what *had* taken place between Teague and P. K. twenty-four years ago to cause such animosity?

Staring blankly at the report, he realized that until this moment he hadn't given a damn.

Now, all of a sudden, he wanted to know.

Chapter 3

As the door closed behind P. K., Adam got up and moved to the window. The rain prevented him from attending to daily chores. The pewter sky promised no relief in sight.

Vonnie. He couldn't get her out of his mind. Seeing her last night drudged up unwanted memories, memories better left alone.

For years he had tried to bury the past under hard work and avoidance of the Taylors.

Today, her memory haunted him.

Clothes had been carelessly turned inside out and left in piles on the floor as youthful passions were feverishly indulged. Murmurs of love words that were meaningless in definition penetrated the darkness; sound was enough.

"Oh, Adam . . ."

"I never knew it would be like this . . ."

"Me either . . ."

Her hands stilled as she gazed up at him. "Honest? You mean you never . . . ?"

"No, never," he admitted. "I hope . . . well, I'm nearly certain . . . I'm doing it right. . . ." It was too good to be doing it wrong.

"Oh, I think you are," she assured him.

Hands stoked fires of passion that had lain waiting for the fanning wind of unrestraint until young bodies were drenched with perspiration.

Although it was their first time, they caught on quickly. Their hunger was unquenchable, their passion insatiable.

As dawn broke, a light breeze drifted through the window to cool sweaty skin. They drew a sheet that had been worn soft by many washings over themselves and fell into an exhausted sleep, vowing that only death could part them.

Only when the heat of the noonday sun woke them did reality rear its ugly head.

Adam awakened with the sense that he wasn't alone. When he realized that it was Vonnie's leg resting against his thigh, her breast soft against his arm, he silently groaned.

Turning his head on the pillow, he lay with his eyes half-closed, studying her young face. A tangle of black hair cloaked the sheet and lay across the mattress. A fringe of dark lashes fanned her pale cheeks. Her slightly parted lips were swollen from his kisses. Light-pink patches along her jaw, on her neck, and over the soft swell of her breasts testified that his beard had abraded her sensitive skin. He lightly touched one of the places with a fingertip.

She was so young. She looked about twelve.

She was only fifteen he reminded himself.

"Vonnie," he whispered, as he lifted her hand to kiss it.

Running his hand along his jaw, he wondered what P. K. was going to do when he told his father he had married Vonnie Taylor. And what was going to happen to Vonnie once her parents learned what they'd done? No one would understand. His father had never listened to reason, especially where a Taylor was involved.

He had to think of something. He couldn't stand leaving her.

A new thought hit him. What if there was a baby?

Oh, Lord. He didn't know much about sex, but he knew how babies were made. And last night could produce four—maybe five. . . . He groaned, his hand shaking.

Feeling a need to protect her, he gently drew the sheet over her exposed breasts.

"Ummm," she murmured softly.

Five kids with Taylor blood.

He was a dead man.

Her violet eyes fluttered open; she blinked slowly, trying to focus. Then, she blinked again before her eyes went wide with surprise.

"Adam?"

"It's late," he said. "We have to get up."

She sat up, drawing the sheet with her.

"Oh, dear." She pushed trembling fingers into her tangled hair as she looked around.

When she'd turned back to him her eyes were a mixture of confusion, wonder, and fear.

"Did . . . did we really get married? I feel . . . sort of like yesterday was a dream."

"We got married."

All of a sudden she looked ready to burst into tears.
"Oh, dear."

He swallowed, wishing he could reassure her. But he didn't feel very sure himself. "It's all right. We'll go tell our parents right now."

"We can't tell your father. P. K. will rip my hide off," she murmured. "And render me in hot oil."

Vonnie slid off the bed, taking the sheet and wrapping it around her as she backed across the room.

"Oh, my stars! What are we going to do?"

Adam sat up and she averted her eyes from him, a high flush coloring her cheeks.

"Vonnie, it'll be all right. I . . . I love you. Everything will work out. P. K. and Teague will be mad, but—"

"Mad? Adam, mad? They'll be furious!"

She bit her lower lip so hard he thought she'd bite it clean through. He tried to console her, but she resisted.

"Vonnie, we're married. There's nothing they can do."

"Adam, I'm scared. Daddy will have the marriage annulled."

"I won't let him." He tried to take her into his arms, but she pushed him away. She suddenly seemed distant, not at all like the woman he'd made love to all night.

"No, Adam. We made a terrible mistake."

"Just calm down."

Panic rose in his throat as she stood against the wall, trembling, her eyes shining with tears.

"They must never know," she said.

Her gaze met his, and he would have done anything to erase the fear and remorse from her eyes.

"My clothes—" She looked at the hastily discarded items scattered around the room and groaned. "I've got to get my clothes on."

She began picking up her belongings, shaking them right side out with one hand, tossing his onto the bed as she came across them.

"Everything's such a mess," she murmured, staring in dismay at the tangle of garments.

"Vonnie."

"I don't have a brush for my hair. I need a bath."

"I'll get water."

Suddenly her legs gave way and she sank to the floor, the sheet and her rumpled clothing forming a pool around her.

"Hey!"

Tears streamed down her cheeks as he pulled her to his bare chest. "Vonnie, stop acting like this. You're making me crazy."

"They can never know," she whispered. "We'll just pretend it never happened."

The meaning of her words were gradually sinking in. Adam frowned. "Pretend we didn't get married?"

"Yes, it's the only answer. No one has to know, Adam, except us. Daddy can't know—he'd be so disappointed in me . . ."

"Vonnie." *Hurt shadowed Adam's eyes.* "We love each other."

"We're too young to love each other," she said. "Daddy will kill me—I'm too young to get married. So are you."

He was stunned. "You're more worried about what your father will think than how I feel?"

She looked up. "He'll kill you, too, Adam. I mean it— he'll be wild with rage."

"No, I agree he doesn't like the Baldwins . . ."

"He hates the Baldwins, Adam."

"Well, why in the hell didn't that occur to you last night!" Adam reached for his pants.

She blinked up at him, tears spiking her lashes. Burying her face in her hands, she cried harder.

He glared at her. *"Is that your answer? To bawl?"*

"I can't face Daddy and tell him I married you, Adam. I can't."

Yanking on his pants, Adam buttoned them angrily. *"You're such a daddy's girl. You'd forfeit my love for his pride?"*

Nodding, she sobbed harder.

"Well, son-of-a-bitch."

"Maybe when we're older—"

Stuffing his shirttail into his jeans, he refused to look at her. His pride was irreparably damaged. *"Get dressed. I'm taking you home."*

"Adam . . . I do love you." She gazed at him, tears filling her eyes. *"I'm sorry—"*

"Get dressed." The contempt in his voice stung her. His failure to understand only made her cry harder.

They'd managed to get home without being seen. On the way they'd convinced Tate Morgan and Nettie Donaldson to say their horses had thrown a shoe forcing them to stay overnight. Within months the two families sold their ranches and moved on. Adam and Vonnie's secret was safe.

Days passed, then weeks. He worried that she might be carrying his baby, but the threat passed.

Shortly after that, P. K. was thrown from his horse during roundup and was trampled. His leg was badly injured, and he required complete bed rest. It had been weeks before he was able to ride again. During that time Adam was forced to take charge. In a sense it had been a good thing. Long hours and hard work kept his mind off Vonnie.

From that time on, Vonnie went out of her way to avoid him. Even in church, she sat as far away from him as she could and disappeared as soon as the last "amen" was uttered. He finally stopped going to services because seeing her only fueled his anger.

Vonnie spent more and more time at home. She perfected her talent for sewing and soon was sought after for her remarkable gowns.

Time passed. It was almost two years before they found themselves alone together at a party, and by then there was nothing to say about that summer, about that one night that was etched permanently into their memory. They pointedly ignored one another.

It was as if the marriage had never taken place.

Chapter 4

"Another one?"

"Another one," Vonnie affirmed, watching Garrett Beasley ring up five spools of white satin thread. "And I'm going to need sixteen more yards of Duchesse lace, Mr. Beasley."

"I'll order it right away." His eyes twinkled. "Getting it here, now that's another thing."

"Do you think—"

"I'll send the order out first thing tomorrow morning. You know I will."

Vonnie smiled at the store owner's little joke. Mr. Beasley had a real talent for making customers feel special.

"There you go, little lady," he said, adding the thread to her purchases. "Heard you're making the Wilson gown?"

"Yes, when it's finished I'll bring it by and let you see it."

Rumors about the gown had been in all the newspapers. Hammond Wilson, a prominent Phoenix million-aire, doted on his eldest daughter, Emily, and had commissioned Vonnie to make the *point de Flandre* gown for a handsome sum. The pure-white lace with graceful, rhythmic patterns of leaves, flowers, and scrolls was widely regarded as the most beautiful of the pillow laces. The accompanying Flemish Duchesse bridal veil was destined to become a Wilson heirloom treasure.

"Business must be booming," he said. "Had a man stop by earlier in the week asking about you. Seems they've heard about your bridal gowns way up there in New York."

"Yes, business is good." Almost too good, she added to herself, thinking about the bolts of cream satin stacked on her cutting table.

"Sounds like the Bennett wedding is going to be quite a shindig," he continued, transferring a bolt of tulle to the cutting table. "Twenty yards, you say?"

"Um, better make it twenty-five, just to be sure."

"Twenty-five it is."

While he measured and cut the silk net, Vonnie browsed. Outside, the sun was just beaching the horizon. Most of the stores were closing, while the bars and bawdy houses were just starting their business day.

Beasley's was one of the first delicatessens in the state. The idea that you could buy ready-to-eat products and dry goods at the same time was a real hit with the customers.

Closing her eyes, she inhaled the wonderful mix of cured hams, loose spices and fresh pies, freshly ground coffee, and hot cinnamon buns.

The countertops brimmed with a colorful variety of foods. Glass cases full of cakes, pickles in trays, and a big tub of sweet creamery butter added character to

Beasley's Grocery. Sitting beside buckets of salt herring and salt mackerel were barrels of crackers, cookies, nuts, and other dried condiments. There were big bushels of apples and a crock of mincemeat. Bunches of long bolognas and fat cheeses wrapped in netting dangled from the ceiling. The store was marvelously chaotic.

"Yep, seems like everybody's decided to get married at the same time. Looks like Adam and Beth will be next," Beasley continued as he cut the fabric.

"Looks that way," Vonnie said.

"Fine young men, those Baldwin boys. Fine young men."

Vonnie picked up an ornately carved music box and carefully wound the little key at the back. A boy and girl in a swing turned slowly to the strains of "I'll Take You Home Again, Kathleen."

"Yes, Beth and Adam make a handsome couple," Beasley rattled on as he wrote the price of each item on the back of a bag and totaled it. "Reckon P. K.'s hopes are high on having his first grandchild by this time next year—"

"Um, I'll also need six packages of seed pearls, Mr. Beasley."

If he thought anything about her interruption, it didn't show.

"White or ivory?"

"The white, I think."

He tore a long sheet of brown wrapping paper off the roll he kept under the counter. "How're your folks doing? Saw Cammy the other day."

"Good, thank you."

"And the birds?"

"We have a new batch of babies."

"Is that a fact? My goodness, those birds must be interesting to raise."

"They are indeed."

The community knew how proud Teague Taylor was of his ostriches. Little did Teague know that when he won the pair of adult, pure North African ostriches in the poker hand he had hit the jackpot. When he'd come home dragging the two birds behind him, rumor had it Cammy was miffed over having another pair of mouths to feed but had quickly changed her mind. The birds developed into a profitable business, with over a hundred birds now at the Flying Feather. The feathers and meat provided the Taylors with a comfortable income.

The store owner looked over his glasses at Vonnie. "What's that your father calls the chicks?"

"Waddlebutts." Vonnie laughed, thinking of the newly hatched ostriches. They were curious things, playful as week-old kittens, but when they walked across their pens, it was clear why Teague had pinned them with the nickname.

"Waddlebutts. That Teague. He's quite a character. Always has been." He tied the string on the package of material. "That about do you for today?" He wrapped the buttons in a second package.

"That should do it. Thank you very much."

Anxious to be on her way, Vonnie paid for her purchases. She'd gotten a late start today, and Mr. Beasley had stayed open later than usual to accommodate her.

Twilight was gathering when she stepped onto the sidewalk. Nogales wasn't a large town, but it had made a name for itself as a stop for gold miners on the way to California. Its influence had remained Mexican even this long after New Mexico, of which the Arizona Territory was then a part, declared its independence from

Spain in 1821. The terms of the 1848 Treaty of Guada-
lupe Hidalgo, which ended the war between the United
States and Mexico, gave the U.S. possession of the area
as far south as the Gila River, the river on which Nogales was established.

In 1856, petitions were sent to Congress for New
Mexico and Arizona to become separate territories, but
Congress ignored the requests because many of the
people in the proposed subdivisions favored slavery.
Most Arizona settlers came from southern states and
considered themselves part of the Confederacy. Finally,
the Confederate government established the Territory of
Arizona in 1863, with the territory's gold, not the will
of the people, being the main motivation.

Fort Whipple, established to protect the few white
settlers, became the capital, but boundary disputes between Arizona and New Mexico continued. Nogales became a stopping-off place for pioneers going west from
the southern states after the Civil War. Some stayed,
others surrendered to the harsh desert climate and returned back east, while still others sold out and continued west, believing the stories of "gold nuggets as big
as your fist just laying on the ground" that circulated
constantly.

At the same time, the soldiers were nearly ineffectual
against the likes of Geronimo and Cochise. Geronimo
had surrendered to General Nelson Miles earlier. Thinking the danger past, settlers again flocked to the west
and began stocking the ranges with cattle.

Cattle.

Cabeza Del Lobo.

Adam Baldwin.

Why did her thoughts always stray to Adam?

Franz Schuyler was slowly making his way down the

sidewalk, his stool hooked over one arm and his long-handled lighter held like a scepter. He lit the gas lanterns, one by one, until the dusty street resembled a brick-paved avenue in a city. The magic the lamplight worked had always been a delight for Vonnie. Franz was like some wizened elf who quietly went about his work without fuss or bother. With a touch of a wand, the town's gas lanterns sprang to life.

"Evening, Franz," Vonnie called.

The old man had always been a favorite character of Nogales. Of Dutch and German descent, his parents had cursed him with a funny little body. Squat and decidedly rotund, he reminded Vonnie of Santa Claus from the books Cammy had ordered from back east. His snow-white hair and twinkling blue eyes made her want to sit on his lap and recite her Christmas list. Wouldn't that have raised a few eyebrows!

The lamplighter glanced up and waved. "Shopping again?" Franz called in a cheery voice. He made his way down the street toward her, carefully trimming and lighting each of the lanterns. The sun had disappeared now, and the mellow lantern light gave the street a golden glow.

"My, my," he said, standing back to admire her. "Has anyone told you that you get prettier every day?"

Vonnie's smile was one of deep affection for the man who, she was sure, was not as old as he appeared to be. "No, but it's sweet of you to say so."

"It's true," he contended.

"You say that to all the girls," she accused.

"Not to all of them," he denied. "Only the prettiest ones."

They laughed together in comfortable friendship, then

turned toward the north as a cooler breeze suddenly sprang up.

"Nice weather today," he commented.

"Yes, it's been so hot." At times it seemed the sun was cruel. "How's Audrey?"

Sadness touched Franz's eyes, and he shook his head slowly. "Not good, little one, not so good."

"I'm sorry," Vonnie said, resting her hand on his sleeve.

Audrey Schuyler was dying, slowly but surely. Everyone knew it. But with a quiet dignity she bore the knowledge that she hadn't many days left. Audrey and Cammy Taylor had been friends since childhood. Vonnie couldn't remember a year when the Schuylers hadn't been at the Taylor house for Thanksgiving and Christmas. Audrey's special cherry-rum fruitcake was something they all looked forward to sharing on Christmas Eve.

But the fruitcake wouldn't be there this year. For the past few months, Audrey had steadily lost ground, and Cammy Taylor refused to accept her friend's terminal illness. She still clung to the belief that a miracle would occur and Audrey would be spared.

"But," Franz sighed, his smile returning, though it was a bit dim. "Any day you wake up is a good day, isn't it?" He touched the packages she held. "Guess you're making another beautiful wedding dress?"

"Yes. Janie Bennett's. She's getting married next month."

"Ah, yes." Franz nodded. "I saw the young lovers at the party the other night. Edward appears smitten to the gills."

"He is. Hopelessly so," Vonnie conceded with a laugh.

Setting his stool and stepping up, he touched the wand to the lamp above her head and smiled wistfully. "Ah, to be that young again."

"Franz," she said impetuously, "if Audrey feels up to it, why don't you come for supper Wednesday night? Mother would love it. She's been wanting to bake an elderberry cobbler, and what's an elderberry cobbler without you around to eat it?"

Franz chuckled delightedly. "Well, I don't know what would stop us. A man can hardly pass up an offer like that. I'll tell Audrey. She'll feel better just thinking about it."

"Wonderful. We'll expect you Wednesday."

"Wednesday, we'll look forward to it," he affirmed.

She accompanied him as he slowly made his way along the sidewalk. His wife's lingering illness had taken its toll on him. Where he once stood straight and proud, he now was slightly stooped and worn. Her heart ached for him. What would Franz do without Audrey? There were so close, marrying young, and had no children; they had no one but each other.

"Oh, and Vonnie?" Franz called over his shoulder.

"Yes?"

"Tell Cammy to put enough sugar in the cobbler this time." He flashed a grin over his shoulder that reminded Vonnie of a younger, happier man. "Last one was right-down sour."

Shaking her head at his good-natured teasing, Vonnie waved and laid her packages on the seat of her waiting buggy. She had to hurry. Cammy would be fussing, and Teague would be upset with her for being late.

The light breeze faded quickly, leaving a stillness over the town. Nogales was more fortunate than places further west. The river afforded a sufficient supply of water, which was imperative in the desert. The mountain ranges were farther apart here, but the vegetation was better for cattle, and the wide valleys and basins offered protection for the stock. Still, ranching was hard work. Many failed by not knowing the land and anticipating the effects of the scorching heat. A man had to learn to pace himself. Therefore, there was a kind of languorous atmosphere over the town.

Reaching the Flying Feather Ranch, she glanced toward the ostrich pens as she left her buggy for the stable hand, Roel, to unhitch.

"Mom?" Vonnie called out, dumping her packages on the mahogany deacon's bench sitting in the foyer.

The Taylor house was a large, two-story cedar, built by Vonnie's grandfather, Reginald Edimious Taylor, and his sons. The Italianate Victorian house, with its slightly pitched roof, square towers, and round-arched windows, represented more than a home; it was a tribute to the Taylor men's ingenuity and quality craftsmanship, which had earned them a living in those days.

"In the kitchen."

The click of nails on hardwood floors signaled that Suki, the family mutt, was approaching to extend her usual greeting. Excitedly leaping in the air, she demanded Vonnie's attention.

"Down, Suki ... yes, I'm happy to see you, too." She rubbed the dog's ears, then gave her an affectionate pat. "Come on. Let's go find Momma."

The aroma of rhubarb filled the air, and Vonnie followed it to the kitchen at the back of the house. The spacious cooking and eating area was her favorite room in the house. Fourteen windows kept the room light and cheery all year round, and she never tired of the panoramic view. Cammy Taylor was at the stove, dishing up thick slices of fried ham.

Cammy, a small, frail-looking woman with the figure of a young girl, looked up. Her laugh was a tinkle, her eyes bright as a bird's, and she was never certain of anything—except that she'd loved Teague Taylor since she was a girl of fourteen.

"I was afraid you wouldn't make it home before dark."

"You know Brigette. She can smell the barn a mile away. She was high-stepping by the time we reached the lane. Daddy not in yet?"

"No, I've called him twice, but he's still out at the pens."

Vonnie hung her bonnet on a peg and went to the hutch to get the everyday china. "Umm, smells good in here."

"Daddy wanted a rhubarb pie, so I made one."

"I saw Franz earlier," she said, gathering the silverware to set the table.

"You did? Did he say how Audrey is today?"

"Not good, I'm afraid."

"Well, after supper I'll have your daddy carry a big piece of pie over to her. She loves rhubarb. Always did, even as a child."

Folding napkins, Vonnie placed one beside each plate.

"I invited them for supper Wednesday night."

"Wonderful. The fresh air will do Audrey good. She stays closed up in that house too much." Dumping collard greens into a bowl, Cammy carried them to the table. "That daddy of yours—Vonnie, go tell him his supper's getting cold."

Just then, the back door opened, and Teague Taylor

came in, stomping his feet. Her daddy had always reminded Vonnie of P. K. Baldwin. They were from the
same hardy stock; whipcord thin, skin leatherlike from
the sun, hair a steel gray, eyes that squinted permanently into the future.

"Well, well," he said, glancing at Cammy, then at
Vonnie. "If it isn't the two prettiest little gals in Pima
County."

"Oh, go on with you," Cammy said, waving a long
fork in his direction.

Vonnie was amazed that after thirty-five years,
Teague Taylor could still make her mother blush.

Vonnie smiled, enjoying her parents' spirited antics.
Her mother and dad had a loving relationship, an affectionate and teasing kind of love that made her long for
a marriage just like theirs.

Cammy carried a bowl of potatoes to the table,
brushing past Teague on the way and bumping him
pointedly with her hip.

With a sweep of his arms, Teague scooped his wife
off her feet and held her to his broad chest in a bone-
crushing hug. Protesting laughingly, she swatted at him,
demanding to be put down.

Their playful gestures made Vonnie envious. Teague
and Cammy had that rare relationship that weathered
any crisis that came their way. She never recalled hearing either of them raise their voice with one another.
Theirs was a marriage of respect and mutual trust. If
she could ever find a man who would make her half as
happy as Teague made Cammy, she'd marry him on the
spot.

But then, that's exactly what she had done.

Kissing her soundly, Teague set Cammy back on her
feet, then hugged Vonnie.

"How you doing, Puddin'?"

"Good, Dad. How about you?"

"Lord, if I felt any better, you'd have to tie me down!" Pumping a wash pan full of water, he splashed his face and reached for a towel. "Get that lace you wanted?"

"I did. And the buttons. Mr. Beasley's ordering more Duchesse for me. Should be here in plenty of time to finish the Wilson dress."

"Duchesse, huh? I suppose that's something all womanified and frilly?"

"Something like that." She grinned. *Womanified.* "How are the birds?"

"Looking good, ladies. Real good."

Cammy slid a pan of biscuits from the oven. "Harold Jenson stopped by this afternoon. Said there was a man over in Phoenix interested in buying a pair."

"He want adults?"

"Harold thought he did—and Lewis Tanner stopped by again. He wants that fifty acres, Teague. He's offering to pay top price for it."

Teague grunted. "I'll bet he does."

"Honestly, Teague, you ought to consider his offer. We don't need the land."

"We sure don't need Lewis's dirty money. Besides, you know he hates the birds. He'd like nothing better than to see us sell out to someone who'll run cattle."

"You'll do what you want, anyway, but I think it's worth considering."

Teague changed the subject. "That's the third person this month wanting birds. If I keep selling at this rate I won't have enough roosters to service my hens." He rubbed a bar of soap to a high lather and scrubbed his arms to the elbows. "Wouldn't want to wear the roosters out, now would we?"

"Teague," Cammy sent a warning look in Vonnie's direction.

Vonnie pretended the salty reference flew right over her head.

"Daddy, I saw Franz when I was in town."

Teague kept scrubbing. "Did you?"

"He sends his best. He and Audrey are coming for supper Wednesday night."

Teague rinsed his arms. "Well, your momma will enjoy the company. Hand me a towel there, will you, Puddin'?"

Vonnie stepped to the hutch to get a hand cloth. "Franz said to tell you to get enough sugar in the cobbler this time, Mom."

"You tell Franz Schuyler that *I'm* baking the cobbler, not him."

Handing the towel to her father, Vonnie grinned. "You tell him yourself."

"Don't think that I won't."

Drying off, Teague studied his daughter. "Heard you danced with Adam the other night."

Vonnie glanced up. "Mom."

"Oh, don't get all flustered. I remarked to your daddy that it was a shame there was such bad blood between him and P. K. Adam's made a fine man. Not only handsome, but responsible and levelheaded. A woman could do worse."

Teague tweaked Vonnie under the chin as he moved to the table. "You stay away from the Baldwins. If I catch you anywhere near one of P. K.'s boys, I'll tan your hide."

The teasing tone was gone from his voice.

Vonnie busied herself with cups and saucers. "Adam's engaged to Beth, Dad."

"That's Leighton Baylor's problem, not mine." He looked at his wife. "What smells so good?"

"Rhubarb pie," Cammy announced.

"Rhubarb? You little sweetheart!" He pecked her on the cheek as he walked by. "If we weren't already married, I'd marry you again." Patting her bottom, he eyed the heaping plate of ham. "I could eat a horse."

"Sit down, I'm taking up the gravy right now. Vonnie, honey, hand me a—" Cammy suddenly frowned. "Teague? Teague, what's wrong?"

Teague's face had suddenly turned white as a sheet, and his mouth was tight with pain.

"Daddy?" Vonnie looked up as she was about to place a fork on the table.

Shaking his head as if he didn't understand himself, his left hand drifted to his chest, his fingers curling into his shirt. A puzzled look came into his eyes, one of surprise.

"Teague?"

"Daddy?" Vonnie reached out to steady him as anguish marked her father's face. His gaze met hers, his eyes suddenly full of fear. She had never seen her father afraid before, and a cold wave of panic moved over her.

His mouth opened, but no words came out. Then his legs buckled, and he slumped to the floor, both hands against his chest.

Screaming, Cammy dropped the platter of meat. The pieces of ham scattered across the floor, mingling with the shattered china.

"Dear God! Teague!" Sinking to her knees, Cammy cradled her husband's lifeless form in her arms. "No no no," she whispered over and over. "You can't do this—

you can't do this—you can't leave me—don't leave me, Teague—"

Kneeling shakily beside her father, Vonnie reached for his hand, hoping to find a pulse. There was nothing.

In the blink of an eye, Teague Taylor was gone.

Chapter 5

Mourners started arriving for the funeral an hour early. Buggies filled the yard of the Flying Feather Ranch, and the kitchen table groaned under the weight of food brought by friends and neighbors. Cammy had withdrawn into herself, and Vonnie was concerned about her mother.

Drying her eyes, she watched the guests' arrival from the front window of the parlor. She'd retreated here to escape the soft words of sympathy that were beginning to grate on her nerves. Everyone was well-meaning, but nothing could soften the pain of the loss that cut so deeply through her. Cammy hadn't come from her room yet today, and Vonnie was even more worried about how she was going to get her through the funeral. Her mother and father had been so close.

"Vonnie?"

She turned from the window. "Yes, Mrs. Lincoln."

"The preacher's here. Uh, Cammy hasn't come down yet. Should someone go see about her?"

Moving from the window, Vonnie dabbed at her eyes with a handkerchief. "I'll go. Tell Pastor Higgins I'll be with him in a few minutes. Has everyone had coffee?"

"Everyone's fine. You just see to your mother. Is she doing all right?"

"Not very well, Mrs. Lincoln," Vonnie said. "She and Daddy were—"

"I know, dear." Eugenia Lincoln and Cammy had been neighbors for years. Mrs. Lincoln had lost her own husband five years earlier. "It will take time, but one day she'll begin to take up her life again. Oh, the pain will still be there, but it will lessen. One day she'll begin to remember the good things about her life with Teague."

"Thank you, Mrs. Lincoln." Vonnie smiled, dabbing at her eyes again. "Your friendship will be good for her."

"I'll do whatever I can," Eugenia said, patting Vonnie's arm.

A moment later, Vonnie knocked lightly on her mother's door. When there was no response, she opened the door gently.

"Momma?"

The shades were drawn down tight, making the room almost totally dark. It took a moment for Vonnie's eyes to adjust, then she saw her mother half reclining on a fainting couch in the corner.

"Momma, the service is about to begin."

Cammy hadn't dressed yet, and her hair hung in a tangled mat over her shoulders. She looked as if she had aged twenty years in the past two days.

"Pastor Higgins is here, and all our neighbors and friends. You should come downstairs."

"I can't . . . I can't go through this."

Vonnie knelt beside her chair, her fingers gently reaching to stroke her mother's trembling hand.

"You must, Momma. They've been so good to come—to offer their help and sympathy."

Cammy turned lifeless eyes on her. "What good will words do? Teague is gone. Nothing will ever be the same again."

"I know you feel that way now, Momma, but you can't hide up here for the rest of your life. As painful as this is, we have to face it, together."

"I can't be with those people. Not now—please, leave me be."

Vonnie's patience was stretched to the breaking point.

"Momma, Daddy wouldn't want you to grieve like this."

Cammy covered her eyes with her hand and held a sodden handkerchief to her trembling lips.

"He shouldn't have left me."

"He didn't have a choice. He didn't want to die, Momma."

Cammy began to sob, and Vonnie was sorry she'd been sharp with her. She had spent more than thirty-five years with Teague Taylor, and part of her was gone. She had a right to grieve. Vonnie had been a surprise gift to Cammy after nearly ten years of believing she was barren. When Vonnie came along, her parents had doted on her. The three became nearly inseparable. Vonnie understood that her mother would grieve deeply, but this retreating to her room, to inside herself, alarmed her.

"Momma, I'll help you get dressed. What about the blue? Daddy loved the blue dress on you."

Vonnie began to search through the armoire for the dress she'd made her mother in the spring. "I sewed it special for Easter, remember? And Daddy commented on how nice you looked in it."

"Vonnie—"

"Try, Momma. The burial is in thirty minutes. You've got to be there." She took a deep breath, fighting back tears. "For me."

Resigned, Cammy got up, weak from not eating.

Somehow she managed to get dressed and brush her hair into a semblance of order. Cammy leaned heavily on Vonnie's arm as they descended the stairs. Mrs. Lincoln was in the foyer and saw them first.

"Cammy," she murmured, coming forward to meet them. "Teague would say you look like a bluebonnet in the summer."

"Oh, Eugenia," Cammy broke down, going into her friend's arms.

Vonnie let Mrs. Lincoln take charge of her mother, watching them go into the large parlor together. Murmurs of condolences floated out to her as Vonnie retreated outside.

It was a beautiful day—sun shining, a light breeze. She lifted her eyes to the heavens and whispered, "You're going to have to help us get through this, Daddy."

For a moment she imagined that she felt Teague's strong hand on her shoulder, urging her on.

Moving toward the small family cemetery, which Teague had prepared in a grove of birch trees about a hundred yards from the house, she gathered her fortitude around her like a shroud. Teague's parents were buried here. They'd lived with Cammy and Teague until their deaths when Vonnie was two. And Great-aunt Alice and Uncle Sill were here. Vonnie pushed open the gate, pausing momentarily as the gaping hole in the ground where her father would be laid to rest jarred her senses.

Tears sprang to her eyes, and she sagged against the weathered gate as the enormity of the past twenty-four hours inundated her.

She remained at the grave site, grieving alone. As she started back toward the house, the funeral party was already spilling out onto the lawn, parting to stand aside as six pallbearers carried the freshly planed pine casket toward the cemetery. Cammy, still firmly in Mrs. Lincoln's grasp, followed her husband's body, a linen handkerchief to her eyes. Vonnie watched the strangely quiet procession make its way across the wide lawn.

Ed Hogan had come. Teague had bought feed from him for years. The Newton sisters were there because they were simply good neighbors. Cammy took a kettle of chicken soup to the sisters when they had come down with pneumonia last year. Teague had gone with her and cut a cord of firewood when he noticed their supply was running low.

There was Pastor Higgins, and his wife Pearl, and Franz and Audrey. Hildy Addison, Mora, and Carolyn were there arriving last night to be with her.

And then there were the Baldwins. They'd come as a matter of courtesy rather than friendship, Vonnie was certain. It would have looked impolite if they'd been missing, since most of the town had seen fit to pay their condolences.

The five men stood well back from the group now surrounding the casket. Andrew, two years younger than Adam, had disliked Teague intensely. Vonnie knew he'd had a crush on her since school, but he'd detested her father. They'd been in the same class throughout their childhood. He and Adam had even fought over her once when they thought P. K. wasn't looking.

Her eyes slipped to the woman who was standing beside Adam. *She* should be standing by him, not Beth. He should be by her side, to console her, to hold her, to love her. . . .

"Dear friends," Pastor Higgins began as the assemblage gathered around the open grave.

Vonnie moved to one side of Cammy as Mrs. Lincoln closed in on the other. Cammy clung to Vonnie's arm like a lost child.

"We are gathered here today to say good-bye to a loyal friend, a loving husband and father, a good neighbor—"

Andrew Baldwin held his hat in both hands, his eyes lowered. He studied his feet and the casket, but Vonnie could feel his frequent glance.

"—and we know that one day we will see our friend again and we will then rejoice together. Let us pray. Our Father—"

Bowing her head, through brimming eyes, Vonnie viewed Adam standing beside Beth. P. K., Andrew, Pat, and Joey stood nearby. P. K., like her father, was a pillar of the community. The men had more in common than just being neighbors. They were two of a kind, the breed of man who had carved a place for families to live out of the desert, who proved that perseverance and providence, yoked by sweat and ingenuity, could build a good life.

Alike in spirit, they were alike in appearance as well—tall, rangy, broad shouldered, faces weathered, near the same age.

She studied Adam from below lowered lashes, trying to block out the pain. He stood with bowed head, his hat held in both hands in front of him. The sun brought out the blond highlights in his brown hair. If she had been taking inventory, she could have noted that he'd not bothered to get a haircut in several weeks. His hair had a tendency to curl when he let it grow, and now it was waving against the collar of a blue shirt that matched his eyes. Buff pants fit his long, muscled legs like a glove.

Suddenly the memory of the boy she'd loved emerged. At seventeen, Adam had been larger than most of the boys his age. He'd done the work of a grown man since he was thirteen. Everyone knew that he and his brothers would one day inherit Cabeza Del Lobo.

The other boys accepted that. Each had his own duties. Andrew was in charge of the hired hands, while the others worked the horses and cattle. Vonnie had heard her father comment to Cammy that P. K. was staying closer to the house more and more these days. Stiffening of the joints, he'd said, made the days long for P. K. Whatever the differences between the two men, her father's concern for Adam's father had been genuine.

Once she'd asked what had happened between the two men to cause such anger. It would be natural, she'd thought, for the two men who were responsible for Nogales becoming a thriving community to be friends, or at least business partners. But such was not the case. P. K. and Teague rarely looked at each other when forced to be in the same place at the same time, much less socialized.

Yet when she asked about the reason for their feud, she was made aware in no uncertain terms that the subject was a closed one, and, if she were wise, she wouldn't press the issue.

"—Amen."

Pastor Higgins motioned Vonnie forward, and she carefully took a handful of dirt and sprinkled it on her father's coffin.

Oh, Daddy. What are we going to do without you?

The moment was so emotional, she felt her defenses crumbling. Holding onto her mother's arm, she helped Cammy sprinkle dirt on the coffin.

"I'll be stopping by in a day or two," Pastor Higgins murmured as he grasped their hands a moment later. "My prayers are with you. Should you need anything, don't hesitiate to send for me."

Vonnie's eyes were bright with tears. "Thank you, Pastor. It was a lovely service."

Suddenly she wished everyone was gone. She wanted to be alone, to cry and grieve with her mother.

One by one the mourners passed by, the women hugging first her mother then her, the men shuffling by uttering a few barely audible words. The death of a friend made them feel too exposed to linger.

Everyone had said their words of comfort when P. K. approached. For a moment he didn't say anything, just looked down at the ground. Eventually, he cleared his throat and looked up.

He opened his mouth to speak, but words failed him. Reaching for Cammy's hand, he squeezed it briefly before moving on.

"I'm sorry, Vonnie," Andrew said, taking her hand in his.

"It was kind of you to come, Andrew."

"Vonnie," Pat said, uncertain of what he should say when it was his turn.

"Thank you for coming, Pat."

"You're welcome, ma'am. . . . I'm real sorry."

Ma'am, Vonnie thought as he moved on. It sounded so old.

Joey just nodded his head and followed his brothers out the cemetery gate.

And then it was Adam's turn. Beth clung to his side, holding his arm protectively. Taking Vonnie's hand, he held it for a moment. The small show of respect made her pain even more unbearable. "I'm sorry, Vonnie."

She swallowed, overwhelmed with the desire to lean against his broad chest and sob her heart out. She realized her foolishness long ago. She should have gone with him that day, stood up to Teague, but she hadn't. Now she had lost him forever.

"Thank you," she managed.

His thumb moved lightly across her knuckles. He'd held her hand just this way, his thumb brushing back and forth, the night they stood before an ill-prepared judge and were married.

For a moment she swayed lightly against him, overcome by emotion. Her forehead rested against his chest, her eyes closed. She felt his need to put his arms around her, to hold her, but he didn't. What had been between them was over. The love they'd once shared was gone.

When Adam had started courting Beth, Vonnie knew P. K. was pleased. Beth was the kind of woman P. K. appreciated, one who was agreeable. Nothing ever upset her. She was flexible; she adjusted. Whatever Adam wanted, Beth was willing to accommodate. She would be the ideal wife.

When it was apparent she'd lingered too long, Vonnie suddenly straightened, embarrassment flooding her cheeks. How *could* she have weakened like that, leaning on Adam and making a spectacle of herself? Beth would think her shamelessly forward.

Always thoughtful and good-hearted, Beth was the first to the bedside of a sick person, the first to lend a hand at church with any event. Sometimes her giving nature rasped on Vonnie's nerves like fingernails on starched cloth, but she would never do anything to hurt Beth.

Quickly regaining her composure, Vonnie's hand dropped to her side. "Thank you, Adam. I appreciate your coming. I must admit I was surprised to see your father here."

Adam's eyes followed P. K. as he walked away from the grave site. "I wonder if he didn't care more about Teague than he's willing to admit."

"If he did, then it's too bad he never told him," she said. "For all concerned." Their eyes met briefly before he looked away.

"I'm so sorry about your father," Beth said, slipping her hand into Vonnie's. "If there's anything I can do, you just must let me know."

"Thank you, Beth. Tell your mother I appreciate the chicken she sent over."

"I'll come by tomorrow and—well, we'll all have a nice, long visit." She tilted her head, smiling encouragingly. "Would you like that?"

"That's kind of you, Beth. Momma is so upset. I'm not sure that she'll be up to visiting. Mrs. Lincoln is going to stay with us a few days to help out, but I'd like your company. The house seems so empty without Daddy—"

She faltered, a lump forming in her throat. The realization that her father would never again come in the back door and call for Cammy hurt. Never again would he hug her and call her "Puddin'." Never again would the aroma of his pipe float through the big house he'd helped build with his own hands.

It seemed so senseless, a man struck down before he could enjoy his declining years. A man who'd worked hard deserved to put his feet up by the fire for a few years at least, didn't he?

As the crowd began to dissipate, Beth directed Adam toward the Baylor buggy. Cammy was surrounded by several well-meaning matrons who went on about how sad it was that Cammy was "left alone" in her prime. In clucking, sympathetic voices, they invited her to join their quilting club on Thursday afternoons. It was little more than a gossip group, Vonnie knew, but it would be good for Cammy to be with friends.

Vonnie's gaze moved over the mourners, most of whom were heading back to the house to eat lunch from the food brought in; all except the Baldwins. The five men had ridden away immediately after the ceremony.

It was evening by the time the farm quieted down. The house was so still that Vonnie couldn't stand it. She decided to go check on the ostriches. Suki followed her outside and scampered around her feet, demanding attention, as she walked toward the pens that were built two hundred yards back from the house.

"Settle yourself," Vonnie scolded the dog. "You'll upset the birds acting like that."

The ostriches were accustomed to seeing Suki, but they were easily disturbed by anything out of the ordinary. The dog's erratic behavior would alarm them.

Ten pens were built in a row, with a pair of adult ostriches in each. The little "waddlebutts" were kept separate, each hatch together in a pen until they were big enough to begin pairing.

The most recent hatch was only about a week old, but they were a handsome group. Vonnie liked watching them. They ran back and forth in the pen as if on a very important mission, their brown-gray feathers just covering bodies balanced on legs that looked far too thin to support their egg-shaped abdomens and long, thin necks. Their large eyes were as bright and curious as buttons as they split their time pecking at various bits on the ground and watching her approach.

"Hello, babies," Vonnie crooned, counting the chicks to make sure they were all there.

Some of the young ones came to the fence and peered up at her, a couple of them pecking at the woven wire fence in curiosity. She slowly walked around each pen, checking that no wires were loose or slipped and that the edges were all anchored into the ground. The material used for the pens had to be specially made with the squares of wire small enough to keep the adult ostriches from poking their heads through and choking, yet large enough so the little ones could get their heads out if they poked them through.

They weren't the dumbest birds in the world, she knew. They just seemed like it sometimes. Curious, they'd try for anything that captured their attention, sometimes getting their heads hung in the fence. More than once, Teague had lost his hat to the lively birds.

If frightened, they'd run pell-mell into the end of the fence, breaking wings, necks, or legs in their hasty flight. And they were temperamental. Just like humans, some were gentle, some had a temper. Some could be handled and petted, others didn't want to be touched at all.

They could be persuaded to move to another area, not herded there. An adult ostrich could run like the wind, reaching unbelievable speeds. A man on a fast horse would have difficulty catching one, once it got going.

Tears brightened her eyes. But, oh, how her father had loved these funny-looking creatures. Did they miss the sound of his voice, the gentle touch of his hand?

Suddenly Vonnie detected a shadow from the corner of her eye.

"Who's there?"

She peered into the twilight, a frown creasing her forehead. Goose bumps raised on her arms.

"Who's there?" she called again.

A figure stepped from behind a tall cactus at the edge of the pens.

"Andrew?" she said, relieved when she recognized him. "You frightened me."

A person could get himself shot lurking around the ostrich pens. The hands knew to shoot first and ask questions later.

"Sorry," he said.

Andrew Baldwin was nearly as tall as Adam, with the same wavy brown hair. He was the most serious of the four boys. He'd walked with a limp ever since she could remember, the result of a fall from the loft of the Baldwin barn, that had broken his leg. The injury had never healed properly. Andrew was rumored to be the brother who'd read all the books in his father's library, a feat P. K. himself had never accomplished.

"Just stopped by to see how you're doing," Andrew said, "and decided to take a look at the birds."

"You gave me a bit of a start," Vonnie admitted. "I'm surprised to see you out this late."

"I wanted to talk to you today—There were a lot of people around, and you were talking with Adam."

"I'm glad you came," she said simply.

"Wanted you to know if there's anything I can do to help—"

"Thank you, Andrew. I appreciate that."

Andrew was the odd one of the Baldwin group. Where Adam was most like his father, Andrew was broody and quiet. No one really knew what was going on in his mind.

The sound of a horse coming at a fast clip drew their attention. Vonnie identified the tall figure astride the big bay immediately.

"Looks like we have company," she murmured, watching Adam dismount.

"Andrew," Adam acknowledged his brother as he approached. "I didn't expect to see you here." His eyes swept Vonnie curiously.

"I wasn't aware I needed your permission to be here," Andrew returned.

Vonnie glanced from one brother to the other. A thread of tension ran between them, and she wondered why.

"Dad's looking for you," Adam said curtly.

"Is he now? He sent you to find me?"

"I don't believe he thinks you're over here." Accusation colored Adam's voice.

The two brothers stared at one another.

"Then I suppose I'll go report in," Andrew stated coldly.

"Thank you for coming by—" Vonnie's words faltered as she watched him limp to where his tethered horse waited.

Swinging into the saddle, he looked back at her, then touched the brim of his hat briefly.

A moment later he disappeared into the thickening darkness.

Turning around, she looked at Adam, puzzled.

Chapter 6

Removing his hat, Adam ran his fingers through his thick hair. The air hummed with awareness between them. It had been years since they'd really been alone.

"What was that all about?"

"Who knows?" he said. "He's hard to figure out."

Vonnie studied Adam's profile in the pale moonlight. He still had the power to render her breathless. "What brings you here this time of night?" she asked.

"I was checking on a stray. Since I was in the area, I thought I'd stop by—see how you're doing."

"Really now?" She wanted to laugh. "Since when have the Baldwins ever been interested in a Taylor's welfare? I thought coming to the funeral would have stretched the 'doing what's right' quotient for the day."

Adam let the remark pass.

"I guess now that Daddy's gone, P. K. wants to put on a good front for the community, show he's a real human being after all?" She hated the sting in her tone, but that's how she felt. The odd thing was, she was more mad at herself then at him. *She* was the one who hadn't been willing to fight for their marriage.

"I know this has been a rough time for you," he said.

"You're right." She turned away, staring at the birds. "My father dropped dead in the kitchen in front of me, and your father's taking advantage of our misery to show he has no hard feelings for a man who's dead? How magnanimous of him."

"Whatever was between your father and mine is dead and buried. Let it lie."

His words stung.

"Thanks for stopping by." Turning away again, Vonnie started back to the house.

His voice stopped her. "Vonnie, I didn't come over to start an argument. Can't we have a conversation without all this animosity?"

Sighing, she dropped her guard. What purpose would it serve to argue? She was being unreasonable and petty at a time she needed his strength more than she needed retribution.

"Of course, you're right. I am upset. Thank you for stopping by. . . . Mother and I are coping. We both . . . appreciate your concern."

When she looked up, she saw compassion in his eyes. A subdued understanding. "I'm sorry about your father, Vonnie. I didn't know him, but I'm sorry for you and your mother's loss."

Pulling her wrap closer against the night air, she studied him. It was the child in her that needed his acceptance, or perhaps it was the woman in her that needed his love.

"I don't know what Momma will do."

"It won't be easy for her."

Maybe if he had been less kind it would be easier. Resentment flared again.

"I think you're here because your father is concerned about propriety, not because you have any real concern for me."

"No," he corrected her. "P. K. doesn't know I'm here, and he doesn't give a damn about propriety."

She bit her lower lip, wanting to believe that he was there for no other reason than he cared for her. Cared deeply.

His voice dropped to a low timbre. "I'm here because I want to be here, and I thought you might need me. That's the only reason."

Her eyes were bright with tears when she finally looked up again. "Well, go home. I don't need you, Adam."

Shaking his head slowly, his eyes met hers in the moonlight. For a moment, time faded, and they were two young lovers caught in the web of desire. "I'd hoped you wouldn't make it necessary for me to remind you."

"Of what," she whispered. But she knew.

"I wanted to fight for us, Vonnie. You didn't."

Closing her eyes against the pain, she looked away. "I was young, Adam."

"You've had seven years to reconsider." Grasping the reins of his horse, he prepared to mount. "We'd appreciate if you'd let us know when you sell the birds. P. K. knows someone who might be interested in buying a pair."

"Sell the birds? What do you mean, when I sell them?"

He looked down on her from his perch in the saddle.

"When you sell out. You can't raise those birds by yourself."

Her chin lifted a notch. "I don't intend to sell my birds. I still have Roel and Genaro, in case you haven't noticed."

She saw the muscles tighten in his jaw.

"With Teague gone, I didn't think you'd be keeping the place. I thought you'd want to move your mother back to San Francisco to be with her family."

"Momma and I are staying right here," Vonnie said. "My seamstress work is good. Daddy had some money put away, and with the bridal gown orders coming in, we'll do fine."

He looked at her in a cold, aristocratic way.

"The birds were Daddy's pride and joy," she added, defending her decision.

In the past, maybe she hadn't taken a personal interest in them, but now they had taken on new significance. The birds had been special to her father, and he'd seen a future in raising them. She would feel guilty if she sold out after all the hard work he'd put into building the herd. Besides, Adam Baldwin certainly would not make a decision like that for her.

"I'm keeping the birds."

Stubborn, Adam's expression said. *As stubborn as your father, if not more.*

You are as bullheaded as P. K., hers implied right back.

"Well, the offer holds. When you want to sell out, let me know."

"In a pig's eye," Vonnie murmured.

Ignoring the less-than-charitable refusal, he wheeled his horse and rode into the darkness.

Vonnie watched him go, listening to the fading hoofbeats. She suddenly felt very alone and hated the fact that he could still make her feel that way.

Rapping lightly on her mother's door, Vonnie pushed it partially open.

"Momma, dinner's on the table."

"I'm not hungry, dear. You go ahead and eat, I want to rest a little longer."

"You can't stay up here in this room forever," Vonnie said, moving to the window to lift the shade.

Two weeks had passed since Teague's death, and Cammy was getting worse every day. She was withdrawing, wrapping herself in a shroud of grief. She rarely left the room she'd shared with her husband. Her face was lined with anguish, and she wept uncontrollably at times. The house was like a tomb.

"Vonnie—don't—the light hurts my eyes," Cammy said, turning her face away from the window.

"Momma, you have to try."

Mrs. Lincoln came each morning to coax her downstairs, thinking up reasons for them to take a short drive or go into town, but Cammy resisted all her efforts. She spent her days in a chair beside the bed, usually remaining in her dressing gown, sometimes listlessly allowing Eugenia or Vonnie to help her dress.

Each morning Vonnie brushed her mother's hair and wound it atop her head, but Cammy never showed an interest in how she looked these days. Already frail, she had lost more weight. Her clothes hung on her alarmingly sparse frame. She spent her days staring into space as if nothing mattered—and to her it didn't.

"I've got a surprise for you today, Momma. We're going to visit Audrey." Vonnie hoped a visit with

Audrey Schuyler would make Cammy realize how fortunate she was to have her health.

Health was precious, and only when one lost it, or saw it being slowly drained away, did they realize their own good fortune. It had probably been her mother who had told her that.

"What dress would you like to wear?"

"I'm not up to visiting today," Cammy said.

"I think the pink flowered one with the pretty torchon-lace collar," Vonnie said, ignoring her mother's protest. "It'll put the color back in your cheeks."

"No, Vonnie. I don't want to go."

"Franz says Audrey has been feeling better the last couple of days. Here, let's just slip off your gown. . . ."

Ignoring her mother's feeble objections, Vonnie maneuvered her arms into the dress sleeves like a rag doll.

"Dear, really—I don't feel up to going anywhere—"

"There, don't you look pretty! Here, let's put this shawl about your shoulders in case it's a bit cooler when we return. I've had Roel hitch the team to the buggy—"

"I don't think so, dear, really—"

Vonnie sighed deeply. She would have liked a good cry herself. She smoothed the shawl across her mother's back. "Now, we're almost ready to go. It's a lovely day out there—the temperature's nearly perfect. Hard to believe Thanksgiving's just around the corner."

Vonnie bustled around the room, gathering up the things needed for the afternoon outing. Audrey would be just the one Cammy needed to set her priorities back in place. Teague was gone. No amount of crying could bring him back. They both missed him unbearably, but somehow she had to make her mother care again about living.

She had to virtually pull Cammy out the door and down the stairway. Oblivious to her weak protestations, Vonnie propelled her outside and into the waiting buggy.

"Thank you, Roel," she said, accepting the reins to the team. "We'll be home before dark."

"Sí, señorita, hasta luego."

Giving the reins a slap against the horses' rumps, Vonnie set the team on its way.

"My, my, my," Franz said, greeting them warmly as they hitched the horses to the railing of the Schuylers' front porch. "What a nice surprise. Audrey will be delighted to see you. Come in. Come in!"

He ushered them into a small but neat living room where Audrey was resting on a sofa, a yellow crocheted throw over her thin legs.

"Oh, how wonderful it is to see you!" Audrey said, holding out both hands to Cammy.

Vonnie relaxed as her mother reached out to Audrey and the two old friends clasped hands. Cammy seemed to momentarily shed the melancholy that had plagued her for weeks. In fact, as she and Audrey talked, Cammy seemed to almost be her old self.

The two women conversed in low tones, and Vonnie settled herself in a chair nearby. Franz escaped to the kitchen, returning shortly with a tray holding a teapot and four china cups.

"Would you pour?" he asked Vonnie.

"Of course."

She performed the small ritual, automatically adding two teaspoons of sugar to her mother's cup.

"Just look at our little Vonnie," Audrey said, accepting Franz's help to sit up straighter so she could sip her tea. He fussed over her, fluffing her pillow, making sure she was comfortable. "Thank you, dear. . . . I remember so well the day you were born, Vonnie."

Cammy and Audrey were like sisters. They spent part of nearly every day together when they were first married.

Though Teague and Franz served in the war together, it was the women who were close and shared every part of their lives.

"You were the sweetest baby. A thatch of black hair that never changed. A little button of a nose." Audrey smiled gently. "And a little rosebud of a mouth. And you never cried. Not really. Just a beautiful baby in all ways."

Her eyes brimmed with emotion for the child that she loved like her own.

Sipping her tea, she then lay back against her pillows a moment to rest. A distant look came into her eyes.

"Franz and I wanted children. A whole houseful. But, it wasn't to be."

Vonnie made an appropriate remark. It seemed Audrey always talked about her disappointment of not having children. It appeared to weigh on her mind heavily these days.

"Well, I guess the good Lord took me at my word." She smiled. "When Franz was gone to war, so many months passed without hearing whether he was alive or injured. I got down on my hands and knees and prayed every night that he'd be spared. I promised, 'God, if you'll just bring Franz home safe, then I'll never ask another thing of you.' "

"And you never did," Franz said, his tone tender. "You've never asked for anything."

One could hear the sadness in his voice and knew

that if he could give Audrey anything it would be the return of her good health, so they could have many more happy days together.

"But," Franz added, a twinkle returning to his eyes, "you did want your piano back."

"Franz," Audrey scolded. "I did not—it was such a frivolous thing."

Although Vonnie had heard the story numerous times, she played along. "A piano?" she asked.

"A Steinway," Franz said. "Her father bought it for her. Oh, how she loved to play. But, we lost everything after the war, and we had to sell it in order to make ends meet." He smiled warmly at his wife, adoration glowing in his eyes. "She did love that piano."

"It was nothing, really. Other people gave more," Audrey insisted. "So many lost families, husbands, sons. What's a piano compared to someone's life? I never missed it. Ever."

"Audrey Schuyler! You're such a fibber!" Franz teased. "I've seen that look in your eye when that piano's mentioned. It meant a great deal to you," he contended.

"Go on now," Audrey said, swatting at her husband as he caught her hand and held it. They held hands for a moment like young lovers.

A knot formed in Vonnie's throat. *Oh, to have a love like that,* she thought. The kind of love that weathers the hard times and flourishes in the good times. The kind that only grows sweeter as the years pass.

"My wife didn't just play the piano," Franz said. "She caressed it. She attended the Sorbonne, you know, and would have played concerts had I not begged her to marry me."

"Begged?" Audrey scoffed. "More like I chased him down shamelessly and pleaded with him to marry me!"

Franz laughed. "When we married, her parents gave her the Steinway as a wedding gift. It was a beautiful instrument, one of a kind. Pearl keys, a fine finish, and a tone that couldn't be matched. When she played, even the birds stopped their singing."

"Why did you sell the piano?" Vonnie asked.

"Like many families after the war, land lay without crops, homes were burned, there was no food. When I came home, there was no work." Franz patted his wife's hand lovingly. "So, we had to sell Audrey's beautiful piano."

"Judge Henderson bought it," Audrey said. "Paid a handsome price for it, too. Enough to keep us going until we could get a good garden in and put food aside. It was a few months before Franz could get work, so selling the piano was the only choice."

"Ach," Franz inserted. "The judge bought it for his daughter, but that Carolyn had no touch. She just pounded it—I've heard her!"

Vonnie lifted her cup to mask a smile. Carolyn *was* quite atrocious at the keys. Tone-deaf, Teague said when he heard her. But Carolyn was possessive about that old piano. She wouldn't hear of it being sold.

"Yes, no one could match my Audrey. When she played, it was like the angels touched the keys. That Miss Henderson, she flitted away from that piano and on to some new fancy, just like she does the boys," Franz said.

Audrey laughed at Franz's irritation, and Vonnie joined her.

"Young people," Audrey said, "are more fickle than when we were girls, aren't they, Cammy?"

Cammy looked up. "Pardon?"

"I said the young aren't like we used to be, are they?"

"No," Cammy murmured. "I suppose not."

The afternoon passed by uneventfully. The talk turned to local gossip. For a while, Vonnie endured the conversation centered on the community's newest engagement, that of Adam and Beth. After a while, she quietly excused herself and disappeared into the kitchen to make more tea.

It was growing late when Vonnie finally stood up. "We should be going, Mother. It will be dark soon."

Nodding quietly, Cammy set aside her teacup.

"So soon?" Audrey protested. "Why it seems you barely got here."

Cammy smiled wanly. "I must confess that I tire easily these days."

"It's been so good to see you," Audrey said, reaching a hand out to her old friend. "Come back soon."

"I will," Cammy said, leaning to kiss a sunken cheek.

Catching her face, Audrey held it momentarily. Gazing up at Cammy, she said softly, "I pray for you each night. Teague is in a far better place, you know. It's you who's hurting."

Cammy's newfound resolve momentarily crumpled. "Oh, Audrey . . . I don't see how I can go on without him," she said brokenly.

"Of course you can." Audrey squeezed her hand tightly. "Teague Taylor would be *ashamed* of you if you didn't try."

Audrey's strength was depleted. Vonnie felt guilty for having stayed so long. Franz walked them out to the buggy.

"I hope we didn't tire Audrey too much." Vonnie

helped Cammy into the buggy, then arranged a warm blanket around her legs.

"Not at all," he returned. "It's good for her to see old friends. You come back. Soon."

"We will," Vonnie promised. She turned, kissing Franz on the cheek. "The visit has been good for Mother, too."

The sadness in Franz's eyes reminded Vonnie that Audrey's days weren't long, and he was already grieving.

It was late as they turned down the lane to the Flying Feather. Much of the trip had been made in silence, mother and daughter involved in their own personal thoughts.

"You know, Momma, we're lucky to have each other."

Cammy studied the horizon, a glint of moisture in her eyes. "I know."

Gathering twilight bathed the countryside as carriage wheels sang along the road.

"When Audrey goes—and I know she's not here for long," Cammy admitted. "It's just so sad to think of Franz and what her passing will do to him. He would do anything for her."

"I know, Momma." Vonnie didn't want to think about it, herself. Franz and Audrey were so much a part of each other—as Teague and Cammy had been.

"People are kind. They want to say something to help—they say, 'Oh, I know how you feel,' but in fact, they haven't the slightest idea how it feels—the pain—" Her hand came up to touch her heart. "The pain never goes away." Biting her lip, she struggled for composure. "When Audrey's gone, Franz will be alone, but I have you."

She patted Vonnie's knee and then left her hand there, as if to reassure herself that her daughter was indeed beside her.

They were nearly home before she spoke again.

"You know, after your father came home from the war, he never wanted to talk about it. Always just said it was too painful."

"I know." That had always puzzled Vonnie, since most men who'd been in the war were prone to talk about their exploits, or at least brag that they were at Bull Run, or had taken part in some other important battle.

"Daddy didn't talk about it at all, even to you?"

"He told enough for me to understand why he hated it so. He just wanted to put it out of his mind. I remember Franz mentioned something in passing one day, and Teague was rather curt in telling him never to speak of the war in his presence. I thought he was unnecessarily sharp with Franz, but he said it was a time he wanted to forget."

"What was Daddy like, then?"

A smile curved Cammy's lips as she thought about her husband. "Oh, he was a rascal when he was young, that father of yours. Wherever there was a party, he got there early and stayed late."

She smiled and paused. Then her face sobered. "But when he came back from the war, he was a different man. The death, the blood, the loss—I've heard others talk about it. It's not something anyone wants to recall.

"But when he finally began to come around, he was more like the old Teague. Yet he was so changed. Slower to laugh, never touched a drop of liquor after that. After a while he started working again, and began building the farm—" Her eyes grew distant. "We had a good life together."

Vonnie let Cammy out at the front door of the house, then drove the buggy to the barn, where she handed the team to Roel.

"Be sure and give them some extra oats," she called.

The aging ranch hand tipped the brim of his hat politely. *"Sí. Buenas noches."*

"Good night."

Cammy had already disappeared to her room when Vonnie entered the kitchen. She decided not to push the issue. That her mother had ventured out for an afternoon visit was enough for today.

Climbing the stairs to her attic workroom, Vonnie realized that she was too tired to sew, but the Wilson dress still had a few final touches to be added.

Flipping on the light, she took off her coat and hung it over the hook. Cammy still preferred the use of coal-oil lamps throughout the house, but Vonnie insisted on electrical lighting for her workroom. Teague had contacted the Electrical Light and Ice Plant and paid for the wiring as a surprise for her eighteenth birthday. He had teased her, saying since it looked like he had an old-maid daughter on his hands, he wanted her to bring in some money.

Smoothing her hair, she automatically stepped to the window to look down on the pens. The birds were settled for the night. Moonlight drenched the barn and the outbuildings. All appeared peaceful and serene—only the emptiness in her heart testified to the startling upheaval that had so recently shaken her comfortable existence.

She found her thoughts returning to Franz and

Audrey. So much in love ... They would be lost without each other.

So much in love.

"Mmm, I love you, I love you." Hands worked feverishly to touch, to adore. Their hunger was a fever that couldn't be quenched.

"Adam, I could get pregnant," she whispered between breathless, heady kisses.

His hands ran along her bare rib cage, his fingers fondling her breasts. She knew they shouldn't be so reckless, even if the judge had married them. The last thing they needed was a child.

Their hunger was insatiable. He couldn't keep his hands off of her, and she could not resist loving him.

Bending his head, he kissed the tops of her breasts, eliciting from her a helpless whimper.

"I can't get enough of you. ... I want to be a part of you, Vonnie. I can't stop touching you."

"Oh, Adam ..."

Pent-up emotion turned to insane desire. His lips on hers, hands stroking, anxious, hungry ...

Young bodies eager, ravenous ...

Bare skin, mouths everywhere at once.

"Promise me, Vonnie," he whispered hoarsely, *"promise we'll stay together forever."*

"I promise, Adam ... I promise. ..."

Snapping out of her thoughts, Vonnie sat down at the sewing machine and attempted to thread ivory thread through the needle with shaking hands.

Adam, for all purposes, was gone. The marriage was over.

As surely as Cammy had laid Teague to rest, she must now lay Adam's memory to rest.

Her resolve quickly crumbled.

Laying her head on her arm, she bit back bitter tears of remorse.

Chapter 7

Blowing a strand of hair out of her eyes, Vonnie pinned a seam to Jane's slim figure. With a deep, weary breath, she smoothed her hair, tucking the errant strand back into place.

She straightened and circled Jane slowly, examining the wedding dress with a practiced eye. The long train was unadorned. The front of the pure-white satin dress was plain, with three tiny flounces edged with silver at the bottom.

Honiton-point lace was arranged in three flounces, and long trails of orange blossom, with buds and foliage, carried down on either side of the flounced space. Two more trails were brought across the sides at a short distance below the hips, lightly tied together in the center where there was a small droop, and then allowed to fall to the edge of the dress.

The long-pointed bodice was fashioned of white-and-silver brocade, and more Honiton trimmed the top of the bodice to form the upper part of the sleeve. A small wreath of orange blossom was carried all the way around the bust, with a miniature bouquet on each shoulder, and a larger one in the center, mingled with white heather.

The matching Honiton-lace veil would allow Jane's face to be in full view, and would be worn with a small orange blossom wreath placed on her hair.

"Well?" Jane said anxiously.

Vonnie made another slow orbit, while Jane stood on the stool wiggling her fingers.

"Stand still. Don't fidget."

"I'm trying. I'm really trying not to move a muscle. Well?"

Vonnie laughed, unable to stretch out the suspense any longer.

"I think it might be the most lovely dress I've ever made," she finally admitted.

"Oh!" Jane clapped her hands together in delight, then yelped as a pin pricked her.

"Can I see it?"

"No," Vonnie said. "Not until I have these seams stitched in permanently and that last bit of lace tacked to the hem. Then, and only then, will I unveil the mirror."

"I can't stand the suspense a moment longer!"

Laughing, Vonnie took another tuck in the waist seam. "It's a rule," she insisted. "Like the one about a groom not seeing the dress or his bride before their wedding day. It's considered bad luck."

"I don't recall hearing a thing about the bride not being able to see the gown. And besides, it's 'the groom shouldn't see his bride *on* their wedding day,' not *before* their wedding day, silly."

"Whatever," Vonnie said, her mind already racing

ahead to how little time there was before the wedding
and how she was going to schedule Jane's last fitting in
with the rest of the work she had to finish in the next
month.

"Are you all right, Vonnie? I mean, is your mother
doing any better?"

"Stand still," Vonnie murmured around a mouthful of
pins.

"I can't, I'm too antsy."

Vonnie began marking the seam lines in the dress.
"Mother is having a hard time adjusting. It's very difficult for her—she and my father were very close."

Jane sighed. "It's so sad—I hope Edward and I have
that kind of marriage."

"What kind of marriage is that?"

"Oh, you know. The kind where Edward can still
make me blush when I'm old and wrinkled—a grand-
mother."

"Lift your arm. Careful," Vonnie murmured as she
methodically adjusted pins. She tried not to think of
the dreams she'd once had for marriage and children.
She never thought about those things any more. She
couldn't remember the last time someone came courting. Was it Peter Kinsley? My goodness, surely not. It
was nearly a year ago that Peter escorted her to the
Christmas ball.

"There, now step out . . . *carefully*." Vonnie extended
a hand for support. The white silk Honiton pooled over
the stool as Jane gingerly stepped out of the gown.

"It feels heavenly just to move again," Jane said,
stretching her hands toward the ceiling.

"Will you be wearing the dress afterward? Many
wedding dresses are kept and never worn again, but
others are being worn on special occasions these days.

I've seen many modern brides who plan to wear their wedding dresses to dinner parties held after the wedding."

"No, I plan to put it away for my daughter."

"Oh, your daughter, huh?"

Jane smiled. "Edward and I want lots of children."

"I'm sure you'll be blessed with a whole houseful."

Taking her day dress down from a hook on the wall, Jane pulled it over her head, settling it around her hips. She had a beautiful hourglass figure, one that would enhance the wedding gown's beauty.

"The attendants' dresses are simply beautiful, Vonnie. The new cut on the neckline was exactly what they needed." She smoothed her hair, then began buttoning the front of the bodice. "I don't know how you do it. You've such an eye for design and color. You must have been born with a golden needle in your hand."

Carrying the dress across the room, Vonnie carefully draped the yards of silk and lace over the dress form that had been adjusted to Jane's measurements. "I've been making dresses since I got my first doll. I fashioned them from bits and pieces of material and lace Mother gave me. It was just what I always did," she mused.

While most children played with dolls, Vonnie had idolized Charles Frederick Worth, an English tailor who became the couturier, or designer, for the Empress Eugénie, consort of Napoleon III.

Teague had provided her with any information he could order about the famous designer, hoping to encourage her gift with needle and thread.

Worth had been the first designer to show dresses made of fabrics of his own choosing. Before, dressmakers used fabrics provided by their patrons. He was also the first to display his designs on live mannequins, or models.

"I just sort of drifted into dressmaking, and then my sewing evolved into designing and sewing bridal gowns. I've been very fortunate that my gowns have been so widely accepted," she admitted.

"Fortunate to be accepted?" Jane made a face. "Most women would die for a Vonnie Taylor gown!"

Vonnie looked around her sewing room as if seeing it for the first time. Long tables she used for cutting materials lined two walls. It was here she drew patterns and measured hems.

Floor-to-ceiling shelves lined the other two walls, framing the one large window that looked out across the Taylor acreage. Separate shelves held various bolts of silk and lace, and cut dress pieces with patterns still pinned to the material. Her father had made a large peg board to hold spools of thread and to hang her scissors and measuring tapes on.

One long shelf was divided into boxes that contained laces and ribbons and other trims, including feathers from the ostriches.

Her reputation for creating exquisite hats was unparalleled. She had also been successful dyeing feathers for more flamboyant trims to adorn capes and cloaks.

Drawers beneath the cutting tables were divided, one to hold buttons, another beads and pearls. The work area was efficient, easy to keep neat, and allowed her to accomplish the sometimes tedious work with a minimum of effort.

"Well, I think you deserve every bit of recognition you get. You saw the announcement of Carolyn Graham's wedding in the New York newspaper, didn't you? It made special note that her gown had been 'designed by Vonnie Taylor of Arizona.' Why, I felt almost a celebrity myself, just knowing you." Grinning, Jane leaned closer. "But, just between you and me, I know my dress is going to be much prettier than Carolyn's."

Jane's lively chatter was suddenly interrupted by a loud ruckus from the barnyard.

"What on earth," she exclaimed, whirling to look out the window.

"Oh, no!" Vonnie bolted out of the sewing room and down the long stairway, leaving a puzzled Jane calling after her.

"What? What's all that noise? Vonnie, where are you going?"

The distinct squawk of birds, mixed with Suki's barking, was enough racket to be heard in the next county as Vonnie raced out the back door and ran toward the ostrich pens.

The big birds were racing frantically back and forth across the pens, throwing themselves against the wire. Dust, mixed with bits of feathers, clogged the air. The sound was deafening.

Glancing around for help, Vonnie realized Roel and Genaro were in town. Who knew when they would return?

Running to the fence, she paused, unsure of what to do.

The adult birds stood erect to nearly eight to nine feet and weighed close to 350 pounds. When calm, they had a kind of humping walk that reminded one of a camel's gait. But when disturbed, they could move in a ground-covering sprint that left roadrunners in their dust.

"Suki! Suki! Quiet," Vonnie demanded, trying to catch the wildly barking dog to calm her.

Two of the birds had their heads caught in the wire,

too frantic to recognize that by turning to one side they'd easily slip free.

"Suki! Sit!" she demanded again, running toward one bird who was in danger of decapitating himself.

"Shhhh," she soothed, trying to calm the kicking bird.

Vonnie jumped back at every thrust. This was turning into some kind of strange dance—bird kicking, Vonnie jumping back, then leaping forward to persuade the bird to turn its head and free itself.

"You stupid, stupid—Ow!" she screeched as an ostrich, having somehow gotten out of the pen, made an attack from the rear. He pecked first, then kicked, missing Vonnie by inches.

While he missed her, he did manage to kick loose a section of fence. Sensing freedom, the other birds poured through the break like water over a dam.

Plastered to the fence so tightly, she knew there must be permanent wire imprints on her backside, Vonnie watched as her father's "babies" leaped over the barrier and, quickly gaining maximum speed, disappeared over the horizon.

Leaning weakly against the posts, she watched the cloud of disappearing dust, unable to believe what had just happened.

"Vonnie! Are you all right?"

Jane, having managed to finally get her shoes on and laced, came running out of the house. "What is going on?"

"I—I'm not really sure," Vonnie managed. "Something disturbed the birds . . . and then . . . well, everything was happening at once. Oh dear—they're gone!"

"Gone?" Jane lifted her hand to shade her eyes. All

she could see was a dissipating cloud of dust some two miles in the distance.

"Gone." Vonnie dusted off her gown, coughing as feathers tickled her nose.

"Well, I do declare, I've just never seen anything like it! Birds, feathers, all that dust . . ." Jane suddenly burst out laughing. "I thought you were being trampled to death!"

"And that's funny?"

Shaking her head negatively, Jane held her hand over her mouth to stifle her mirth.

"Well," Vonnie surveyed the cloud of dust, sighing. "I sure hope they know their way back."

Teague had told her once that the birds were territorial, which meant they would eventually find their way back home. She hoped he was right.

Though she rarely had anything to do with their actual care, their deep-throated roar, much like a lion's mixed with a strange hissing sound, had become familiar to her. They were odd creatures, their size and pecularities intimidating.

She and Teague had an agreement. "You don't expect me to take care of the birds," she told him, "and I won't expect you to pin lace on wedding gowns."

"Agreed," he had quickly replied with a grin.

She didn't have the patience to baby the birds the way her father did. He would go out to talk to them at least three times a day, and got up in the middle of the night to check eggs when the birds were laying.

He watched to make sure the males were on the nests at night, and that not too many eggs were broken. He attended the birds like an expectant father until they hatched chicks that were hen-size from birth and grew into big birds in six months.

Raising ostriches was tedious work. It required the understanding that there was little one could do to control the circumstances, and Vonnie liked to be in control of a situation. But the situation was definitely out of control now.

With a last anxious glance over her shoulder, she followed Jane back into the house.

"Keep that wire tight," Adam called, watching as Joey nudged his horse forward a half step.

The Baldwins were stringing a new strand of wire along the north property line today. Adam kept a close eye on the dark clouds that had hung low in the west all morning, threatening rain.

It was the rainy season, and Arizona had had more rain in the past thirty days than it'd had all year.

As Joey held a roll across the front of his saddle, making sure the horse kept the wire firm, Adam and Pat stretched and nailed the new strand to posts.

The building storm made the air thick and heavy. Around nine, they'd shed their shirts, and now muscled, bronzed backs bent to the work under the hazy sun.

"Think we can beat the rain?" Pat called.

"It should hold off another couple of hours." Adam stood back, running his forearm across his face to wipe away the sweat.

The men glanced up as the sound of rumbling thunder rolled over the knoll.

Baffled, Adam squinted toward the horizon and tried to evaluate the cloud of thick dust coming in their direction.

Pat came to stand beside him, his eyes fixed on the bewildering sight. "What do you think it is?"

The three men stared at the strange stampede as it

drew closer. Long-necked birds covered the ground at a phenomenal pace, leaving floating bits of feathers and gouged earth in their wake as they headed straight toward the brothers.

The grazing cattle idly lifted their heads, their eyes widening as they spotted the bizarre entities bearing down on them.

Bolting, the cattle stampeded, trampling anything in their path to get out of the way.

"Get the horses!" Adam shouted.

Wild-eyed, the horses whinnied, reared, then broke into a gallop and converged on the stampeding cattle.

Joey ran after them, then quickly abandoned the pursuit as the birds bore down on him.

Diving headfirst for cover, the three men crouched low, watching the strange scene playing out below them. Awkward birds screeched and bellowed while leaping with their ungainly gait across the ground like crazed ballerinas.

Beef cattle, unnerved by the sight of giant, leaping feather dusters, turned heel and ran bawling over the horizon, followed in hot pursuit by the birds who were suddenly outrunning them.

"What in the *hell*?" Pat said, wonderment in his voice.

Spitting dirt out of his mouth, Joey sat up. "Did you see that—are those the Taylors' birds?"

"Whose else could they be?" Adam snapped.

"Well, hell's bells, that beats all I've ever seen." Pat sat up, reaching for his hat.

Rolling to his feet, Adam settled his hat low on his forehead. "Come on, we have to get those damned birds away from the cattle before they run them to death."

"The cattle are in Mexico by now," Pat guessed.

"Then we'll have to go to Mexico and get them."

Pat and Joey grumbled as they got to their feet, smacking their hats against their thighs to knock a layer of dust off both.

"We're going to have to run down our horses first."

"Hellfire."

"Beats all I've ever seen."

"Why would anyone want to raise those crazy things?"

The three men struck off on foot. It promised to be a long morning.

Three hours later, Adam rode into the Taylor farmyard. Swinging out of the saddle, he strode across the front porch and knocked on the solid door.

He waited, about to assault the door again when it opened. Jane Bennett stood in the doorway.

"Where's Vonnie?"

"Hello, Adam. What are you doing here?"

Dispensing with pleasantries, he repeated. "Where's Vonnie?"

Jane's amazed gaze took in his dusty clothes and dirt-streaked face. "I—I don't know. She was out at the pens a little while ago. There's been an incident with the birds. . . . I'm staying with Mrs. Taylor. She—she's in her room and—"

Whirling, Adam stepped off the porch and rounded the corner of the house, striding angrily toward the ostrich pens. There was an ominous silence about the place this afternoon.

Rounding the barn, he saw the empty pens, and the gaping hole in the fence.

"Vonnie!" he shouted.

The sound of chickens clucking near the henhouse came to him.

"Vonnie!"

"Stop *shouting*, please."

Glancing around, he didn't see her anywhere. Rounding the corner of the barn, he saw a comely bottom trying to extricate itself from a broken piece of fence on which a dress was firmly snagged.

Anger momentarily drained out of him; rage was replaced by a rush of white-hot heat so intense it startled him.

"Blast, blast, blast the cursed, blasted luck!"

Adam's lips curved into an unwilling smile as he heard her muttered swearing.

Tipping his hat back on his forehead, he grinned. "Something wrong? Did I hear someone complaining?"

"Yes, there is something *wrong*, and you're going to hear much worse if you don't get me out of here!"

Bending over to get a better look up her dress, he agreed. "Yeah, looks like you might have a little problem there."

"My back is about to break, Adam! Get me loose!"

"I don't know . . . the view's interesting from this angle—"

"Adam!"

Stepping to the fence, he extricated her from the snare. "You wouldn't have been in that fix if you'd used the gate instead of climbing the fence."

"I don't need advice from you, thank you."

"I wasn't giving advice; I was stating a fact."

"For your information, I was trying to repair the fence, not climb it."

He glanced toward the barn. "Where are Roel and Genaro?"

"I don't know. They went into town earlier—I haven't seen them since early this morning."

Straightening, she refused to look at him as she pinned back her falling hair.

Leaning against the fence, his blue eyes skimmed her lightly. "Having a bad day?"

She sighed. "A bad life."

"What happened?"

"I've lost the entire herd of birds."

His anger would have been easier to maintain if she hadn't looked so charming with her hair falling down, a streak of dirt across her sweaty face, her dress soiled and torn from the experience. To this day, she could reduce him to a mooning, callow boy. Just the sight of her filled him with memories of the hot summer days in Liken's pond, the earthy passion they had discovered there.

Crossing his arms, he viewed her sternly. "I found them."

She looked up. He stood, weight on one leg, his hands resting on his hips now. His shirt, clearly the worse for wear, was open down his chest. Dirt mixed with sweat streaked his face, and his damp hair curled over the nape of his neck. No man had the right to look that good when covered with dirt and reeking of sweat.

"You know where they are?"

"I believe I do."

"Thank goodness." Relief pulled her mind back to the business at hand. "Where are they?"

"In Sonora."

"Oh, dear." Her heart sank.

"Yes. Oh, dear."

"I . . . I don't know what happened. They suddenly began running as if they were scared to death, and before I knew it, they were beating themselves against the fence. . . . Since I didn't work with them, I . . . You know, my father—"

His features hardened. "Those birds are a menace. If you can't take care of them, then you damn well better get rid of them."

Her hands fisted at her waist, and she could feel the blood rush to her cheeks. "Is that why you're here? You came all the way over here just to tell me to get rid of my birds?"

"Three of your damn *birds* just straddled three of my prize beef, while the other couple of *dozen* terrorized the rest of the herd."

"Oh, my."

"It took me, Joey, and Pat three hours, Vonnie, *three* hours to round them up again!"

"I'm sorry . . . I have no idea what spooked them—"

"Could it be the dog?" he mocked.

"Nonsense! The birds are used to Suki. It wasn't the dog."

He stabbed the air in front of her with his forefinger.

"I don't care what spooked them. Don't let it happen again!"

The atmosphere between them was electrically charged, not only with the approaching storm, but with seven years of pent-up frustration.

"Well, pardon me!"

"The hell I will! You keep those birds in their pen!"

"You don't tell me what to do, Adam Baldwin!" She kicked dirt on his boots.

Slamming his hat back on his head, he turned and stalked off, rounding the pen in angry strides.

"Come back when you can't stay so long!" she shouted at his fading back.

"Keep those birds in their pens or I'll have ostrich and dumplin's on my dinner table."

"Ooooh!" Kicking a clump of dirt angrily, she stomped back toward the house to finish Jane's fitting.

Ostrich and dumplings. Just let him try!

Chapter 8

"Damn it, Joe, keep those birds together!"

Joey urged his horse forward as another ostrich decided to take a right turn out of the group.

"There goes another one!" Pat shouted.

Adam kicked his horse and galloped after a bird who had his eye on the far horizon rather than on the Flying Feather.

Adam bit back a curse as two adult males made a break for it. Galloping ahead of them, he cut the birds off, turning them back toward the Taylor ranch.

"If we had to herd these pests another mile, she'd get them back in toe sacks," he muttered.

"I don't know why Teague wanted the birds anyway," Pat complained, pulling his mount abreast of Adam's.

"Could be because they made him a lot of money."

"Maybe so, but damn, they're big," Pat's eyes traveled the full height of the African male, whose size was stupefying. "I wouldn't cross one."

"I don't know how Vonnie's going to handle them," Adam said.

An ostrich suddenly leaned forward to pluck the hat off Adam's head. For a moment, a game of hat tag ensued among the birds until one fumbled, and the hat hit the dust. Chaos broke out as the three men scrambled to retrieve it.

The hat was flattened. The ostriches fled.

Climbing off his horse, Adam picked up the hat and dusted it on his pants leg. Settling it back on his head, his eyes surveyed the birds, which were, at least momentarily, moving in the right direction.

How did Vonnie think she was going to handle the nuisances with Teague gone?

From what he heard, she had her hands full with her mother. Alma had mentioned the gossip she'd heard in town. Cammy Taylor wasn't doing well. In fact, she had practically taken to her bed since Teague's death and was hardly responding to anyone.

Vonnie was capable, but with her dressmaking business doing so well, he didn't see how she could oversee the birds, too.

"Joe," he shouted suddenly, "that one's making a break for it!"

Swinging back into the saddle, Adam spurred his black into a full gallop as a female flapped her short wings and made a dash for freedom.

The sudden ruckus launched the other birds into a faster gait, and their awkward lope began to carry them across the ground at an alarming rate.

It took over thirty minutes to cover the final five hundred yards to the pens.

Leaving Joey and Pat to get the birds settled, Adam rode on to the main house.

Swinging out of the saddle, he stepped upon the porch. Pulling off his hat and running his fingers through his damp hair, he rapped on the door, then wiped his sweaty face on his shirtsleeve.

Vonnie opened on the first knock, her wide violet eyes reflecting surprise when she saw who it was. The welcome on her face cooled immediately. "Yes?"

"Your birds are back."

Her gaze slipped to the pens where Joey and Pat were herding the birds into the runs.

"Well, I haven't gone looking for them because they're territorial, you know." Her nose lifted a notch higher and she had to stop herself from reminding him how little knowledge he had about the birds. "I knew they'd come back on their own—"

At his dubious look, she added, "And if they didn't, then I was going to send someone to look for them. . . . Roel and Genaro should be back any moment."

She looked tired. It was obvious she'd been sewing. Wisps of hair had strayed from the loose knot at the nape of her neck, and curling strands framed her face. Bits of lace dotted her dress. Deep circles shadowed her eyes. She looked exhausted, and Adam's gut twisted with the renewed realization of how difficult things were for her right now.

"Get someone on that broken fence as soon as possible. Pat and Joey will repair it enough to hold the birds tonight, but it's only a temporary fix."

"I'll have Roel mend the hole the moment he gets in."

"They're in the pens," Pat said, riding up to join them. Joey followed close behind. "Don't know if they're in the right ones or not."

"I'll sort them out," Vonnie assured them. "Thank you for bringing them back."

"Finding them wasn't too hard." Joey laughed, settling his hat more firmly on his head out of habit more than need.

At that moment, Suki rounded the corner of the house in a trot. More friendly than a watchdog should be, she decided to investigate Adam's boot.

Vonnie seemed anxious to get back to her work.

"Well, again, thank you." Glancing at the dog, Vonnie noticed the animal was worrying the hem of Adam's trousers.

"Suki, stop that," she admonished as Adam pushed the dog aside with his boot. She could see that he wasn't particularly fond of the dog's attentions.

Getting bolder, Suki's exploration progressed up Adam's leg.

Stepping away, he tried to distract the dog by throwing a stick.

The dog wasn't interested in a stick.

"Could I get you gentlemen some lemonade?" Vonnie asked, trying to ignore Suki's persistent and embarrassing sniffing.

"Sounds good to me," Pat said, starting to dismount.

"We don't have time," Adam said as he pushed Suki aside for the fourth time.

Pat climbed back into the saddle, surprised by the bite in Adam's tone.

"Anything else we can do for you, Vonnie?"

"Thank you, Joey. You've all done quite enough already."

"Well, Alma will be waiting supper for us. You coming, Adam?"

"I'll be along in a minute."

Tipping the brims of their hats respectfully, the boys reined their horses and rode off.

Suki blissfully resumed her busy exploration.

"Damn it, Vonnie, what is wrong with your dog?"

The dog was making a real bid for Adam's attention now, dipping in front of him, then jumping up to paw his leg.

"She's female." Vonnie smiled, leaning against the door frame. "I would think you would be used to females trying to get your attention."

Their gaze met and held. There was only one female he'd ever wanted attention from, and she damn well knew who it was.

"Suki, stop it." Vonnie opened the door, shooing the dog into the house. "I know you don't want my gratitude, Adam, but thank you anyway for bringing the birds home."

Avoiding her eyes now, he shoved his long fingers inside the belt of his trousers while he studied the horizon. His actions were familiar. Something was bothering him.

"Was there something else, Adam?"

"Yes."

Now what? Somehow knowing she didn't want to hear this, she took a deep breath and braced for the worst.

Clearing his throat, he looked away again. "I talked to Clive Henderson this morning about our situation."

Her gaze anxiously flew to his. "You told him?"

She was alarmed, thinking about Carolyn. That girl couldn't keep a secret for five minutes. The whole county would know about the marriage in a matter of hours.

"He assured me he will handle the matter discreetly."

"I see."

"It will take a few weeks."

He shifted his weight nervously.

Vonnie returned his gaze. What was he feeling inside? Did he care at all about what was happening? How had they let this go on so long anyway?

"There will be papers for you to sign—"

"I'll do whatever needs to be done." She continued to meet his eyes. Did her gaze reveal her resentment, sadness? "Have you told Beth? About us?"

"No."

"Adam, you have to tell her. She would want to know."

"I don't think it's necessary. There's no use upsetting her. If you'll agree to sign the final papers without a fuss, that will take care of the legalities."

Legalities. Was that all their marriage had been?

"I . . . won't make a fuss."

"Good." Twisting the brim of his hat in his hands uneasily, he cleared his throat again. "I'll let you know when the papers are ready."

"That would be very decent of you." The words came out faintly snappish.

A bead of sweat trickled between her breasts, and she pressed her hand against her bodice to soak it up. His eyes followed the motion.

When she looked up, she caught him staring at her. "Was there something else?"

"No, that's it."

She swallowed against the pain in her throat. This was what she'd wanted. It would be over once and for all. No ties to Adam Baldwin. Not ever again.

"Vonnie."

"Yes?"

"I don't know much about birds, but a couple of yours seemed a little . . . well, droopy. They were acting strange. I don't know anything about ostriches. It was hard to tell, but a couple of them looked sickly."

"I'll have Genaro check on them."

"Well." He put his hat on, then fit it more snugly on his head. "I'll be going."

"Good night."

"Good night."

She leaned against the door frame, watching him ride away. A sob caught in her throat. As he disappeared over the rise, she closed her eyes against the aching emptiness inside her.

After a while, she straightened. The ostriches. He said a couple were acting strange.

Exactly what did strange mean? She glanced in the direction he had just ridden.

Strange to him?

Stepping off the porch, she walked to the pens. Dusk had fallen. After their afternoon adventure, the birds were settling down for the night.

They should be separated, but it was more than she could cope with tonight. Tomorrow she would separate the pairs from the young ones and . . .

She paused, peering closer through the fence.

Was that one looking a little droopy?

Her heart hammered as she stepped closer to examine a midsize chick standing closest to the fence. The bird looked back at her with large expressive eyes.

Please, she prayed silently, *don't let any of the birds get sick. They're too expensive to lose. Especially now.*

"Vonnie?"

Vonnie whirled in response to her mother's call.

"Yes, Momma?"

"Why are you out there in that heat? And you without a bonnet on your head. Get into the house, child, before you have sunstroke!"

Frowning, Vonnie moved away from the pens. "It's all right, Momma. It's getting dark."

"Dark? Why, child, it's broad daylight! You come on in now—and tell your daddy I'm waiting supper on him! That man—he just doesn't know when to stop. Tell him to come in here and get washed up. Hurry now!"

Vonnie watched as she closed the door, then through the open window, saw her shuffling back through the kitchen.

"Oh, Momma," she murmured. Self-pity overwhelmed her. Her life was falling apart, and she didn't have a shoulder to cry on. If only Cammy was here for her. She couldn't tell her about Adam and the marriage, but at least she could feel safe again.

Safe and loved.

It had been a long time since she'd felt that way.

Chapter 9

Late Saturday afternoon, Adam was totaling a column of figures when the library door opened. He glanced up, then, recognizing Andrew's distinctive step as he limped into the room, returned to his work.

"Am I interrupting?"

"No. What's on your mind?"

Penciling in the column total, Adam closed the ledger. It was unusual for Andrew to seek his company. The loner of the four Baldwin boys, more withdrawn and serious about life in general than Pat and Joey, Andrew was the balance weight to the younger boys' impetuousness. As a child he rarely engaged in boyish pranks, and, as a result, he often drew P. K.'s wrath and seldom his favor. P. K. expected his boys to be boys.

As his sons grew into manhood, it was hard for them to live up to P. K.'s expectations. He wanted them to be men. His kind of men. Men's men.

Removing the spectacles he'd worn since childhood, Andrew cleaned the lenses with a handkerchief before settling them back onto his nose. Nearly as tall as Adam, with the same Baldwin leanness, he was a handsome man, save for the fact he rarely smiled.

The chair squeaked as Adam leaned back, lighting a cheroot.

"Books closed for the month?"

"Yes. Just balanced out. You'll need to look them over, but we seem to be in good shape."

"Has P. K. seen them yet?"

"No," Adam hesitated. "I'm not sure he's that interested."

P. K. still ran the ranch, but the day-to-day matters had been left to Adam.

Andrew's gaze sharpened. "It looks as if he's finally about to turn the reins over to you for good."

"I doubt it."

Drawing on the cheroot, Adam studied the specially made boot that accommodated his brother's shortened leg. Andrew had never accepted his affliction, nor was he charitable to those who singled him out for pity. He was also the brother who most resented Adam's favor with P. K., and most resented Adam's sense of responsibility toward the younger brothers.

The difference P. K. made between the two boys was a sore spot between the brothers since early childhood. P. K. preferred his oldest son and made no bones about it. Adam, his firstborn, was the child who most favored his wife in looks and temperament. When the reins of power were handed down, it was understood that Adam would assume control of Cabeza Del Lobo.

Adam resented the favoritism as much as his brothers did. He certainly didn't seek it. It created an insurmountable barrier between himself and Andrew, yet he was unable to alter his father's partiality. The younger boys learned to live with it and used it to their own advantage, seeking Adam's interference when P. K.'s fury was vented upon them. Andrew had never accepted it.

"Teague Taylor's death seems to have gotten to him." Andrew limped to the sideboard to pour a glass of scotch. The boot made a harsh, grating sound against the pine floor. "Maybe the old man's finally realizing that he's not invincible."

"He's not exactly a kid anymore."

Andrew took a bracing sip from the glass, grimacing as he let the scotch slowly trickle down his throat.

"Think Vonnie will keep the birds?"

"The birds?"

Andrew's lips curled with a mirthless smile. "You've forgotten the ostriches?"

Adam grunted. "Hardly. It took hours to cut them out of the herd and get them back to the Taylor ranch."

"Yes," Andrew mused, staring into his glass. "It seems she has her hands full."

Swinging out of his chair, Adam moved to the file cabinet. "She's a big girl. She can handle it." *And stubborn as a Missouri mule,* he silently added.

"I'm surprised to hear you say that. I always thought you had a thing for Vonnie Taylor."

Closing the file drawer, Adam sat down again. "Name one red-blooded boy in Pima County who didn't."

One of Andrew's rare smiles slipped through, and Adam caught it.

He grinned. "Didn't you?"

"Yes," Andrew confessed. "I suppose I did."

"Suppose you did?" Adam repeated, pinching his lower lip between thumb and forefinger as he studied his younger brother. "If I remember right, it was in the eighth grade you cornered her outside and kissed her."

Ignoring Adam's teasing tone, Andrew took another sip of scotch and stepped to the window. "You think she'll keep the birds now that Teague's gone?"

"If she's smart, she won't."

Adam looked past his brother to the mountains in the distance. They were bathed with the gold of the sunset, but they would soon be touched by purple, then black, as night swept over the desert.

Andrew continued staring out the window, a pensive look shadowing his features.

"What do you make of her—now that she's grown?"

Adam looked up.

"Who?"

"Vonnie—what do you think of her?"

The question caught Adam off guard. Andrew usually had his own opinions about people and kept them to himself, rarely expressing an interest in what anyone else thought. As far as women were concerned, he'd never been seriously interested in one, at least not that Adam knew about.

He'd always thought it was because of the limp and Andrew's mistaken belief that a woman didn't want to be seen with an "invalid." Adam believed that many a woman would be proud to be on Andrew's arm, but his brother refused to believe it.

As he grew older, Andrew had ignored the fairer sex, choosing instead to bury himself in his books. Women ceased to be an issue as far as Adam could tell.

Vonnie Taylor was the only girl Andrew ever mentioned. Even as a boy, Adam knew his brother had a crush on her.

"I think she's a beautiful woman."

Turning away from the window, Andrew smiled.

"What a pity. She isn't interested in you anymore, is she?"

Adam knew his brother well, and the edge in Andrew's voice caught his attention. He knew Andrew had resented Vonnie's open attraction to him. He didn't blame his brother; he'd have been jealous as hell if he thought Vonnie favored Andrew over him. But that had been a long time ago.

A knock sounded at the library door, interrupting the conversation. It was immediately opened by a bustling Alma. She carried a tray with two pieces of pecan pie, cups, and a pot of steaming coffee. "Supper's running late, tonight. I've brought something to tide you over."

Adam glanced at the laden tray. "You spoil us, Alma."

Pinching Andrew's cheek as if he was still a youngster, she smiled widely. "*Sí*, but you are worth it."

Oblivious to the earlier tension in the room, the housekeeper set the tray onto the desk and added a drop of cream to Andrew's coffee, before bustling out again.

Adam reached for a cup and took a sip of the hot coffee.

"Why the sudden fascination with Vonnie?"

Andrew's gaze swung to confront him, and Adam recognized the familiar tightness around his mouth.

Meeting his brother's eyes over the rim of the cup, Adam continued. "You just being neighborly, or are you really concerned about her?"

Adam cut a bite of pie and chewed it slowly. It struck him as odd that Andrew had been at Vonnie's the night Teague was buried. No more curious than his own unexpected arrival, he supposed, yet it wasn't like Andrew to show such compassion. Not even for Vonnie.

"No particular reason. I'm just curious about what

she plans to do now that her father's gone, and her mother's no longer responsible."

Adam lifted his brows. "Who told you her mother was no longer responsible?"

"I overheard some of the hands talking. Is it true?"

Pensive now, Adam looked away. "I don't know."

"Why not?" That sharp edge was still in his voice. "You've been over there often enough lately. You should know what's going on."

"Well, Andrew, I don't know what's going on at the Taylors'. It's none of my business."

Staring into his cup, Andrew grew thoughtful.

"What does Beth think about you spending so much time at the Taylor ranch?"

"I wasn't aware I was spending an undue amount of time over there." The conversation was taking a nasty turn. "I took her damn birds back. You got a problem with that?"

"A problem?" Andrew laughed hollowly. "Is the 'gimp' not allowed to be concerned about a neighbor?"

"Damn it, Andrew, if you've got something on your mind, spit it out."

"Things never change, do they? Adam's top dog, Andrew's the pitied one."

Shoving his cup aside, Andrew got to his feet and limped from the room.

As the study door closed behind him, Adam realized the rift between Andrew and himself was deepening, and there wasn't a damn thing he could do about it.

Beth Baylor arrived at Cabeza Del Lobo around six, anticipating a quiet dinner with Adam, his brothers, and father.

Alma's eyes crinkled in a friendly grin when she

opened the door and found Adam's pretty young fiancée standing before her.

"Oh, how *bonita* you look."

Beth was wearing a dark-rose dress with a tight waist, a cascade of lace descending from the top of the neck to the waist. A band of lace decorated the edges of the short, close-fitting jacket, matching that on the hem of the narrow skirt and overskirt. Her hair was piled high on her head.

"Adam's in the study with Andrew," Alma said. "I'm sure they won't be long. I am in the kitchen. You can join me there, or perhaps you'd like to sit in the parlor—"

"The parlor, please." Beth peeled off her gloves and handed them, along with her bag, to Alma. "Ummm, something smells wonderful."

"I put a leg of lamb in the oven earlier," the housekeeper told her, leading the way toward the back of the house. "Would you like some tea?"

"I'd love a cup, thank you. It was so dusty on the way here."

As Beth passed the study doors, Andrew burst out, greeting her with little more than a cursory glance.

"Andrew, my goodness, you startled me—"

Her greeting fell on deaf ears as Andrew brushed past her and slowly ascended the stairs to the second floor.

Pushing open the library door, she found Adam leaning back in his chair, staring out the window. He turned when she tapped lightly on the door.

"Hello. I know I'm early—hope you don't mind."

Adam stood up, grinding out the cheroot. "Hello, Beth. I didn't hear you come in." Moving around the desk, he brushed her lightly on the cheek with his lips.

"It's so nice that we're having lamb for supper."

"Lamb?"

Detecting a hint of disapproval, she was immediately concerned. "You don't like lamb?"

"It isn't my favorite."

"Oh, dear. You don't like lamb? Does Alma know— no, I'm sure she doesn't or she wouldn't have prepared lamb for supper. Well, not to worry, darling. I'll just zip off to the kitchen and ask her to prepare something other than lamb for your supper. What would you like? Steak? Chops? Chicken—do you like chicken? Broiled, baked, stewed?"

Adam felt his hackles rising. "Don't worry about it, Beth. Alma knows I'm not partial to lamb, but the others enjoy it so I can—"

"—Eat it, but you're just being nice," she chided. "Really, darling, I don't care to cook at all." Moving closer, she tripped her fingers lightly along the front of his shirt. "After all, it won't be long before I'm responsible for all your meals. The practice will do me good."

"Really, Beth—"

"—It's not necessary," she finished for him. "But it is! I couldn't eat a bite knowing that you weren't enjoying your meal." She leaned forward, giving him a light peck on the mouth. "Just relax. I'll go out into the kitchen and get things started."

"Beth, I wouldn't do that—Alma doesn't—"

"—Like anyone in her kitchen." Beth sighed. "I'm sure once I explain the problem she'll welcome the intrusion. She'll want you to be pleased, won't she? Now, you just relax and let me do my duty."

Adam released a mental sigh of relief when the door closed behind her.

He wished, just once, she'd let him finish his own damn sentence.

Beth was back momentarily, and Adam bit back a

smile. She looked like a hen that had just had her tail feathers singed.

"Alma says that you can eat what everybody else is eating, or you can go hungry. 'This is not a cantina.' Those were her exact words. She says she will cook one meal and one meal only.

"She actually was quite rude," Beth complained. "And I had decided to fix burritos—do you like burritos?"

"I can eat them."

"But do you like them, Adam?"

"I don't know, Beth. Do *you* like them?" He didn't think Spanish cuisine was standard fare at the Baylor table.

Smiling, she said, "I do if you do."

"But do you *like* them, Beth? That's the question."

"No," she said pensively, "I believe the question was, do *you* like them?"

This conversation was getting on his nerves. "They're all right."

Beth made a pretty face. "Just 'all right'? It's a woman's place to accommodate her husband, and I desperately need to know your food preferences."

"I don't want to be 'accommodated,' Beth, I just want to know if you like burritos."

The subject was right-down asinine, but for some reason he felt compelled to see it through.

"Dear me, *I* think we'd better change the subject," she reproached. Perching herself on the edge of the chair, she wagged her finger playfully at him. "Someone is getting cranky."

Adam struck a match on his thumbnail, his eyes boring into hers.

"Besides, burritos are not important. There's something far more meaningful we need to discuss."

Adam sat back down at the desk, waiting for the announcement. The bombshell wasn't long in coming.

"I'm asking Vonnie to make my wedding dress."

Seeing the astonishment on his face, she clapped her hands together gleefully.

"Isn't it wonderful? I know it's extremely extravagant, but father said I could. Now, the question is: Do you want me to arrange for Vonnie to make the shirts for the men, or do you—"

Adam interrupted. "Beth, I don't think that's a good idea."

Beth paused, blinking at him. "Why? That's what Vonnie does—she makes exquisite bridal gowns."

"I know, but in view of everything that's happened recently, I don't think it's such a good idea. I understand that—"

"—Her mother isn't doing well. I know. Cammy isn't adjusting to Teague's sudden demise, but honestly, darling, I can't imagine anyone but Vonnie making my dress. Why, she's simply the best there is. I wouldn't dream of having anyone else make the gown."

"I don't think you should expect Vonnie to take on any more than she already has—especially now."

"Darling! I wouldn't 'expect' her to do it, although we've been friends for ages. She'll *insist* on doing it. Don't you see? I want the dress to be absolutely perfect, and Vonnie's the only one I would trust to do it. You'll see, she'll be thrilled I asked her—why, she'd be *crushed* if I didn't!"

Adam hardly thought Vonnie would be crushed.

"I'm only thinking of her—"

"—Welfare. Of course you are, and that's so thoughtful of you, darling, but really, Vonnie and I will work it out. Now, about the shirts, do you want her to make them?"

He didn't want Vonnie to make the shirts. Or Beth's wedding gown. He attempted to divert Beth again.

"Beth, Vonnie's got her hands full with the ostriches, her mother isn't doing well, and I think—"

"—It'll be too much for her? Heavens, no, it won't! She'll welcome the extra money, what with her father gone and all."

Adam put the cheroot out. He could see Beth had her mind made up.

Beth smiled. "You'll see, darling. It will be the most beautiful gown in the world. Do you like pure-white silk or off-white silk?"

"Either one."

"Or maybe more of a vanilla," she mused. "No. A yummy milk white—cream, maybe, no, magnolia white—snow white!

"Yes, snow white with eggshell lace—no, oyster colored . . . or perhaps a nice ecru . . ."

Two birds were dead.

The startling discovery left Vonnie shaken. Genaro and Roel came to the house early with the grim news.

Vonnie hung on the fence, her fingers caught in the wire, watching the ostriches pace the length of the pens. What had caused the birds' deaths? Thankfully, they were not adults, but still it was a costly loss.

The birds walked around the pen, oblivious to what had happened. Large eyes blinked slowly back at her as they peered over the top of her head. Occasionally they paused to peck at an object on the ground.

It was precisely that pecking that concerned Vonnie.

Somehow, in spite of their best efforts, the birds had gotten hold of foreign material. Bits of bailing wire had been found caught in the deceased birds' throats.

Bailing wire!

Teague would roll over in his grave if he knew that. The pens were patrolled by Genaro and Roel each day to avoid exactly that kind of threat.

The birds were never exposed to rocks or pieces of glass or string that they could pick up and swallow. The birds could easily choke to death on foreign matter.

Vonnie had even taken to raking the pens herself, picking up any tiny object that might attract the curious creatures. Had they picked up the killing material when they were on the loose?

Teague had lost a few of the birds to illness or bad weather, but never through neglect. She pressed her face against the wire. Her father had been gone less than a month, and already she had managed to lose two of his prized stock.

Drawing a deep breath, Vonnie vowed to be more alert. She would talk to Genaro and Roel, and they would all redouble their efforts to protect the birds.

"Suki, I'm not very good at this," she confessed to the dog.

Suki yawned widely and sat down on her haunches.

The sound of an approaching horse drew Vonnie away from the fence. Shading her eyes with one hand, she groaned aloud when she recognized the rider, Sheriff Lewis Tanner. Crooked as a dog's hind leg, and the very last person she wanted to see.

Tanner, a stocky man with a white handlebar mustache, drew his bay up alongside Vonnie. She fanned dust away from her face, irritated at his thoughtlessness.

"Morning, Miss Taylor. How are you, this fine day?"

"Good. What brings you out this way?"

Though Lewis Tanner was a neighbor on the south, owning fifty acres adjoining the Taylor land, there was little neighboring going on between the two families, especially since Teague's death. For years, Lewis had wanted to sell his property, but claimed the birds were a hindrance to the sale.

"Got a serious prospect for my property."

"That's good," Vonnie said, hoping he did. Getting rid of him would brighten her mood considerably.

Suki growled, and the saddle leather creaked as the sheriff shifted his bulky weight, eyeing the dog warily.

"Thought so myself, until my prospect saw the birds," he said, nodding toward the ostriches.

"What does my stock have to do with you selling your property?"

Suki growled, and the sheriff's horse shied away. The sheriff's bulk shifted from side to side in the saddle.

"Well, now, ma'am, seems my buyer don't much like the idea of having those strange-looking birds around."

"They're not 'around' your property, Sheriff."

Suki growled again and got up to sniff curiously at the sheriff's horse.

"No, but heard they got loose the other day and created quite a ruckus. Heard the Baldwins had to bring them back."

"That was an unusual circumstance, I assure you."

The sheriff's horse shook its head at the dog and sidestepped nervously again.

"Suki, get away," Vonnie reprimanded quietly.

"Unusual or not, the fact is they're a nuisance, ma'am. Now, I can't sell my property with them here, so I thought with your papa gone an' all, you might be thinking about selling out?"

"Selling out?"

"Your pa's gone, Miss Taylor, and I hear tell your ma ain't doing so good. Now, since it don't appear that you can handle those birds, I thought you might just get out while the gettin's good." Leaning over, he spat a stream of tobacco on the ground. Wiping his mouth on his shirtsleeve, he smiled. "When you think about it, what choice you got?"

She took offense at his presumptuousness. What made the men in this area so darned interested in her business, anyway?

"Keep them?" she guessed, realizing too late that the sheriff had no sense of humor.

Lewis Tanner had a reputation for meanness, and he was indiscriminate about whom he vented his temper upon. It was well-known that his friends were men who should be in the sheriff's cells instead of in his parlor drinking moonshine liquor. There were those in Nogales who wanted Tanner out of office but, fearing swift retribution, no one was willing to challenge his authority.

"Well, little lady." Lewis looked into the distance as if carefully weighing his next words. "If you insist on bein' stubborn about this, I'll have to warn you. Keep your birds where they belong. It'd be a shame if more popped up dead—"

Before he could finish his threat, Suki jumped up, barking wildly, leaping at the sheriff's boot and startling the horse.

The ostriches flinched at the noise, then began pacing the pens, flapping their wings nervously.

Glancing anxiously at the birds, Vonnie saw that the sheriff was trying to bring the big bay under control.

"Down! Down!" she shouted at the leaping dog. "Suki!"

"Remember what I said," Tanner shouted from the back of his plunging horse. With a distinctive lack of grace, he gave his horse its head and galloped off.

Suki followed after him to make sure he left.

Leaning wearily against the fence, Vonnie closed her eyes, her mind going over his thinly veiled threat. He would do what? Throw foreign objects in their pen?

"What in the tarnation is going on? Was that Lewis Tanner?"

Vonnie looked up, surprised to see Franz standing not five feet away, his weathered face lined with concern. She hadn't heard Franz arrive. She must be unusually tired.

"Yes, it was him, all right."

Walking toward her, Franz frowned. "What did that snake want?"

"To cause trouble, I think."

"Is there anything I can do to help?"

"Not unless you can bring two birds back to life, make Momma come out of her room and stop crying over those old photograph albums, sew a wedding dress . . ."

"Ah, poor child. Since your father died, everything's fallen on your shoulders. Maybe I can help. The birds? Chores? I would be happy if I could do something for you."

Vonnie straightened, pushing her hair back off her face.

"Oh, Franz, you've got your hands full with Audrey and your own chores. I couldn't ask—"

"You didn't ask. I'm volunteering."

Vonnie weighed the merit of his generosity, knowing it was prompted by their long-standing friendship. She knew he would feel hurt if she didn't accept his offer.

"I'd be ever so grateful if you could help me. Since Daddy's gone there are so many things that need to be done, and I simply don't have the time to do them all."

"Good. Good." He seemed genuinely pleased by her acceptance. "Tell me what I can do first."

Together, they walked toward the house.

"Well, there's a mound of canned fruit that needs to be put on the shelf, water to carry to the birds. They drink a lot when it's this warm."

"I can help Genaro and Roel keep them watered."

"Then there's the step on the back porch. It's about ready to give way."

"I'll get the hammer and nails. Shouldn't take long to fix it."

"There's a loose shutter on the front window, and the wind blew a shingle off the roof last night."

"And then there's the cellar," Franz added. "Teague kept meaning to get to it, but he never did."

"Oh, yes, the cellar. I would appreciate it if you could clean it, so I can get the rest of the vegetables stored."

"Don't worry your pretty head another minute. Franz is here."

She left him at the steps and went inside to work. In her sewing room she felt more in control. Familiar things surrounded her—the smell of machine oil, her materials, buttons, threads.

The colorful bolts of cloth soothed her; the sight of lace on satin restored her fortitude. Sewing was something she understood, something she could control. When nothing else made sense, she sought refuge in her work.

But this time it wasn't working.

As she sat down at the treadle sewing machine, her

mind was clouded. Would her mother ever get over Teague's sudden death?

It was too soon for the grieving process to be completed, but she was so worried about her. Cammy sat in her room for hours on end, staring out the window. The few times she had ventured downstairs she sat in the parlor, weeping and pouring over old photographs of Teague. It was as if half of her, the important half, had been stripped away.

Vonnie sat, the card of buttons forgotten in her lap. Didn't she know a little of how her mother felt? Hadn't she mourned her break with Adam?

Adam.

Why couldn't she get him out of her mind?

Chapter 10

The days crept slowly by. Emily Wilson's gown was mailed, and Janie Bennett married Edward Lassitor.

Rising shortly before dawn each day, Vonnie dealt with the housework before fixing Cammy's breakfast, then going to her sewing room.

She had established a routine of cleaning one room of the house each day, and today the chore was the kitchen.

Every Monday, she straightened the cabinet and shelves and put things in order the best she could, but the jars of canned vegetables that she and Cammy had put up this summer were always in the way. The shiny jars of tomatoes, corn, green beans, and pickles stood row on row, filling the holding room just off the kitchen. The rest stood on tables at the back of the kitchen where the canning was done. Franz was busy with other, more immediate tasks, so he hadn't finished in the cellar so they could be stored.

Vonnie paused, her hands tightening around a jar of

green beans. With Teague gone, the reserve of food would last forever.

Perhaps she would give some to Franz. Audrey was too ill to do any canning this year.

Loading a woven basket with jars of tomatoes, Vonnie elbowed the back door open and made her way to the cellar door and down the steps, where she found Franz diligently at work.

He industriously wielded a broom, clearing the rafters of accumulated cobwebs, brushing stacks of crates and discarded tools.

"Hey! Slow down," she teased. "It doesn't all have to be cleaned today."

Apparently willing to take a breather, Franz propped the broom on the dirt floor and leaned on the handle. Vonnie noticed how twisted and painful his joints looked this morning. Her first impulse was to tell him to let the work go, but then she knew he'd be embarrassed by the gesture. He liked to think he could still outwork any man his junior.

Besides, she certainly needed his help. The cellar was filthy, bug infested, and she only came down here when it was absolutely necessary. Both she and Cammy had always avoided the dank vault like the plague. If they needed anything, Teague had retrieved the stored goods.

The sound of a carriage pulling into the yard caught her attention.

"Someone's here," she murmured.

"Leave the basket," Franz said. "I'll put the jars away for you."

The job wouldn't be that strenuous, she decided, so she readily set the basket down.

"Thank you, Franz. I don't know what I would do without you."

He nodded and tugged his cap.

Flashing him a smile, Vonnie ran quickly up the stairs. A carriage stood at the railing. Beth Baylor and Hildy Addison were climbing the steps to the front porch.

A flash of resentment went through Vonnie when she saw Beth, but she forcefully pushed it away. After all, Beth didn't know she was engaged to her husband, and after the divorce, what Adam chose to tell her was his business.

As usual, Beth looked as pretty as a picture. Her vanilla nansook suit was trimmed with a deep flounce. The overskirt and waist ran in narrow tucks. Narrow and broad white lace bows of black and white grosgrain ribbon comprised the remainder of the trimming. The perky Italian straw bonnet perched on her head was trimmed with cream-colored serge ribbon and a black ostrich feather.

Beth Baylor was the epitome of fashion, and here was Vonnie, flushed from housework, the odor of the dank cellar clinging to her.

"Hello," Vonnie called out, refusing to give in to her irritation.

"Vonnie!" Hildy turned, spotting her dear friend. "Were you in the cellar?"

"Yes, putting away canned goods. I'm ready for a break. How about some lemonade?"

"Wonderful!" the girls chorused.

Following her into the kitchen, the two women chattered like magpies. Beth and Hildy seated themselves at the large, round oak table while Vonnie prepared the drinks.

"What brings you all the way out here today?" Seat-ing herself opposite them, Vonnie poured lemonade into tall glasses.

"Oh, Vonnie, I am just ecstatic! Father said I could ask you to make my wedding dress!" Beth blurted, hardly able to contain her excitement.

Vonnie's heart dropped like a stone. The idea Beth might ask her to make the gown had crossed her mind, but she had hoped against hope that the girl would decide on another seamstress, Eleanor Regan, in nearby Tuboc.

"Isn't it wonderful?" Hildy exclaimed. "I'm so pleased for Beth. I know you'll design something absolutely stunning for her."

Oh, Lord, Vonnie agonized. Beth doesn't know what she's asking! Make her wedding dress? She'd sooner try eating an ostrich at one sitting.

"Now, how does this sound?" Beth said. "I saw this perfectly marvelous picture in a catalog of a white *peau de soie* with a full-trained, untrimmed skirt. It had this darling, short, seamless bodice trimmed with lace on the front, set off by a wonderful lace jabot sort of draped diagonally across—sort of like this—" She crossed her hands across her bustline.

"Oh my," Hildy squealed. "It sounds gorgeous!"

"Simply sumptuous. Then it has this wonderful tulle veil, hemmed at the edge and fastened with orange blossom and a small cluster of the flowers on the corsage."

"Yes!" Hildy squealed with ecstatic approval.

Vonnie felt her throat closing as she reached for her glass. A pox on Adam Baldwin! He could have spared her this persecution by telling Beth the truth when he asked her to marry him. Beth would be discreet. After all, she wouldn't be particularly fond of others knowing about her fiancé's past folly.

"Well?" Beth asked. "Doesn't it sound thrilling?"

"Thrilling," Vonnie managed.

Leaning forward, Beth covered Vonnie's hand with hers, a look of concern coming into her cornflower-blue eyes. "I know how terribly busy you are right now, but as I told Adam, I wouldn't dream of letting anyone but you make my gown. Your work is unequaled."

Vonnie glanced up. "Adam knows you want me to make your gown?"

"Yes," Beth said, with a puzzled look.

"Well, I . . . um, don't know, Beth. What with Daddy's death . . . and the birds—" Vonnie said lamely.

Edging forward in her chair, Beth's gaze searched Vonnie's imploringly. "But you can work it in, can't you? A woman's wedding is the happiest day of her life, and if I weren't wearing one of your gowns, why . . . why, it just wouldn't be the same."

Beth had no idea of the spot she was putting Vonnie in. They had been friends since grammar school—how could she tactfully refuse to make the dress without a more plausible excuse than she was too busy?

"I . . . it's just that there's so much work right now. I've got orders stacked on my cutting table, the birds are taking more time than I imagined, and there's Mother—"

"Oh, yes." Beth patted her hand consolingly. "I understand she isn't feeling well."

"Daddy's death has just devastated her. She can't seem to get her life back in order."

"Of course," Hildy murmured. She glanced at Beth. "How thoughtless of us to try and put more on you—

it's just that we love you and value your work so highly—"

"I appreciate that, Hildy, Beth. But I really don't know how I could take on more work right now. . . ."

"I understand completely," Beth said. "I'm disappointed, but I understand your dilemma. It's just that Adam and I so desperately hoped—"

Avoiding her eyes, Vonnie fidgeted with her glass. "Have you and Adam set the date?"

"No, not yet, but soon, I'm sure." Gathering her purse and gloves, Beth mustered a brave smile. "The wedding won't be until after the first of the year—I'd like to leave the invitation open . . . at least for a few days." She viewed Vonnie hopefully. "Promise you'll at least think about it? It would mean so much to me."

"Beth," Hildy cautioned. "Vonnie shouldn't be pressured right now. If she can't make the gown, she can't."

"Of course. It was inconsiderate of me to press," Beth relented. "Is there anything I can do to help you, Vonnie? I would like very much to make this transition easier for you."

In spite of a multitude of reservations, Vonnie felt herself softening.

"I'll think about making the gown, Beth. It would mean that I would have to bring in Nelly Fredicks and Susan Matthews to help. I couldn't possibly finish the dress alone by the first of the year—the additional cost—"

"Oh, the cost isn't important," Beth assured her. "If Nelly and Susan could help, that would be wonderful."

Right now the nagging feeling of empathy was worse than the thought of making the gown—she felt as if she were letting Beth down on the most important day of her life. But it just seemed so unfair. How could she make the gown that Beth would wear to marry Adam?

"Well, we must be running along," Beth said, still visibly disappointed. Picking up her bag, she smiled waveringly. "I've a thousand things to do before the wedding."

Where is your graciousness, Vonnie chastised herself, *your sense of compassion? This isn't Beth's fault. It's Adam's.*

Vonnie walked the two young women to the door and watched as they drove off down the lane. Upon parting, Beth and Hildy made vague references to getting together again soon.

Vonnie hoped she hadn't offended them; they were good friends, cherished confidants. It was just that Beth's request had taken her by surprise, and she'd handled the situation badly. She returned to her work, depressed and distracted.

The remainder of the day didn't go any better. With Franz cleaning the cellar and putting away the canned goods, Vonnie decided to work. A half hour into the project, the needle on her Singer sewing machine broke. Her order of needles hadn't arrived the last time she went to town, and this was her last one.

She laid the dress aside in frustration, and there was a knock at the door. She answered the summons to find an agitated Sheriff Tanner pacing back and forth on the porch.

An already bad day was only getting worse.

"Sheriff."

"Miss Taylor," he said, thumbing his hat to the back of his head. "Wondered if you had time to think over our prior conversation?"

"Concerning the birds?"

"Yes, ma'am. I hope by now you see the wisdom of selling out."

"No, I haven't changed my mind," Vonnie said, folding her arms against her body and leaning against the door frame. "I see no reason to sell my stock."

"Well, now, that's too bad." His eyes pointedly studied the outbuildings, pens, and surrounding acreage. "Lot of work here for a little gal like you. Genaro and Roel are getting on in years. You think you can keep a place like this going on your own?"

"I have men dropping by every week looking for work. Young, strong men. Keeping responsible help shouldn't be that difficult."

She didn't know why she was against the idea of selling. Plain perverseness because the sheriff was being so pushy, she supposed. At times it would be a relief to be spared so much responsibility.

No, it wasn't the request, it was *who* was doing the asking, that got under her skin. Teague had frequently said he had no use for Lewis Tanner; consequently his prejudice had rubbed off on her.

"Well, like you said, your ma ain't doing well and all. Seems to me selling out would be to your advantage. Heard you got relations in Frisco. Why not sell out, take your ma to California, and let her get back on her feet? The change would do her good." He smiled, his mustache pulling even with his chin. "I think if you give it some serious thought, you'll see I'm right."

She fought the thread of fear that went through her and held his challenging gaze.

"This is my mother's home. She doesn't want to leave. If you want to sell your property you're entitled to do so, but I'm not selling mine."

The sheriff's face tightened. "I can't sell my land because of your damned birds," he growled, pointing a sausage finger at her. "You, little lady, are getting on my nerves!"

Vonnie remained firm. "I won't be pressured into selling my land, or my birds. Or into moving. Is that clear?"

He took another tack.

"If it's finding a buyer you're worried about"—he rubbed a hammy hand down his face—"then I'll buy your property."

She laughed in surprise. "You?"

"My buyer will take a larger parcel, but he won't buy with those birds here."

"I don't want to move."

"I'll give you $500 an acre, plus $10,000 for the house and outbuildings."

She mentally figured the sum in her head. "That's . . . why, that's . . . $75,000!" An unbelievable amount of money.

With that kind of money, her and her mother's future would be secure. They could live in comfort anywhere. They could even buy a small house in town, where Cammy could visit her friends, and she could set up a small shop . . . no, with that much money, she would never have to sew another seam if she didn't want to. . . .

But what would she do with the birds?

And how would Vonnie convince her mother to leave the house she'd lived in with Teague all her married life?

Impossible. Cammy would never agree to it.

"You have to admit, with Teague gone, a couple of women can't run this place. It makes no sense."

"This is our home," Vonnie contended.

"You're just being stubborn. You know I'm right. Take the offer."

"I don't think so," she said reluctantly, wishing he hadn't made the proposition so tempting. Seventy-five thousand dollars was a fortune.

"Take a week," he said agreeably. Too agreeably. "Think about it. Talk it over with your mother. You'll see it's a very generous offer."

Yes, it was generous. Too generous. How did a sheriff get that much money?

"You'll not get another one to match it." He fished his meaty hand in his pocket. "I took the liberty of having an agreement drawn up. I'll leave it with you. You sign it, send it to me at the sheriff's office, and I'll have your money within a week."

He extended the paper to her and, after hesitating, she took it. Taking it wasn't the same as agreeing, she told herself.

"Sign it," he urged again. "And get on with your life."

"Good day, Sheriff," she said, none too graciously.

After a pointed hesitation, the sheriff turned on his heel and went to his horse. Hauling his bulk astride his mount, he gave her one last glance, then rode away.

Vonnie stepped back and slammed the door, then leaned against it and closed her eyes, fighting the tears that threatened. Furious with herself for letting the sheriff get to her like that, she pounded the door with her fist.

"Blast you, Adam Baldwin. This is all your fault!"

It was irrational, but somehow it seemed to her, at that moment, that the whole rotten day was Adam's fault.

"Blast you, Adam," she repeated. "*Why* didn't you love me enough to fight for me?"

There. She'd said it. To herself, assuredly, but she'd said it. The thing that had been gnawing at her for seven years. And now that she'd said it to herself, she was going to repeat it to Adam.

Her decision made, she grabbed her bonnet and rushed out of the house without thought of consequence.

Quickly saddling her horse, she rode at a fast clip toward the Baldwin ranch with Suki following, her tongue lolling out as she loped along behind.

Knowing that Adam would be working outside, Vonnie checked the barn first. She found him there, mucking out stalls.

Dust motes floated in the air. The fragrance of freshly cut hay mixed with that of horse manure and seasoned wood. Her eyes adjusted slowly to the dimness inside the barn.

He'd shed his shirt, leaving bronzed shoulders bare. The muscles in his arms flexed tightly as he worked with his dark head bent. Long legs were encased by worn denims that hugged his behind—best-looking one in Pima County, without a doubt.

She stood in the doorway for a moment, just staring at him.

Turning, he saw her. "What are you doing here?"

His low voice brought her out of her trance.

Lifting her chin, she took a deep breath, then said, "I have something I want to say, Adam."

"Oh?" He leaned on the hay fork. "This should be interesting."

His amusement fed her fury.

"Only the lowest, vilest kind of animal would have his fiancée ask his wife to make her wedding gown!"

He sobered. Straightening, he carefully leaned the pitchfork against the stall.

"I didn't want Beth to ask you to make her dress."

"Well, she did."

"And you think I encouraged her to ask you?"

"Why else would she?"

"Well, let's see. Because you're friends? Because you make beautiful dresses? Because you're the best seamstress around? Any of those reasons ring a bell with you?"

She hated it when he was logical.

"Then why didn't *you* head her off? Why didn't *you* tell her I was too busy?"

"Because *I'm* not running your business," he returned. "You tell her you can't do it. Make up a reasonable excuse, or tell her the truth. You've got too much work as it is."

"You're darned right I've got too much work, the birds—"

"Sell the damned things."

Vonnie fumed. "What?"

"Sell the damned birds!"

"I can't. They're Daddy's—"

"Vonnie, Teague's gone. The birds are yours. You're hanging on to them out of pure stubbornness."

"Me? Stubborn?" Stung and looking for a fight, she planted her hands on her hips. "I'd rather be stubborn than a coward, Adam Baldwin."

"Coward!" he bellowed, his own anger boiling to the surface.

"Only a coward would run whining to the sheriff about my birds."

He swore. "Where did you get that cockamamy idea? I don't need Lewis Tanner to take care of my problems. Seems like you need somebody, though, since you can't keep those birds in their pens."

"That wasn't my fault!"

"Then whose fault is it?" He towered over her angrily.

"Yours!" she shouted, suddenly remembering why she'd come here in the first place. "Everything . . ." Her breath caught. "Everything's your fault!"

A puzzled look crossed over his face.

"My fault? How is your being unable to keep your birds in their pens my fault?"

The words burst into her throat. Before she could stop them, they rolled out unchecked.

"Because you wouldn't fight for me. You didn't love me enough to fight for me!"

She could have cut her tongue out. How could she have said that? But now that she'd started, she couldn't stop.

"What are you talking about?"

"You didn't love me enough to fight for me." Horrified, she heard her voice break. Oh, no! Now she was going to turn into a blubbering, silly twit!

He looked as if she'd slapped him.

"Where in the *hell* do you come off accusing me of that? If you recall, lady, I wanted to fight for you. *You* were the one who said you wanted 'to pretend the marriage never happened.' "

"I was fifteen. You were older—you should have known better." To her horror, she was crying.

Anger tightened his features. "I loved you more than anything. It killed me to walk away from you that day. I did it because that's what *you* wanted."

A sob caught in her throat. "*You* know the meaning of the word 'love'?"

"Oh, no you don't. You're not laying this on me. The problem was you didn't love me."

"I did," she whispered. "I did, Adam." A sob caught in her throat again.

Turning away, he clenched his fists and raised his eyes toward the barn loft. She could have sworn he was counting to ten.

She needed proof—proof that he had cared about her seven years ago. "What were we doing the first time we kissed?"

Turning back, he looked at her. She could never remember him looking so virile, so attractive—so forbidden.

"What were we doing?"

"You don't remember, do you? How can you say you cared when you can't even remember—" She remembered every day, every hour, every moment they had spent together.

"We were standing under the juniper near Liken's pond."

"Where were we when we had our first fight?"

"At the Doughertys' barn dance. You thought I paid too much attention to Lucinda Brown. It was"—he pinned her with a challenging look—"eight-thirty on a Friday night and it was cold out. Unusually cold. I'd just gotten you some cider and you turned on your heel and walked off with your nose in the air."

Her voice dropped to a whisper. "The day I sprained my ankle?"

"You insisted on trying to jump off the haystack, and you landed wrong. You were wearing a blue-sprigged dress with white lace and some other sort of frilly stuff around the collar. And," he leaned close, dropping his voice to a sensual tone, "I remember you were just about to outgrow it because it fit your breasts so tight I could count your breaths."

Her face flamed in embarrassment.

"I had to take you home on my horse, and if I remember right, we took the slow way and I was late getting home. P. K. was angry, but I told him a snake spooked my horse, and it threw me and I had to walk home. I missed supper that night."

The air in the barn was suddenly deathly quiet.

"Why didn't you just tell him we were married?" she whispered.

His jaw firmed, and she could see obstinacy flare in his eyes. "He didn't ask."

Furious, Vonnie shoved at his chest, throwing him off balance.

"Didn't ask!" She shoved him again. "Why would he ask?" He fell back another two steps and she followed, planting her hands in the middle of his chest and shoving again. "We lied about where we were so no one would ask!"

"Vonnie, have you lost your mind?"

She shoved him again. "Maybe!" She certainly had been pushed to the brink lately. First Lewis Tanner trying to run her off her land, and then Beth asking her to make her wedding gown. Wedding gown! *Peau de soie,* no less! She'd make it out of black crepe!

Before she could shove him again, Adam grabbed her forearms and pulled her. The pitchfork caught his foot and he fell, taking her down with him.

She squealed as they fell into the hay, then grunted as she landed on top of him. She immediately tried to roll to one side, but Adam held her tightly. His voice was husky as his eyes bore into hers.

"Remember Dade Simmerman?"

Her mind was spinning. "Dade Simmerman? You bloodied his nose."

"Because you went with him to the harvest dance."

"I didn't go to the dance with him. You only thought I did—and I let you."

His eyes caressed her. "Wicked wench. You were there, and you were dancing with him."

But I wanted to be with you, her heart cried out.

"Remember our wedding night, Vonnie?" His voice was deceptively soft. "No matter how many times we made love," his mouth lowered to within inches of hers, "you always wanted more. You couldn't get enough of me, could you?"

"And you couldn't get enough of me."

"Shall we see how seven years has altered things?"

She refused to rise to the bait. She struggled to break his hold, but he rolled her roughly to the side, pinning her tightly against him. She could feel the full impact of his awakening arousal pressing into her lower back.

"Let me go."

"That would be too easy. You, or the memory of you, has kept *me* prisoner for seven years. Why should I let you walk out of this unscathed?"

They lay for a moment, listening to the sound of their uneven breathing.

"Let go of me, Adam," she said in a tight voice.

"I'm not touching you improperly."

"What do you call it if you're not touching me 'improperly'?" She was painfully aware of his state, as he intended her to be.

"Simply pinning you down until you cool off."

His hand rested tightly just below her breasts. His breath was warm and pliant against her ear. The prospect of her "cooling" down anytime soon was unlikely.

"You're engaged to be married."

"You don't have to remind me of that."

Gradually her struggles ceased. They lay for a moment, no longer fighting each other. Outside, the hens clucked as they scratched beneath a hot sun. A cow sounded in the distance. Overhead, a fly buzzed in the hayloft.

"I'm sorry I wounded your pride," she said quietly. "I know you will never forgive me for that."

The anger in his voice was gone; now there was only resigned acceptance.

"You wounded more than my pride."

"I never meant to—when I woke up that morning I was scared." Her voice sounded small, vulnerable in the large barn. The close proximity of their bodies was torture. "I've relived that morning after our marriage a thousand times. If I could change one moment of that day, I would, Adam. But I can't."

"That's nice to hear, but it changes nothing."

Releasing his hold on her wrists, he let her go.

Getting to their feet, they avoided eye contact. Brushing the hay off her clothes, Vonnie murmured, "I still think you should have ordered Beth not to ask me to make the dress."

She walked out of the barn, head held high, and mounted her horse.

She glanced back once to see that Adam watched from the barn door as her mare broke into a gallop, heading back toward the Flying Feather.

Kicking an empty feed bucket into the corner, he reached for the pitchfork.

Suki skittered out the door and turned to stare at him.

Turning on the dog, he thundered, "Go home!"

Startled, Suki hung her head and trotted off.

Adam stabbed the pitchfork into a pile of hay and stalked out of the barn.

Chapter 11

A faint blush of light filtered through the window-pane around six. Rolling to her side, Vonnie struggled to adjust her eyes to the light.

The pane needs cleaning, she thought drowsily. Maybe she would ask Franz to do it.

No, she couldn't keep imposing on Franz. He had been over every day to help. There was a limit to his kindness.

Dressing quickly, she knocked on Cammy's door before going downstairs.

"Momma?"

When there was no answer, she opened the door a crack. Cammy sat in front of the window in her dressing gown, as if she planned to get dressed, like she did every morning as long as Vonnie remembered. Vonnie knew that was not her intention today. After a while, she would crawl back into bed and sleep the day away.

"Momma, it's a beautiful day. Let's go for a ride. Maybe go see Audrey."

"No. I'm . . . not feeling well," Cammy said, passing the tips of her fingers across her forehead in a gesture that was becoming all too familiar.

Vonnie suppressed a sigh.

"At least get dressed. I'm making pancakes for breakfast. You love pancakes."

"I'm not hungry—" Cammy began.

"Momma, if you don't come downstairs," Vonnie threatened in exasperation, "I swear I'm going to dress you like a rag doll and personally *carry* you down!" It must be a hint of Teague's temper surfacing that made her impatient with her mother today. But, Vonnie reminded herself, Teague never lost patience with Cammy.

Cammy's lower lip trembled. Opening her mouth, she quickly closed it again. Her mouth curled down at the corners as tears welled in her eyes.

"I'm a burden on you."

"Momma," Vonnie said, kneeling beside Cammy's chair and taking the thin, cool hands in her own. "You're not a burden to anyone. It's just that I worry about you. It's not like you to sit up here and do nothing. Daddy would be heartbroken to see you like this. He liked you doing things, active, enjoying life. You know it's true!"

Cammy studied Vonnie's face as if seeing it for the first time.

"You're right," she said. "You're right. Teague would be disappointed with me, wouldn't he?"

"Yes, he would."

Cammy's fingertips caressed Vonnie's cheek. "I'm sorry, darling child. I *have* been a burden—I just miss your father so. He's been gone so long."

"It's all right to miss him, Momma. I do, too." Every day was a trial without Teague's revitalizing authority. No thunderous sound of his laughter, no voice calling out unexpectedly, "Puddin', get out here! There's something I want you to see!"

"He was such a good man," Cammy whispered. "So good—I don't know what's wrong with me lately—it seems I just can't . . . think clearly."

"I know, Momma, and it's understandable, but you've got to try. Begin by getting yourself dressed and coming downstairs to breakfast, because I'm making the best blueberry pancakes you've ever tasted."

"You just do that," Cammy said, her eyes brightening, "and I'll eat a whole big stack of them."

Hugging her tightly, Vonnie felt tears stinging her own eyes. This was going to be one of Cammy's good days.

"Ten minutes, Momma."

Tripping downstairs, she wished she could feel more positive about her mother's recovery. Just maybe she was beginning to pull out of her grief. Oh, the sorrow wasn't lessened. She knew that. But maybe Momma wouldn't drown in it.

Ten minutes later, Vonnie had the big iron skillet hot and the pancake batter mixed.

"Where are those hotcakes?" Cammy asked, stepping into the kitchen, pretending to sniff the air.

She was wearing a yellow dress that had been one of Teague's favorites, and Vonnie felt so relieved, laughter bubbled up inside her.

"Just sit yourself down there at the table," she said, pouring a cup of coffee for her mother. "And get your mouth set for a feast."

Fifteen minutes later, their plates nearly licked clean,

mother and daughter lingered over cups of coffee. For the first time in weeks, the atmosphere in the kitchen felt normal. Comfortable, effortless, relaxed.

"This is good," Cammy said. "I didn't know how much I'd missed sitting at this table with you."

"I've missed you, Momma."

"I haven't been myself lately, have I?"

Vonnie smiled. Cammy had always possessed an inner strength that many admired, and it wasn't likely to change, but during the weeks since Teague's shockingly sudden death, she had wavered—perfectly understandable for a woman who had lost a vital part of herself. Hopefully, they were putting that behind them now. Together, they would go on without Teague, remembering the joy he brought into their lives.

Sighing, Cammy stared at her hands. "It's been so . . . difficult. Your father and I have been together so long—"

Vonnie squeezed her hand, then jumped when someone pounded on the back door.

Startled, Cammy sat up straighter. "Who would come visiting so early in the morning?"

"I don't know," Vonnie said, going to answer the impatient knocking. Opening the door, she saw the hired hand, his face a mask of concern.

"Roel? What's wrong?"

"*Buenos días, Señorita* Taylor. Two of the birds, they are looking real sickly this morning—you said to watch them close, so I thought you'd want to know about it as soon as possible."

"Two of them?" Vonnie breathed. "Momma, I've got to check the birds—"

"You go ahead," Cammy said, waving Vonnie out the door. "I'll take care of the dishes."

"Thanks, Momma."

Vonnie followed Roel out to the pens. She immediately saw that he was right. Two of the ostriches were "drooping." Standing alone in separate corners of the biggest pen, they appeared dull and listless.

Entering the pen, Vonnie approached the rooster nearest her. The adult male was smaller than the hen, with prettier feathers. His bright red legs meant he was breeding now.

"Quiet now," she crooned, not sure she knew what she was doing. "I just want to look at you a bit."

Slowly edging closer, she held out her hand, until she reached the ostrich. Very carefully, she circled around him, keeping an eye on the bird but out of reach of his feet in case he decided to kick. This morning he was too ill to be combative.

Smoothing feathers that suddenly seemed dusty and ugly, Vonnie examined the bird. Just the day before, the animal had seemed perfectly healthy.

"Roel, did anything disturb the birds last night?"

"No, *señorita*. I'd have heard them."

"This bird has several cuts, bad ones, on this side of his neck. Get me the salve from the shed, will you?"

"*Sí*, immediately."

Roel returned with the jar of salve, and Vonnie thoughtfully applied it to the fresh cuts. Moving on to the other bird, she examined it and found the same situation. She treated him accordingly.

When she was finished, she handed the salve back to Roel and then walked the full length of the pen, running her bare hand along the wire.

"Ouch!" she cried softly, shaking her hand and flinging drops of blood across her skirt.

Investigating the injury, she found a deep cut across

her index finger. Wrapping her finger in her handkerchief, she bent down to examine the fence.

"How can this be?" she exclaimed softly.

A short piece of wire was wrapped around the fence where two pieces came together to form a square. Just enough of the ends had been left sticking out to catch and slice, but not enough to be readily seen. It would take someone running their hand down the fence, as she'd done, to find it.

"Or the birds rubbing along the fence," she muttered to herself.

"Roel, come here."

"*Sí?*"

"See this?"

Bending closer, Roel studied the jagged end of wire.

"*Sí*, but I do not understand. I checked this section of fence just yesterday."

"Walk every bit of fence, running your hand along every inch. Wear gloves or you'll cut your hands. Find every bit of ragged wire, and remove it, immediately. This wire was intentionally rigged to injure the birds."

"*Sí* . . . but who could have done such a thing?" Roel asked, straightening.

"That's a good question," she mused. "A very good question."

While they both walked the fence, Vonnie thought about the question. *Who* would want to hurt the ostriches? Sheriff Tanner came to mind first. He wanted her to sell the birds. Failing that, he wanted her to sell him her land. Either way, the birds would be gone, and that was what he wanted.

But would he go this far?

Yes, she decided. Lewis Tanner would go as far as he needed to achieve an end.

The question now was, what was she going to do about it?

Every day after that, Vonnie went to the pens first thing each morning, running her hands along the wire to make sure there were no barbed spurs to harm the birds. Either Roel or Genaro performed the same ritual at dark, as well as listening for any disturbance during the night.

Cammy was less inclined to seclude herself in her room lately, but her apathy had returned. Once again she retreated into her own world.

For once, Vonnie was too distracted to worry about her mother. Between watching the birds and trying to keep up with her sewing, there was scarcely a free moment.

One Sunday morning, Vonnie convinced Cammy to dress and attend church with her.

Out of habit, they sat in the same pew they'd occupied since Vonnie was born.

Automatically holding the songbook for Cammy, Vonnie kept her eyes averted from the Baldwin pew. Beth stood smiling up at Adam, looking for the world like an angel as her lilting soprano blended harmoniously with his baritone in a spirited rendition of "Blessed Assurance."

The times she'd sat in this same pew and watched Adam and Andrew make faces at her ...

More than once, P. K. had thumped his sons on the head with his knuckles to settle them down.

The music faded as she relived the times they'd met out back of the church. . . . The kisses, the fumbled urgencies, the delightful awakening of inexperienced urges . . . the hasty intervals of hot, sweet desire. So brief, so passionate.

Guiltily, her mind snapped back to the service as the pastor stood and opened his Bible.

After the sermon, everyone stood around greeting friends and neighbors. It was a social hour, the hour of righteous atonement.

As Vonnie and Cammy made their way outside, they ran into Judge Henderson, his wife, Maddy, and daughter, Carolyn.

"Camilla, it's so good to see you out and about again," Maddy exclaimed, "and Vonnie, you look lovely. One of your designs?"

"Yes, it is." Vonnie's hand self-consciously smoothed the skirt of her dress. The striped, changeable, rose silk trimmed with black velvet bands and Vandykes of white Irish guipure lace was striking, she knew. The buffalo felt hat trimmed with black velvet and black ostrich feather gave the ensemble a French look she had copied from a catalog.

"It's been so long since we've seen you," Maddy chided. "You must come for tea this afternoon. We'll have time to visit and catch up on things. We'd so love to have you."

"Why, that would be lovely," Vonnie said. "Wouldn't it, Mother?"

"I don't know, Maddy," Cammy said vaguely. "Maybe not this time—"

Maddy wasn't prepared to take no for an answer. "Nonsense. Shall we say four o'clock?"

Cammy glanced imploringly at Vonnie.

"That's very kind of you, Maddy. Of course, we'll come." Vonnie said. "We'll see you at four?"

"At four. We'll be looking forward to seeing you."

Grasping Vonnie's hand, Carolyn grinned. "I have so much to tell you." Bending closer, she whispered. "Have you heard that Priscilla Nelson is seeing Lem Turner?"

"No!" Vonnie gasped. "Since when?"

"Since last week."

"I thought Lem was seeing Nola Richards."

"So did I, but apparently he isn't any longer—I'll tell you everything at tea this afternoon."

"I'll be there," Vonnie promised.

Vonnie and Cammy made their way to their buggy, stopping frequently to speak to old friends.

They ate a quiet dinner of roast chicken with mashed potatoes and green beans, and afterward, Cammy wandered into the parlor while Vonnie washed the dishes. She found her mother there looking through the picture album. For a week now, that had been her new quest. Looking through the picture album, and crying.

"Oh, come see, Vonnie. Look here."

"Momma," Vonnie chided. "Why don't we put the album away? You should rest for a while before we go to the Hendersons'."

"In a while," she promised. "Come, sit with me—there's something I want you to see."

"I've seen the pictures a hundred times, Momma."

"Please." Cammy patted the seat beside her. "Share a moment with me."

Sighing, Vonnie sat down beside her mother and glanced at the photo she indicated. It was of Teague, dressed in a Confederate uniform. Her father looked so young. He had been good looking—vitally attractive until the day he'd died. How she missed his calm, insightful presence.

"Doesn't your father look handsome in his uniform?

See how wonderful he looks? Why, he's barely aged at all, don't you agree? I must remember to tell him so—though it will surely embarrass him."

Vonnie's heart fell. In spite of all her hopes, her mother was living more and more in the past. She had begun to talk as if Teague were just away on a trip and would walk through the door at any moment.

"Why, I told your father just the other day that when I look at him in his uniform, I fall in love with him all over again."

"You mean you talk to Daddy . . . in spirit, don't you, Momma?"

"Yes dear . . . in spirit," Cammy answered vaguely.

Turning the page, her fingers caressed the worn photographs taken when she and Teague were first married.

"He knows that after I met him I never looked at another boy. He used to laugh at me, but it's true! I fell in love with him immediately. I was just fourteen. . . . I'd never met a boy who could make my heart pound with giddiness like Teague did."

Tears glistened in her eyes. Her fingers touched the brown-tinted photo. "When will he be home, Vonnie? He's been gone such a long time. Almost as long as when he put on this uniform and marched away."

"Momma—" Vonnie started, and then stopped.

She could tell Cammy a hundred times that Teague was never coming back, but her mind just could not comprehend that the heartbeat of her life was gone, never to return.

Sometimes she envied her mother's fantasy. At least the strength of her love sustained her.

"Momma, you must rest before we visit the Hendersons."

Cammy looked up, anxious. "Oh, my. Leave again? What if Teague comes while we're gone?"

"He won't," Vonnie assured her.

"You'll leave a note for him, won't you? In case he should? I wouldn't want him to come home and not know where we are. He worries about us, you know. Why, when you were a baby he'd wake up nights stewing about you, wondering if you'd marry properly, if the man would treat you good."

Vonnie patted her mother's hand.

"Why don't you go up and change into that blue dress with the white lace collar. You look so pretty in that."

"Yes, I will. Thank you."

After Cammy went upstairs, Vonnie remained on the settee, holding the photo album.

Oh, Daddy, what am I going to do? Momma's so bad, and I don't know what's happening to the birds.

Teague's image stared up at her, cold, unfeeling.

By three, Vonnie and Cammy were in the buggy on their way to tea.

Judge Henderson's three-story house sat at the end of a lovely street shaded by beautiful, old magnolias just off the main street. The wide porches wrapped around three sides, and in the summer one could sit there in the cool of the evening, smell the flowering magnolias, and watch the sun paint the desert muted shades of yellow and purple.

Within the large rooms, the snowy white walls were a perfect setting for the dark, handmade furniture. The hardwood floors gleamed with polished care.

Carolyn's room absorbed the whole front of the second floor. The lush living quarters had been the envy of her friends when, as girls, they'd lain awake in the big four-poster bed and giggled over what boys they were interested in, and who'd been kissed first.

"Here we are," Vonnie said, drawing the buggy up in front of the house. Judge Henderson sat on the porch having an afternoon smoke in a large, white wicker rocking chair.

"Afternoon, ladies," he boomed, getting to his feet to greet them.

"Afternoon, Judge," Vonnie called. "Lovely day, isn't it?"

"That it is," he agreed, ushering them into the house.

"There you are!" Maddy exclaimed from the stairway as they entered the old house. Latching onto Cammy's arm, Maddy squeezed it affectionately. "I'm so glad you've come. Come into the parlor where we can be comfortable. We'll have tea later."

The judge escorted Vonnie into the parlor, where a fire burned brightly in the fireplace. Cammy hadn't said a single word on the trip over, and now she was looking around as if she didn't recognize where they were, although they had been the Hendersons' guests a hundred times.

"I know it might be too warm for a fire this afternoon, but it seems so festive, what with Thanksgiving coming up next week."

"It feels good," Vonnie admitted, still a little chilled from the ride.

"Vonnie, your dress is exquisite!" Carolyn cried upon entering the room.

It got to be a tiny bit embarrassing that each time Carolyn saw Vonnie in a new dress she marveled aloud at her friend's sewing ability.

"Honestly, Vonnie. You amaze me. I can hardly believe that the shy young girl I shared a primer with is now so incredibly talented and dreams up marvelous designs for dresses straight out of her head."

Vonnie simply smiled her appreciation for the compliment and sat next to Cammy by the fireplace.

They made small talk for a few minutes, about the weather, a new mercantile being established in town and how it might affect Garrett Beasley's business. Cammy said little, looking occasionally to Vonnie for assurance. It hurt to see her mother so vulnerable, so uncertain.

Vonnie found herself avoiding the judge's eyes all afternoon. His knowledge of her marriage made her uneasy, although he gave no indication he was in on the secret. He spoke fondly about the upcoming Christmas festivities, and how much he looked forward to holidays.

Carolyn chatted incessantly about upcoming parties and Christmas soirées.

The conversation touched briefly on the recent trouble with the ostriches. It was commonly agreed that it was unfortunate, but would probably never happen again. The injured birds were healing properly.

The chime on the front door interrupted the conversation.

"That must be Franz and Audrey," Maddy announced. "I asked them to join us."

The Hendersons and the Schuylers had been friends nearly as long as the Hendersons and Taylors. It had been the judge who suggested the lamplighter job to Franz.

The four of them, and Cammy and Teague, had spent

many an evening together playing cribbage and commiserating troubles.

Over the years, the three families shared the good and the bad, as old friends tend to do.

They could hear the judge's hearty laugh from the foyer, then Franz entered with Audrey holding tightly to his arm. It was obvious her health was failing, but her smile was as bright as ever when she saw Cammy and Vonnie.

"Momma, Audrey's here." Vonnie's eyes plaintively urged her mother to respond.

"Why, Cammy, don't you look lovely," Audrey said, coming over to place a kiss on Cammy's cheek.

Vonnie glanced at Audrey apologetically when Cammy didn't respond, but Audrey's look clearly said she understood.

Maddy brought tea and served while Audrey and Franz caught up on the recent happenings in the community.

"And Cammy, how have you been?" Audrey asked, trying to draw her into the conversation.

Cammy ignored the question, sipping her tea indifferently. She turned to her daughter and said, "You know, Vonnie, dear, you should see those nice Baldwin boys more often—Adam and Andrew? They're such fine boys—handsome young men. Eligible, too . . ."

"Mother," Vonnie admonished, embarrassment coloring her cheeks. "Adam is engaged to Beth. Have you forgotten?" she gently chided.

"Forgotten? No," Cammy mused. "Well, yes, perhaps I knew that." She looked up again. "Have you ever considered them as proper suitors?"

"Adam and Andrew?" Vonnie couldn't believe this turn of her mother's conversation.

"Yes, they're good men ... your father doesn't care
for them, but he's hardheaded—always has been ... if
you like them, you tell them they can come courting.
You leave your father to me." A smile softened her
face. "I know how to handle Teague Taylor ... always
have, always will ..."

Vonnie apologized, the full impact of her mother's
condition striking her. It was frightening. "I'm sorry ...
Mother is a little distracted today—maybe overtired—"

"It's all right—" Audrey began.

"The cellar is evil."

Vonnie's cup rattled on her saucer. This behavior had
gone beyond grief.

"Mother—"

"It's evil. Bad. *Bad!*" Springing to her feet, Cammy
screamed. "I *won't* go down there. Not *ever*—you
shouldn't make me ..."

Maddy looked uncomfortable. The outburst was so
out of character for Cammy. Reaching for the teapot,
she smiled at the judge. "More tea, dear?"

Clearing his throat, the judge held out his cup. "Just
a little more, Mother."

Vonnie quietly laid her hand on Cammy's arm.
"There's nothing wrong with the cellar, Momma," she
soothed. "Don't you remember? Franz cleaned it for us
just last week."

Her mother's fear of the cellar was legendary.
Cammy had always had an abnormal fear of the tight,
small place.

"I won't go down there," Cammy repeated, her voice
strained and tense.

"Momma, the cellar is as neat as our parlor—"

"It certainly is," Franz declared. "I spent the good
part of a week going over every inch—"

"No!" Cammy sat up straighter with a look on her face that startled Vonnie. She wore a mixture of fear and loathing. "No! I'll never go down there. Never!"

Chapter 12

"Cammy isn't herself today," Franz said, smiling re-
assuringly at Vonnie when she attempted to apologize
for her mother's astonishing behavior. "If it makes her
feel any better, I'll clean the cellar as many times as it
takes to set her mind at ease. Don't you worry about it."

"Have you heard that Beth has chosen rose as the
color of her bridesmaids' dresses?" Carolyn inserted
helpfully.

"No, I hadn't heard that," Vonnie said, wishing the
floor would open up and swallow her . . . and her
mother.

"I thought surely she'd ask you to make her dress,"
Carolyn blurted, then looked as if she wished she'd bit-
ten her tongue. "I mean . . ."

"She did," Vonnie said brightly. A knot formed in her
throat. "But with everything that's happened lately . . .
well, I'm not accepting new work at this time."

There. Hopefully, she sounded convincing enough.

"Oh, my," Audrey crooned, spotting the piano. "My old piano—"

Audrey ran her hands over the fine wood lovingly, her eyes filled with sweet memories. "I never tire of seeing it."

"It is lovely," the judge said. "And I must confess, it's done nothing but gather dust these past few years. That girl of mine played it just long enough to learn a song or two, then got bored with the whole idea."

"Daddy, you have to admit, your nerves calmed down once I stopped playing." Carolyn laughed. Turning to Cammy, she giggled. "He said that piano practice was far too kind a word for what I was doing. He said it was more like premeditated slaughter of fine music when I sat down to play."

Audrey laughed along with the others at Carolyn's self-deprecation, though they all knew it was true. The girl had absolutely no sense of rhythm. Her piano teacher, Vonnie remembered, had given up out of sheer frustration.

"I'd like to buy the piano back," Franz offered quietly.

Clive laughed. "Franz, there isn't enough money on earth to make Carolyn part with her piano. I fear my daughter is a bit possessive."

Carolyn smiled. "Father's right. I have no intention of ever selling it."

"Oh," Audrey said, with regret, "and I'm sure we could never afford to buy it back."

"But you will play for us, won't you?" the judge said quickly, to save Audrey embarrassment.

Audrey, no longer able to deny her hope to once again play her beloved piano, sat down on the bench and lovingly opened the lid to expose the keys. Her fingers lightly touched the ivory, up and down, up and down. Glancing around, she remembered her audience.

"What would you like to hear?" she asked.

Carolyn asked. "What was the song that you always wanted me to play, Daddy, but I absolutely could not do it? Instead I'd have the teacher play it for me, and you overheard it. Oh, what was it?" Her brow furrowed. "It was one by Johann Strauss, right?"

With a smile, Audrey nodded, then her fingers flowed up and down the keys, and a hauntingly sweet melody came forth that captured her audience with its irresistible beauty. The room's occupants were held spellbound, breathless, as she bent over the keys, her body moving with the emotion of the piece.

Vonnie glanced at Franz and smiled at the clear pride in his face as Audrey played on. They listened, recognizing Audrey's love for the music and the match of artist and instrument, from one piece to another, until, exhausted, Audrey straightened from the keyboard and the last notes faded into the late afternoon.

"My, oh, my," Maddy said at last. "You do have a wonderful talent, Audrey. Thank you for sharing it with us."

"Thank you for loaning me the use of your piano," Audrey said.

"Well, I'll make fresh tea," Maddy said, gathering their cups.

While Audrey talked to Cammy, trying to prompt a response from her, Carolyn went to help her mother in the kitchen.

Vonnie took the opportunity to wander out onto the side porch for a breath of fresh air. Judge Henderson followed. The fragrance of the roses Maddy had coaxed to climb the porch post permeated the late afternoon air.

"The divorce proceedings are moving along well," the judge told Vonnie, lighting a cigar.

Taken by surprise, Vonnie glanced anxiously toward the open verandah doors.

"No one knows about it . . . do they?" she asked.

"I assure you, everything is being handled with the utmost discretion," he said, but his eyes danced with amusement. "And I must admit, I can't ever recall another case like this one." He winked at her playfully. "When you put your foot in it, little lady, you really put your foot in it. P. K. and Teague would have had a royal fit." He chuckled. "It would have been worth a king's ransom to see it."

"I fail to see the humor," Vonnie said dryly.

"Forgive me," he said. "I realize the situation is anything but funny to you. Please, be reassured. This will all be over very soon, and without anyone but those absolutely necessary knowing of it."

Vonnie hugged herself, wishing it were over now.

"I do have one question."

Vonnie could guess what it was. "What ever possessed us to do such a thing?"

"No, if my memory serves me, I know what possessed you to do it. My question is why you have waited so long to dissolve the issue?"

Vonnie studied the quiet street, the houses lined along it. Sounds drifted to her—a dog barking in the distance, the breeze rustling the juniper tree in the side yard. She tried to think of a reasonable explanation to a question she had been asking herself.

"I have no idea why Adam delayed as long as he

did," she finally said. "I guess I kept hoping that things would work out for us."

"Work out?"

"Between Adam and me." She hesitated, feeling foolish. "It's my fault. Adam wanted to go to our parents that morning, but I wouldn't allow it. The years passed, and each time I thought about telling Daddy about what I'd done I'd get physically ill. Being in his favor meant so much to me—too much. I know that now." Lifting a handkerchief, she touched her eyes. "Adam's feelings should have come first."

The judge drew on his pipe thoughtfully. "I suppose one might argue why Adam didn't take the matter into his own hand?"

"Adam's not like that. He loved me enough to do as I asked. I asked him to pretend the marriage never happened, and in doing so, I wounded his self-esteem."

Promise me you will stay with me forever, Vonnie.

I will, Adam, I promise . . . forever.

"I was so foolish, Judge. I'm older and wiser now. A woman can't hurt a man's pride the way I did Adam's and not expect to suffer the consequences."

"Oh, my child," the judge said, resting his hand on her shoulder. "I had no idea."

"What? That I'm such a fool?" She bit her lower lip, hard, hoping to stop threatening tears from spilling over.

"Are you still in love with him? After all these years."

Her lower lip trembled.

With a sigh, he pulled her to him, his hand gently patting her back. "Oh, how tangled our lives can become. Are you still in love with your husband?"

Her husband. The words sounded foreign to her. The

marriage had been so brief, she'd never thought of Adam as "her husband."

"I'm not sure what I feel for him. I did love him. Please, Judge Henderson, don't tell anyone what I've just confided. You must promise me. . . ."

"I won't breathe a word of it," he vowed. "But the question remains: what are we going to do about this?"

"There's nothing that can be done. Adam is divorcing me, and marrying Beth." She turned, her back firming with resolve. Bitterness consumed her. She had no one to blame but herself.

"Dear me," the judge commiserated. "You're willing to let the man you love marry another woman? Just like that?"

"You've seen Mother. She can't bring herself to accept Daddy's death. And there's Beth. She knows nothing about all this—I can't destroy her happiness with my mistake. Even if I were to fight Adam on this, P. K. hasn't changed his mind about me. He despises all Taylors."

"Yes," Clive mused. "The senseless feud refuses to go away."

"And then there's the decision of what to do about Sheriff Tanner. He wants me to get rid of the ostriches so he can sell his piece of property adjoining ours, or, failing that, sell his buyer our land. He made me a most generous offer—almost too good to refuse. But I don't want to sell Daddy's land, or his birds. At least I don't think I do. . . ." She paused. "To be perfectly honest, I don't know what I think, or want."

She stared out across the lawn, wishing a fairy godmother could wave a magic wand and make her troubles go away.

"What would you do, Judge?"

"Sell out."

She turned. "Sell out?"

"Sell out. If what you say is true, that you don't intend to interfere in Adam's future, then it would behoove all concerned if you were to take Cammy back to San Francisco so that she can be near her family. Perhaps there, she will adjust to her painful loss. The birds must be a great deal of trouble. Why not start a new life in California? With your talent, you needn't worry a day about finances."

Vonnie paced a step or two away as if to separate herself from the truth.

"I don't know—perhaps that would be best."

"You and your mother will be sorely missed, but I'm confident it's the best all-around solution."

"I keep hoping Momma will get better. She still thinks Daddy's going to come home at any minute. If I take her away before she's accepted that he's gone, I don't know how it will affect her."

"The decision is most difficult, but you must consider what's best for the both of you. How will seeing Adam and Beth together affect *you*? Will you be able to set aside your love and not be hurt when their children come along—"

The mere thought of Adam and Beth having children . . . sharing the passionate intimacy, as she once shared with him, sent a razor-sharp pain through her heart.

"Judge . . . Vonnie . . . are you going to stay out there all afternoon?" Maddy called.

Taking a deep breath, Vonnie turned to go back inside.

"Promise me you'll think about what we've discussed," the judge urged. "I know you've been called upon to have wisdom far beyond your years, but it's all really quite simple. Either you love Adam and are willing to fight to keep your marriage, or you move to California and make a new life for yourself."

Oh, how she wished it were so simple. Yet she knew he spoke the truth. If she remained here, not a day would go by that she wouldn't think of Adam and covet his wife's place by his side.

"I'll give it serious thought," she promised. It was clear she couldn't go on this way.

"I'm sure you'll arrive at the proper decision." Extending his arm, he smiled at her paternally. "Shall we go have that tea?"

Pulling the handkerchief over his face to filter out the dust, Adam spurred his horse into a gallop. He was riding drag this morning while his brothers bunched the herd closer. Moving cattle to higher pasture was a tedious, dusty job, considering the animals had been left to range free all summer.

He'd both looked forward to the chore and detested it, for the same reason.

The ride gave him time to think.

Judge Henderson had told him the divorce was proceeding smoothly. He expected no hitches. Within a few weeks he'd be free to marry Beth.

That was well and good, since she was pressuring him to set a wedding date. He'd avoided the subject as long as possible.

The judge had let him know that he had spoken with Vonnie and assured her the divorce proceedings were in motion.

She had to be feeling pretty good about that.

He recalled how she looked this past Sunday, sitting

in the pew with her mother. Beautiful, self-assured, confident . . .

There was a rumor floating around that Lewis Tanner had made Vonnie a handsome offer for her land. Tanner was heard boasting around town that he had an eager buyer for the Taylor ranch and the fifty adjoining acres he personally owned. The birds were the only hitch in his plan.

The buyer didn't like having the ostriches around. They frightened his stock—and him. Anything that could extend a neck nine and one-half feet long was a power to be reckoned with, and respected.

Adam couldn't deny the birds were troublesome. They'd done a fair job of spooking his own herd a third time. Baldwin beef had been scattered over nearly a hundred acres. It took two days to round them up and cut the birds out of the herd.

When he took the birds back to Vonnie, she seemed almost unconcerned. Told him he should get calmer cattle.

Their conversation ended in a fight, nothing out of the ordinary these days. They both wore their emotions on their sleeves around one another.

Beth had mentioned the trouble Vonnie was having with the birds lately. Jagged fences, strange disturbances, the birds getting out periodically. That had never happened under Teague's care.

Was it lack of experience or calculated interference?

Lewis Tanner wanted to buy Vonnie's land. Why? Did he want it badly enough to sabotage the birds? If he had a buyer as eager as he claimed, how much were they willing to pay? Enough for Tanner to try to force Vonnie to sell? Enough to buy Vonnie out for a healthy price and pocket a hefty profit?

But Lewis wouldn't be able to sell his land as long as Vonnie kept the ostriches.

Hold up, Baldwin. Vonnie isn't your concern, he reminded himself. It was something he had to tell himself far too often lately.

Whistling, he turned a stray back into the herd.

How far would Tanner go? As far as he needed, Adam told himself. The man would do anything for a buck.

Adam had never liked Lewis Tanner. Never liked his way of doing things. He reminded him of his cousin Port. Port was worthless and as crooked as a snake. He'd go out of his way to avoid an honest day's work. Made his living playing poker and cheating at it. He was in jail more often than out.

Port had been married four times, to four women who heaped about as much abuse on him as he did on them. The unions had produced six boys and a scrawny little girl who did nothing to improve society. That was the problem: Port and his clan contributed nothing to society. Rather, they lived on it, feeding off others' generosity.

Lewis Tanner was no different. He used his power to punish and for his own benefit. And, at the moment, it looked like Vonnie was in his way.

If she got one of her stubborn streaks and refused to cooperate—as he suspected she would—how far was Tanner willing to go to make her sell?

Enough to hurt the birds?

Enough to hurt her? He bristled at the thought.

If Tanner thought he'd get away with hurting her, he was sadly mistaken. Adam would personally see to that.

Back off, Baldwin, it isn't any of your damned business.

Giving another sharp whistle, he rode into the herd, determined to get his wife off his mind.

Vonnie had just finished cleaning up their lunch dishes Tuesday when there was a knock at the door.

Glancing in the parlor as she passed, she frowned when she saw Cammy with the photograph album cradled in her lap.

"Momma, close the book, please."

Opening the door, she stepped back, surprised when she saw the caller.

"Sheriff Tanner."

Tipping his hat, Lewis didn't bother to smile. Vonnie could tell this was no social call.

"Shouldn't be surprised to see me. Told you a week ago I'd be back," he snapped at her.

"Told you a week ago not to bother," she returned.

Ignoring the sarcasm, he came to the point of his visit. "Have you reached a decision yet?"

"I have, and the answer is no. I'm not going to sell the land. To you, or anyone else."

Actually she hadn't decided one way or the other until the moment she opened the door and saw him standing there. The last person on earth Teague would approve of her selling the ranch to would be Lewis Tanner.

Tanner's eyes narrowed.

"I gave you a better offer than you'll get from anybody else. More than the land is worth."

"I realize that. And I also have to wonder why."

"Because you've got me over a barrel, damn it!"

She doubted that. Lewis Tanner never let anyone best him. But why was he lying to her? Just to sell his land? She doubted it. He was far from destitute, and the land was like money in the bank. There had to be another reason.

"I'm sorry. I don't want to sell."

Tanner's face flushed with anger.

"You will be sorry," he said. "Real sorry."

Lifting her chin a notch, she confronted him icily. "Are you threatening me?"

Spinning on his heel, Tanner stomped off the porch, mounted, and rode off, leaving Vonnie with a knot in her stomach as large as a fist and a sense of impending doom in her heart.

Slamming the door shut, she leaned weakly against it. *He is threatening me.*

Chapter 13

Straightening his string tie, Adam shrugged into his dress jacket, gave his reflection a final once-over in the mirror, and proceeded down the stairs.

"Having supper at the Baylors'?"

Adam paused at the library door. P. K. was sprawled in front of the wide window that allowed the room a scenic view of the large paloverde grove behind the main house. It was the elder Baldwin's favorite room.

"Yes, I'm on my way to Beth's now. Alma taking care of you?"

"She always has. I'm sure she has some kind of gastric torture planned for my supper. Your brothers are off tonight, too."

"Oh? Andrew?"

"Yes . . . strange thing. He must have found an interest in town, he's gone enough, lately."

It was unusual for Andrew to be away from the house at night. He was more inclined to stay home and bury himself in a selection from his latest book order from back east while enjoying a glass of imported wine.

"Andrew and a woman? She must be a sorceress to get his attention."

"Uh huh. Say hello to Leighton and Gillian for me," P. K. said, sipping his brandy.

"You take it easy on that," Adam warned his father, receiving a scowl in return.

The sun was just setting when he looped his horse's reins over the hitching rail in front of the Baylor house.

Leighton Baylor had carved a niche for himself and his family in the community. The shrewd businessman owned the local lumber yard. As sole proprietor, he had found a way to ship in lumber and other vital building materials, and sell them for a reasonable price while still retaining a healthy profit for himself.

"Momma was about to give up on you," Beth scolded as she opened the door.

"Sorry, as I was leaving, I stopped to talk—"

"—To P. K.?"

Adam nodded.

"Adam," Gillian trilled as she came to the door, wiping her hands on a towel. "What a delightful pleasure. Let me take your hat."

Adam removed his hat and handed it to her. "Good evening, Mrs. Baylor."

"Law sakes, call me Gillian. We're about to be family, dear."

"Gillian," Adam corrected.

"Make yourself at home. Beth, take Adam—"

"—Into the parlor. I am, Momma." Looping her arm through his, Beth smiled up at him as she escorted him through the door. "Daddy, Adam's here."

"I can see that," Leighton said, automatically pouring

a glass of liquor and handing it to Adam. He winked. "You look like you could use this."

Adam took the glass and silently saluted Leighton, a man who wore his success with comfortable ease.

"P. K. sends his best."

"How is the ol' coot?" Leighton chuckled, settling himself in an overstuffed chair and directing Adam to a matching one.

"Fine. He's fine."

"Still favoring that leg of his?"

"It bothers him from time to time. But he manages."

"Stubborn as a donkey. Always was. Wouldn't admit he isn't as young as he used to be, even if that leg gave out on him completely."

"Dinner is on the table," Gillian announced from the doorway.

"Roast beef," Leighton murmured. "Act like you like it."

The dining room was square with a rectangular table set with Gillian's best. Eggshell china with a rim of gold cups so thin that one could almost see through them. Knives and forks matched with gold plates that gleamed brightly beneath a crystal chandelier that must have cost as much as half the houses in Nogales.

The table setting did justice to the silk wallpaper that Gillian had ordered from Boston in the spring. Beth made a point to tell Adam that her mother had taken great pleasure in finding a tablecloth and napkins to match the flowery pattern, so he was to be sure to comment on the striking design.

Should he get it over with and comment now, or wait?

Gillian saved him from the decision. "Leighton, your

usual place. Adam, at the other end." She gestured one way, then another with her hand.

Beth was on Adam's left; Gillian sat to his right. Leighton said a perfunctory grace. Adam could see he was uncomfortable with saying prayers aloud, but bent to Gillian's wish for a blessing at dinner.

After the amen, they immediately began passing dishes of roast beef and boiled potatoes, carrots, squash, string beans, and cabbage.

"Has Beth told you she's chosen rose as the color of her attendants' dresses?" Gillian asked Adam.

No less than thirty times in the past week, he thought.

"Yes, I believe she mentioned it."

Gillian gave him a sly look. "Your favorite color. You mentioned once that your mother was partial to it."

He looked up. "I did?"

"Yes. Do have more carrots, Adam. I made them with that brown-sugar glaze you favor so much," Gillian urged.

"Thank you." Adam regretfully spooned more carrots on his plate.

"Beth made the rolls. You must have more than one."

"Thank you."

"I thought about white flowers. With some greenery—" Beth said.

Adam looked up. "White flowers?"

"For the wedding."

"Oh."

"Butter for your potatoes? Though I'm not sure that's the best choice."

"No, butter's fine," Adam said.

"No, I'm talking about the flowers."

"More roast?" Gillian asked, holding the plate toward him.

"I'll have to think about that," Beth mused. "Cabbage?"

"Thank you, I have some."

"Have you two chosen a date yet?" Gillian asked.

"Well," Beth hesitated. "I thought . . . if Adam has no objections, December 31." She met Adam's surprised look with a warm smile. "At first I thought sometime after the first of the year, but then, this way we can start the new year off right. Don't you agree?"

"New Year's Eve?" Adam said. Wasn't that pushing it? What was wrong with summer . . . or next December?

"Well?" Beth prompted.

"I . . . yes, I guess December 31 is all right."

He was suddenly annoyed. Why couldn't Beth have discussed this with him in private before springing it on him in front of her parents?

"Oh." Gillian clasped her hands. "A New Year's Eve wedding. It will be—"

"—Perfect!" Beth finished.

Beth and Gillian were more like twins than parent and child. Adam looked from one to the other. Was he about to marry a mother *and* her daughter?

Hell, if he had both of them finishing his sentences, he'd never get to say anything!

"Adam, what were those marvelous flowers we saw the day we went driving south of town. Remember? I stepped in a hole and sprained my ankle."

Adam thought a moment. "You sprained your ankle?"

"Yes, don't you remember? I said, 'Now be sure and remember the name of these flowers because I will surely forget,' which I have." She peered at him inquisitively. "What were they?"

"I'm sorry, Beth, I don't recall."

"Oh, you *must*. Remember? I pointed them out to you as you carried me back to the buggy."

He smiled lamely. "Sorry."

"Oh, dear . . . well, it will come to me."

"What about the music?" Gillian asked. "I always say, music makes the wedding. Who will play? What—"

"—Pieces? Oh, my, so many details," Beth sighed. "Adam, you accompanied me to Belle Madison's wedding. Do you remember that song Mrs. Dillard sang? Something about true love and roses and dreams. Very pretty. Remember, we discussed it after the ceremony?"

"Belle Johnson?"

"You know, last month, and Meg Ruger wore that hideous pale-pink dress. It was not a good choice," Beth finished graciously. "It unmercifully blended with her skin and hair until she looked, well, she blended in with the flowers so you couldn't see her at all. How could you forget?"

"Oh, men don't remember things like that," Gillian apologized for him. "More—"

"—String beans? If you two would give the man room to breathe," Leighton said, "he might be ready for seconds."

"Leighton, I'm just trying to make him feel at home," Gillian said. "After all, he'll be our 'son,' soon."

Beth buttered a roll for Adam. "What day was it that we drove out to Paul Sandler's place to look at that team you were thinking about buying?"

"I don't know . . . Thursday, maybe."

"No, it couldn't have been Thursday. That's when I went to see Carolyn. Tuesday. It was definitely Tuesday.

Anyway, did you notice the house? It was so homey, so impressive. Could we think about building one like it?"

"Beth, I suppose we can think about anything we want."

"No, silly, I'm serious. Didn't you just love the Sandlers' house?"

Adam tried to cover his embarrassment. His memory had never been this bad. "I'm sorry, I wasn't thinking about the house. I guess I was thinking about the team. I don't remember what it looked like."

"Adam," Beth said, exasperated. "It had that big, wide porch across the front with four tall windows. You must remember. I told you at the time how much I liked it."

Adam suddenly felt a little panicky. Why couldn't he remember things he'd done with Beth just last week, yet he could remember, with total clarity, even the smallest thing he'd done with Vonnie seven years, eight years, nine years before?

He remembered the dress she wore the first time he kissed her, the first Christmas party they attended together, the way she smelled, wore her hair, the way she laughed.

He only heard part of the question Beth was asking. "I'm sorry, what did you say?"

"I asked if you had thought about having your groomsmen dressed in dark gray with black ties—it would be a wonderful contrast to the rose of my attendants' gowns."

"It doesn't matter. Have whatever—"

"—I want," she supplied, "but it's your wedding, too. I do want you to have an equal part in the planning."

"Beth, the man's ears must be burning. Doggone it! *You* plan the cotton-pickin' wedding!" Leighton said.

"It's a woman's thing. I remember when Gillian and I got married, I didn't know anything until I stood there at the altar waiting for her to come down the aisle."

"Oh, Leighton, you *did* too."

"I did not. Didn't know green from red. Punch from piss water."

"Leighton!"

"Daddy!"

"The point is, the color of the attendants' dresses doesn't matter to a man."

"It does to Adam, doesn't it, sweetheart?" Beth asked. Her smile was so sweet and full of trust that he felt bad for having little interest in the wedding preparations.

Gillian picked up the bowl of potatoes and spooned more onto Adam's plate. "I received a wonderful catalog in the mail yesterday, Beth, that shows a lovely china pattern. I believe there may be a silver pattern you'll like. We can look at it after dinner, and Adam can tell us what he thinks."

There seemed no escape. He was smothering under Beth and her mother's fussing. At this point, Adam didn't care if the bridesmaids paraded down the aisle buck naked.

He just wanted it over.

"We'll take our coffee in the parlor," Gillian announced when dinner was over, "so we can look at those china patterns."

Adam stood up, trailing Leighton into the parlor. Beth helped her mother prepare a tray of coffee and cookies.

"Scotch? You'll need it," Leighton warned. "Once Gillian gets something in her head—Well, she's as sweet as sugar, but when she sets her mind on something, take my word, it's just best to go along."

"Thanks," Adam said, taking the glass Leighton handed him.

"Just set that over there," Gillian told Beth. "I'll put the catalogs over here, near us."

Beth sat by Adam and poured coffee while her mother settled herself opposite them, armed with a barrage of catalogs.

"I thought this one was quite nice." Gillian spread a gazette on the footrest. "And this one, though I like the first just a little better, don't you?"

"Oh, I don't know ... it's nice, but ... oh, what do you think, Adam?"

"I don't—"

"—Care for it either," Beth inserted. "He doesn't like it, Mother. How about this one?"

Adam conscientiously studied the choices. Flowers and leaves, flowers alone, flowers on top of flowers, flowers mingled with flowers, or a small clump of flowers on a plain white plate? Personally, he hated all of them.

"Or this one. I rather prefer it, don't you?"

He looked at the picture. "Grapes and leaves?"

"It's different. It would surely set a fine table. What do you think, Mother?"

"I rather like it," Gillian observed. "And this silver pattern would go quite well with it."

Adam swilled half the scotch Leighton had given him in one swallow.

"I do like that," Beth said, poring over the two designs. "I do. I truly do. A pale-green tablecloth, with lilacs as the center piece. Wouldn't that be lovely?"

"I think so. And with corresponding pale-green napkins—"

"Oh, yes," Beth concurred. "Or perhaps mist green."

Gillian frowned. "Mist green, dear? Are you sure the foliage green wouldn't be more appropriate?"

Beth looked at Adam.

"Foliage green."

"Really?" Her face fell. "But the mist green is so lovely."

"Did I say foliage green? I meant to say mist. Mist green," Adam said.

"Well." Beth compared the two. "No, Mother's right. Foliage is better. Would you mind too much, Adam?"

"Fine."

"You're sure? I can just as easily order mist green as I can foliage green."

"Foliage green is fine with me."

He swallowed the last of the scotch, wishing it were a double.

"Wonderful! Now, for the fabric swatches for the attendants' dresses. I like the taffeta. And with a winter wedding it would be cool enough for it. Don't you think, Adam?"

"I'd—"

"You'd rather I made the decision myself. But I want *you* to be involved with the decisions. It's your wedding, too."

"Taffeta's fine."

"Rose or pink?"

"What's the difference?"

"Well, rose is soft and pink's a little harsher, but if you like rose, then rose it will be—don't you agree, Mother. Pink is a little harsh."

"What does Adam think?"

Setting his glass aside, Adam smiled wanly at his bride-to-be. "I'm sorry, Beth, Leighton, Gillian, but I have to be going. There're a couple of strays that need my attention."

"Oh!" Beth exclaimed. "Couldn't that wait? There are *so* many things to decide. I wanted you to—"

"You make the decisions. Whatever you choose will be fine with me."

"Well, if you must leave—"

Beth laid aside the catalogs and rose to walk him to the door. "I'm sorry you have to leave so early," she said, leaning to kiss him.

Cognizant that he was not acting the part of a besotted, soon-to-be groom, he pulled her gently to him and gave her a long kiss.

As their lips parted, she gazed up at him with troubled turquoise blue eyes. "I know men are uncomfortable with wedding preparations, but I just want our day to be perfect. Forgive me if all this fussing troubles you."

"No, forgive me for being so distracted lately." Kissing her lightly on the lips, he smiled. "You just tell me what I need to do, and I'll do it."

"Thank you, darling."

His lips touched her mouth again briefly. "Those strays won't come back on their own. I'll see you—"

"—Tomorrow."

He settled his hat on his head.

"Tomorrow."

Let her see if she could finish that one.

It was a clear night, moon high and waning as he rode off. He headed toward the ranch at an easy lope, trying to divest himself of the tension that had enveloped him like a wet blanket at the Baylors'.

He'd ridden for several minutes when the sound of an approaching carriage caught his attention.

Drawing his horse to a walk, he turned to look over his shoulder to see who might be out for an evening ride. His forehead creased in a frown when he recognized the horse and buggy.

The approaching carriage whizzed around him, and he got only a brief look at Andrew, finger to his hat in mock salute as he passed with Vonnie Taylor at his side.

Adam stared after the carriage. What the hell did they think they were doing? Where the hell had they been? And what the hell was Andrew doing with his wife?

Had Vonnie waved at him as the carriage bowled on down the road? The sound of her laughter hung in the air, affecting him like salt in an open wound.

Turning off the main road, he kicked the horse into a gallop, taking a shortcut to the ranch in order to avoid another meeting.

He was in a rare foul mood by the time he reached Cabeza Del Lobo.

Leaving the saddle before the horse came to a complete halt, he strode toward the house and immediately went to the library.

Several fingers of scotch later, he sat down at the desk and waited for Andrew's return.

Two hours passed before he heard his brother's uneven gait crossing the porch. The clock in the hall was striking ten.

As he passed the library door, Andrew paused, his eyes casually assessing his brother.

"Taking after Father, I see."

Adam didn't waste words with a retort. "What were you doing with Vonnie Taylor tonight?"

Andrew's brow lifted curiously. "Doing with her? Enjoying an evening ride, why?"

"Well, don't, anymore."

"Don't?" Andrew laughed. "Says who?"

"Don't argue with me, Andrew, just leave her alone, damn it!" Slamming the desk drawer shut, Adam got up to replenish his drink.

"I don't recall having to ask your permission on what I should or should not do with Vonnie Taylor."

"Leave her alone." Adam's voice rose to a near shout.

"Leave her? My dear brother," Andrew said, a warning cloud settling on his features. "Must I remind you that you are engaged to Beth Baylor? What I choose to do with Vonnie Taylor, or she with me, is our choice and frankly, none of your damned business." The air in the room was charged with tension.

Adam poured another drink. "You know how P. K. feels about the Taylors."

"Yes, and it didn't make sense when we were children, and it doesn't make sense now. Whatever was between Teague and P. K. is six feet under now."

Adam made a threatening move toward Andrew. His eyes were unreadable, but there was no mistaking the intent.

"Stay away from her, Andrew. She's off-limits."

Andrew's eyes darkened. "Go to hell."

"Adam? Andrew?" P. K. descended the stairway, his hair standing on end as if he had been jolted from a sound sleep. "What the hell is going on down here?"

Walking back to the desk, Adam sat down. "Sorry we woke you, Dad."

"Do my ears serve me right? Are you two arguing over that Taylor girl?"

He stood at the library door.

Neither Adam nor Andrew answered him.

"Of all the women in the county, you've picked a fight over Vonnie Taylor? Hellfire! Can't you boys control yourselves? You're like rutting stags! Like the serpent in the garden, one little gal you can't have, and I'll be damned if that's not the one you want!"

"Dad—" Adam began.

"Do you think I'm blind? Do you? Don't you think I knew you were making eyes at her all those years, mooning around like a lovesick calf?" P. K. fixed Andrew with a tyrannical look that allowed no discussion. "I warned you then, and I'm warning you now, leave Vonnie Taylor alone!" His voice shattered the quiet night.

He pointed at Adam with the cane he seldom surrendered to using.

"You've got Beth Baylor halfway down the aisle. Get that Taylor woman out of your head! You, Andrew, don't let me catch you with her again. Don't even look in her direction. I won't have it. You hear me? *I won't have it!* Now, both of you, get to bed!"

Andrew turned, shuffling into the hallway.

"Get to bed!" P. K. ordered Adam, before turning and following Andrew up the stairway.

Adam remained seated, resentment burning like a live coal in his stomach.

He was a grown man. A man with the responsibility of running a ranch of more than 73,000 acres, controlling more than a million acres surrounding Nogales, and keeping three brothers in line, and still his father persisted in running his life. When was it going to end?

"Son?"

Adam looked up to see P. K. framed in the doorway. He suddenly looked old. Old, disappointed, and beaten.

"Yes, Dad?"

P. K. was repentant, almost childishly so. "I'm sorry I have to come down so rough on you—you'll understand when you have sons of your own."

Even P. K.'s voice sounded tired, defeated, sad.

"I only want what's best for my boys. Ceilia always said I was too hard on my sons—maybe I am, but I love you, son. . . . I love all my boys. It may not seem that way to you at times, but I do."

The show of affection was uncharacteristic for P. K. and, Adam knew, painful.

There was silence for a moment, then Adam said, "What happened to make you hate Teague Taylor so vehemently?"

For a long moment it appeared P. K. was going to ignore the question. Walking to the window, he looked out over their acreage as he always did when something was on his mind.

He began slowly. "It was a long time ago. During the war, Teague and I served together, warmed at the same fire, ate from the same plate, rubbed each other's feet to keep them from freezing. Closer than brothers, we were."

Adam waited, tense with anticipation, aware the mystery was about to unfold.

"We were on our way home—worn out, sick at heart. Our uniforms, such as they were, were in rags. We'd gone twenty-four hours without a decent meal, and that had been only what we could scavenge from a nearby farmhouse.

"Late in the day, we came upon a family—God, it was hot. So hot you could fry an egg on a rock.

"The family was Irish, a man, his wife, two sons, and a small daughter." His tone was lifeless now. "I don't know how it happened—none of us knows how it happened. One minute we were all looking at each other, then El Johnson suddenly pulled his pistol and fired. . . ."

P. K.'s eyes glistened with unshed tears as he recalled that awful moment. "We could smell their sweat, their blood, their death. . . ."

Adam hesitated to ask questions that sprang to his mind for fear of breaking his father's concentration on those long-past events that had haunted him and driven an irreversible wedge between Teague Taylor and himself.

"We got shovels and buried them—the sight of that little girl—" P. K. turned away, pain searing his features.

Drawing a deep breath, he whispered, "Johnson and Teague scavenged the wagon and found a black velvet pouch containing some jewels. . . ."

The silence stretched. Finally, Adam prompted him again.

"Jewels?"

"Jewelry. Heirlooms . . . things the family wanted to protect from both the North and South. Apparently they'd hoped to keep the little cache safe until the war was over. Of course, they didn't count on running into us. . . ." He drew another deep breath, bitterness seeping through his voice. "Johnson and Teague took the pouch."

"Teague took the jewelry?"

"Teague and Johnson. They split it between them."

"No one else?"

"No one else wanted blood money," P. K. snapped. "Only a ghoul . . . a man with no righteousness, an ungodly, despicable man, would steal from the dead."

Leaning back in his chair, Adam ran his hand over his chin. Teague had the reputation in the community of being an honest man in all his dealings. Granted, in view of his strong personality, he was either well liked or despised; there was no middle-of-the-road when it came to Teague Taylor. But to Adam's knowledge, no one had ever accused him of being dishonest.

"That surprises me. I never took Teague to be that kind of man."

"Surprised the hell out of me," P. K. grunted. "I thought I knew him. Shows how wrong a man can be."

"You're sure Teague took it?"

"I saw it with my own eyes. There's no mistake. He and El took the jewels," P. K. scoffed with irony. "And people have believed all along that he'd made his money with those damned birds."

"But it's unfair of you to judge Vonnie by her father's sins. I don't believe she knows anything about that time in her father's life." If she had, she would have told him. They had been too close. At one time they knew everything there was to know about the other.

"Doesn't matter," P. K. said impatiently. "She's got Teague's blood running through her veins. By the way, another one of those birds got out this afternoon and jumped our prize bull."

"Damn!" Adam swore.

"The bull's fine—the bird lost most of its feathers, though." P. K. chortled. "Had the boys lock him up in the barn. You take him back tomorrow and tell that Taylor woman she's got to sell those birds before I shoot every one of them myself. You hear?"

"You just told me to stay away from her."

"This is business, damn it. Do as I say."

As P. K. left the room, Adam sank back into the chair to light a cheroot. Something didn't ring clear with P. K.'s story, but he couldn't put his finger on what it was.

He could ask Vonnie about it, but he'd swear she knew nothing about what had happened between the two once-best friends, or she'd have said something before.

Drawing on the cigar, he stared out the window. No, something was amiss with the story.

Swiveling around in the chair, he got to his feet abruptly and left the library.

Chapter 14

Sliding the barn door open, Adam studied the ostrich. It was late, but by damn, he was taking the pest back to Vonnie tonight. No six-foot pile of feathers on stilts was going to take up barn space all night.

Why not admit it's her you want to see, Baldwin? You don't give a damn about the ostrich.

I'm returning the ostrich. Nothing more. Taking it back, dumping it in a pen, and getting out of there.

The bird ceased its anxious pacing. Turning, he blinked down at Adam with wise eyes.

After rejecting several options, Adam decided to try looping a rope around the bird's neck to control him. He hoped this one was more cooperative than the ones they had returned a few days earlier. Without Pat and Joey to help, he knew it wasn't going to be easy to get the bird back to the Taylor ranch.

"All right, boy, you and I are going for a little walk.

You don't give me any trouble, and I won't give you any."

Looping a lariat, he began swinging it loosely above his head. He had the bird's attention.

The ostrich was curious enough about the rope that he held his head fully erect.

With a leisurely swing, the loop fell easily over the head and settled at the shoulders.

Taking a half hitch around a post, Adam tethered the bird. Quickly saddling his horse, he began the five-mile journey to the Flying Feather. This should not take long.

It was much later when Adam got there. Details are unimportant. Suffice it to say, if Adam owned the bird it would have been dead on arrival.

As he corralled the ostrich into the courtyard, he caught a shadow from the corner of his eye. He was certain a form darted out of the cellar and disappeared around the corner of the house.

Sitting up in the saddle, Adam squinted, trying to locate the hazy figure. The moon slid behind a cloud, obscuring his vision. By now there was nothing to see.

Frowning, he glanced toward the house, where a light burned in Vonnie's attic workroom. If she were awake and working, he might as well tell her that the bird was back.

Nudging the ostrich to the hitching post, he secured it there, alongside his horse.

Moving to stand beneath the window, he picked up a handful of pebbles and tossed it at the attic window. A moment later, Vonnie looked out.

He motioned for her to open the window.

Lifting the windowpane, she stuck her head out. "Adam," she whispered. "Do you have any idea what time it is?"

Removing his pocket watch, he held the dial up to the moon, which had slid from behind the clouds. "Eleven forty-one."

"*What* are you doing here?"

"Looking for you."

"Great day in the morning." Lowering the window, she disappeared, surfacing at the back door a couple of minutes later. Unlatching the lock, she opened the screen, still grumbling. "Why are you creeping around at this time of night?"

He knew he'd made a mistake when he saw what she was wearing. She was dressed in a man's shirt, probably Teague's, that was too large, and trousers so formfitting they left nothing to his imagination—which was active, to say the least. He couldn't keep his eyes off the pants, or her.

Not an enviable position for a man who was about to be married to another woman.

"I brought your bird home."

He was suddenly as nervous as a schoolboy. He'd known this woman intimately—more than intimately— he knew her body as well as he did his own. Every curve, every soft indentation . . . nothing about her was foreign to him. Her smell, her touch, her anxious murmuring in the throes of passion . . .

That was the whole problem: he had forgotten nothing about her.

Nothing.

Not one, desirable inch of her.

Her brows lifted in a frown. "You have one of my birds?"

Turning, he looked at the ostrich tied to the hitching post.

"Elmer?" She wilted with relief. "Thank goodness. We looked everywhere for him."

"Really?" His eyes locked with hers. "I suppose that was what you and Andrew were doing? Looking for Elmer?"

The brows came up again. "Excuse me?"

"You and Andrew. Earlier this evening when you passed me on the road like a scalded cat. Didn't look like you were searching for any bird."

"Are you referring to the incident earlier this evening when Andrew, who is no more than a casual friend, and I passed you on your way back from seeing Beth?" she asked.

"I'm *engaged* to Beth," he said, as if that marked the difference.

"Well, I suppose you could say that Andrew and I are courting now."

"The hell you are."

"The hell I am," she verified. "Andrew is a grown man. When are you going to stop protecting him? And please quit using that domineering tone with me. You and P. K. have that same stubborn look when you don't get your way."

He ignored her accusations. "Andrew is not going to 'court' you."

Leaning against the door frame, she looked at him. "A Taylor isn't good enough for him, either?"

"No, damn it." Taking a step forward, he forced her to back up. "Because you just happen to be already married. To me."

"Married—" She laughed at his audacity. "You're *engaged* to marry Beth, and that's all right, but you don't like my taking a simple carriage ride with Andrew because there's some sort of legal paper that says you and I are married?"

Her hands shot to her hips. Her curvy hips. Her distracting hips. "I have *put up* with all the 'old maid' jokes, all the questions—'When are you ever going to get married, Vonnie?' 'You're too picky, Vonnie,' 'Time is passing you by, Vonnie.' And I endured it all because I *thought* I was married to you! Apparently you haven't thought the same for the past seven years."

"I never forgot we were married."

"Well, we won't be, not for long," she assured him.

"Where do you want me to put the damned bird?" he snapped.

"Guess," she snapped back.

He got the drift. Lowering his voice, he asked civilly, "Do you want me to put it in the pen?"

"No, I'll take him. I was coming out to ride Elsie anyway."

He had already turned to walk away when her remark stopped him. Turning around, he looked at her.

"You're going to do what?"

"I'm going to ride Elsie. Daddy rode her all the time. It relaxes me to take a ride before I go to bed."

He turned to look at the birds, settled for the night.

"Ride one of those damn things? You're out of your mind."

Her chin went up a notch. "They're faster than horses, you know."

They were faster than bullets, from what he'd seen. And about as safe.

Pulling on a worn pair of gloves, she pushed the screen open. Stepping down off the porch, she clucked to Elmer, who was still tied to the hitching post.

"You've been naughty, Elmer. Genaro's going to fix

that latch in the morning. It's obviously too easy for you to get open. Bad bird."

She led Elmer to his pen as Adam curiously followed behind.

"In you go," she said, opening the gate.

Elmer went in without hesitation.

"How do you do that?" The bird had gone out of its way to aggravate him.

"Some of them are very docile," she said. "Daddy worked with them a lot. Elmer and Elsie are a pair that he's had for quite some time. Carrie and Carl are another. He began riding those four a while ago."

She stepped inside the pen and shut the gate behind her, but didn't slip the latch.

Adam watched with half curiosity, half fear for her, while she walked among the birds, talking to this one, patting that one. Lanterns strategically hung from poles, illuminating the pens. He could distinguish the males by their black markings; the hens had silver-and-brown feathers.

"Down, Elsie." Suddenly one of the females dropped to the ground, and before he could stop her, Vonnie mounted the bird.

Struggling back to its feet, the bird and rider loomed high above him. Sitting far up on the back, clasping underneath the wings, Vonnie laughed, riding easily as the bird strutted proudly around the pen.

"Some men have been known to use the ostrich as a saddle horse," she proclaimed.

"Some men are nuts, too."

"Coward."

"I'm the only sane one here," he muttered.

"Want to try it?"

"No, I don't want to try it."

"Scared?"

"Smart."

"I dare you to try it."

"No thanks."

"Double dare you. Triple dare you! Double, triple, quadruple dare you!"

It was a familiar dare with them, beginning when they were in the third grade. Anything he did, she tried. And anything she did, he had to prove he could do better.

"I've seen you ride broncs and bulls."

"You be careful."

"Elmer knows you now. Try it. He'll get down for you. Mount him as you would anything."

Realizing her slip of tongue, she looked away from his quick grin.

"As you would a horse," she amended.

"A horse, huh?" He studied the nine-foot, gangly creature. "Hell of a looking horse," he muttered.

He hesitated, then his curiosity got the better of him. Sliding inside the gate, he made his way toward Elmer, who was standing near the bird Vonnie was riding.

His eyes slid warily over the bird. "You riding Elsie?"

"Uh huh. She's my favorite. Down, Elmer," she ordered, and the bird obliged by squatting.

Adam awkwardly mounted, clutching Elmer's neck when the bird lurched awkwardly to his feet.

"Oh, hell . . ."

Laughing, Vonnie led the way out of the pen. "Come on, chicken!"

Adam held on, wondering if he had lost his mind. Riding one of the damned things! "Slow down, Vonnie!"

"Burk burrrrk, burk, burrrrk, burk," Vonnie clucked.

"Funny, Vonnie, funny. Where the hell are you taking me?"

"Outside the pens."

"Forget that," he said.

"You'll be fine. I'll control Elsie, and Elmer will follow his lady."

Vonnie let the gate latch behind them, then led the way across the barnyard. They made a strange sight, riding ostriches in the moonlight. Soon they were loping toward an open field where she'd ridden before.

"Take it easy," Adam warned. The sheer height of the bird alone made a formidable perch.

"Okay." Grinning, she flanked the bird and set off. Elmer followed. In a few minutes the birds were running freely.

Adam shouted, but his words were lost in the wind. Once he got the feel of the bird, he relaxed and began to enjoy the ride.

The birds flew over the ground, with both riders holding tightly beneath their wings. The wind rushed by, raising Adam's spirits.

Elsie loped along at a jarring gait, passing Elmer, Elmer passing her, her passing him.

Breaking into a head-on dash, the two birds raced across the open range at breakneck speeds.

Vonnie's laughter came to him as she looked over. His masterful ease in the saddle had resurfaced.

Grinning at each other, they rode for over an hour, racing side by side over the open range.

When they finally rode the birds back into the pen, Vonnie ordered them to squat. As they dismounted, she gave each an affectionate pat, then closed and carefully latched the gate.

Adam leaned on the fence, watching her.

"Well, what do you think about my birds now?"

"I have to admit, they're not what I expected."

Her face sobered. "They're not what I expected either. Daddy always took care of them. Momma and I had little personal contact with them, but now, I realize, like people, they each have their own strengths and weaknesses."

Smiling, she looked up at him. He had never seen her looking prettier. The wind had blushed her cheeks a rosy red, and her hair had come loose, falling over her shoulders in wild disarray. He wanted to kiss her—kiss her and never stop.

"I'm actually beginning to enjoy them, and I've become quite attached to some of them. I guess that's part of the reason I refuse to sell to Sheriff Tanner. That, and he's such a worm. I'm not ready to let the birds go—maybe I never will be."

They began walking back toward the house. Moonlight drenched the farmyard, and a relaxing calm had settled over the ranch. The whirr of crickets was the only sound besides the two sets of footsteps moving in perfect rhythm.

"It's your decision," Adam said. "I can't say I'm overly fond of the birds. P. K. would like to see them go."

"He's upset about them getting out, isn't he?"

"He doesn't want the cattle spooked. You can see his point. We have a fortune in stock."

This year alone they had introduced shorthorns and Hereford bulls onto the ranch, breeding a purebred shorthorn to one hundred cows isolated in one area.

Sighing, Vonnie turned to face him. Her features were drenched in the moonlight. "Adam, I am sorry about the inconvenience they've caused. I don't know how they keep getting out. A lot of strange things have been happening lately."

"Do I have to tell you to be careful?" Should he tell her about what he thought he saw when he first rode up tonight? If he was mistaken, she would worry unnecessarily. "I mean it Vonnie. Lock your doors and be alert."

"Don't worry, I'm careful. Genaro's on night watch. And Franz is here during the day. Except for Elmer getting out this afternoon, nothing has happened for a few days. Maybe it's all just been a coincidence."

Vonnie was silhouetted against the house, and he couldn't see her face clearly. But it didn't matter. He knew her face as well as his own.

"And maybe not. Maybe someone is trying to force you out."

"I thought of that," she admitted. "And the wire incident almost convinced me of it—yet, I can't be sure . . ."

"Wire? What happened with the wire?"

"Someone has been cutting the fence, leaving sharpened ends sticking out, just enough for the birds to cut themselves. They get hurt, they get infected and sick. We've been checking the fences morning and night, but the incidents continue."

"You think someone is purposely sabotaging you?"

"Have to be. It couldn't happen by itself. I think it might be Lewis Tanner, but again I'm only speculating. No one has seen anything suspicious going on—nothing that can be traced to Tanner."

Adam wished now he had pursued the shadow that moved from the cellar. At least he would know if someone were snooping around. They'd reached Adam's horse and he stopped, turning her to face him. They gazed at each other.

"Maybe this is all too much for you to handle."

She smiled up at him. "You've been after me to get rid of the birds. Maybe you're the one causing all the trouble."

He slowly returned the smile. "Have I ever given you any trouble?"

"You've been known to," she confided, her voice barely a whisper now.

She impulsively hugged him. "I'm sorry, of course you haven't. I don't know what I would have done without your 'roundup' services lately."

The hug caught him by surprise. After the briefest moment, his arms closed around her, and they held each other.

Vonnie pulled away and stepped back, apologizing. "I'm sorry. I don't know what I was thinking—I only wanted to thank you . . . on Elmer's behalf."

Her attempt to lighten the moment was obviously contrived, but Adam graciously accepted the effort.

"Next time, I'll ride him home," he said, putting his foot in the stirrup. He hesitated. Stepping down, he took off his hat. Worrying it in his hand, he said softly, "I want you to know, Beth has set a date for the wedding."

He watched her face change. The moon ducked behind a cloud, and the glow left her eyes.

"Oh?" She swallowed. Adam watched her fight to remain detached. "When?"

"December 31."

His voice sounded flat. She gave him a wan smile. "New year, new life."

"Yes," he said. "So they say."

"I assume the divorce will be final by then?"

"Judge Henderson expects it to be over soon."

"Well, best wishes. Or is it congratulations one gives the groom? I can never remember."

"Either one I guess." Neither fit the occasion.

Placing his foot back in the saddle, he mounted. Looking down at her, he felt his insides tighten.

"Why don't you just say it?"

She chewed her lip. *Please,* he prayed, *don't let her cry.*

"Say what?"

"That I'm a despicable son of a bitch for springing Beth on you the way I did."

The words hung between them like a pall. It was the first time the idea had been said aloud, not thought, but openly conceded.

Summoning a smile, she whispered, "I don't think that at all. Beth will make you a good wife. I want nothing but happiness for you."

Pain touched his eyes briefly.

"Adam."

"Yes."

"I did love you."

Their eyes met in the moonlight. "I loved you, too, Vonnie."

"Have a happy life," she whispered.

Nodding, he reined the horse and rode off.

Vonnie was up early the next morning. Beth's dress, or rather the thought of Beth's dress, had kept her awake all night. She was being small and petty by refusing to make her friend's wedding gown.

After all, they'd known each other for years. If she couldn't have Adam, then she should have no objections to Beth having him. It wasn't fair of her to punish

Beth for something that happened between Adam and her.

Dressing quickly, Vonnie twisted her hair into a knot at the base of her neck and went to check on the birds before fixing breakfast. Franz was already at work, rewiring the fence along the back side of the pens to make sure the adult male birds couldn't push free again.

"Good morning," she called.

Franz straightened slowly, and once again she wondered if he wasn't taking on too much work. Still, she knew the small salary she'd convinced him to accept was a help to him and Audrey.

"I have a fresh cherry pie. Audrey sent it especially for you."

"Audrey makes the best cherry pie in the county," Vonnie said, accepting the tin that Franz had wrapped in a dish towel and kept beneath the seat of his buggy. "We'll have some with our lunch. Tell Audrey we love her."

"Enjoy," he said. "Now, I must finish the fence."

Carrying the pie into the kitchen, she stored it in the pie safe, then filled the coffeepot with water and set it on the stove. After stoking up the fire, she turned to the cabinet to get the container of coffee.

"Mother," she called. "Are you coming down this morning?"

Silence reigned upstairs. Cammy had not been down once this week. She had taken all her meals in her room, eating and drinking sparingly.

Jerking open the cabinet door, a scream tore its way from Vonnie's throat as the freshly severed head of an ostrich fell out, striking her in the chest.

Stumbling backward, she gasped, her screams filling the kitchen as the head bounced across the floor.

The back door flew open, and Franz ran in, his face a mask of bewilderment. "Vonnie?"

"Oh! Oh! Oh!" She stood frozen, staring at the bright splash of blood on the front of her dress.

"Ach du lieber mein Gott!" Franz swore, pushing Vonnie out of the room.

Collapsing against the wall in the hallway, Vonnie closed her eyes, her hands lying palm up in her lap. She suddenly felt faint and sick to her stomach. Dear Lord, *who* was doing this to her?

"Vonnie? What is it—Are you hurt?" Cammy called from the top of the stairs.

Realizing she couldn't let Cammy see the ostrich head, or even know about the accidents that had been happening lately, for that matter, Vonnie dropped the front of her apron so her mother wouldn't see the blood.

"A snake—" Vonnie called. "In the wood box. It startled me. Franz is taking care of it."

"Oh, my," Cammy murmured. "Your father will have to be more careful when he brings in wood. Teague? Did you hear that? There was a snake in the wood box. It scared Vonnie out of a year's growth."

"Everything is all right now," Franz said, carrying a towel with the severed head wrapped in it. "I'll dispose of it."

"Th-thank you," Vonnie managed. Her heart was beating so fast she could hardly catch her breath.

Frowning, Franz paused in the doorway. "Will you be all right?"

She wanted to cry. She wanted to scream in rage and in fear, but she wasn't capable of either at the moment.

"I don't know, Franz. I—I never expected it to go this far—"

A frown creased his brow. "Something has happened before?"

"Nothing this bad. I think someone has been putting things in the pens for the birds to pick up and choke on. I lost a couple a few weeks back. They had been out of the pens, though, so I couldn't be sure where the hardware came from. Then there's the sharp wire the birds have been rubbing against. We've had three or four serious injuries. The birds get out on a regular basis, who knows how? . . . And now . . . this."

"Who could be doing this to you?"

"I don't know, Franz. Maybe Sheriff Tanner . . . he wants me to get rid of the birds so he can sell his property. He's even offered to buy me out—for a hefty sum. But I don't want to leave—and there's Momma. This is her home, and I don't think she wants to leave. I just don't know what I'm going to do."

It was getting to be too much. The accidents, the work, the constant pressure.

"I don't know, maybe I should sell out, before it gets worse."

"You can't let Lewis Tanner scare you off your own land! It might not be Tanner at all. It could be anyone. Teague had his enemies, you know." Franz looked thoughtful. "And P. K. Baldwin was his biggest."

"I know, but it isn't just the birds, Franz. It's everything combined. If someone wants the birds gone so bad they would resort to this—" Her eyes surveyed the blood-splattered front of her dress. "—then what would they be willing to do next?"

"It's no secret that some people don't want the birds here," Franz argued. "They don't understand their nature, and anything different is something to be feared."

"You're right. I don't plan to let whoever it is drive

me off my land. And once they get that through their heads, hopefully, the sabotage will stop."

"That's my girl." Squeezing her shoulder supportively, he smiled. "You be strong, *Liebchen*. Soon things will be better. This has been a very troubling time for you."

Her spirits much lighter, Vonnie straightened. She would have to put the incident behind her.

"Thank you, Franz. I don't know what I'd do without you."

"It is my pleasure to be of service," he said, with a courtly bow. "Now, I return to my work."

With her appetite gone, Vonnie fixed a light breakfast for Cammy, then set off to Beth's house.

By the time she arrived at the Baylors', she was thinking more clearly.

"It is so good to see you," Gillian enthused, leading her toward the parlor. "Hildy and Carolyn are having tea. Won't you join them?"

"Yes, thank you."

Gillian chatted as she led the way. "I was so disappointed when Beth told me you wouldn't be able to make her wedding dress. I had so looked forward to having her wear one of your wonderful designs."

"Oh!" Beth clapped her hands together as Vonnie entered the parlor. "Can I dare hope you've decided to make the dress?"

"Yes, that's why I'm here," Vonnie announced. "I will be honored to make your dress, Beth."

"Oh, this is truly wonderful!" Carolyn exclaimed. "We were all just devastated when we thought you couldn't make the gown."

Gillian disappeared, returning with another pot of tea and fresh cinnamon rolls.

"Did you hear, Mama? Vonnie is making my dress! Oh my, the wedding is going to be absolutely perfect now.

"I want you to know that if I can help in any way I will. I don't want you to be overworked. And I'll be there any time you need me for fittings—day or night. Whatever you need, you have only to ask." She paused for a breath. "Don't even hesitate. Just say the word, I'll be there."

Beth was so anxious to please. *When* would she learn not to be so infuriatingly accommodating?

"I'm sure we'll be able to work things out," Vonnie murmured.

"How is Camilla?" Gillian asked, refreshing Carolyn's tea. "I do hope she's feeling better."

"She is in mourning," Vonnie said. "It's been difficult, keeping things from her. . . ." Vonnie paused, realizing her slip of tongue.

"Things? What things?" Hildy asked.

"Oh, just a few strange things have been happening lately. Someone loosened the fence and the ostriches got loose. Then it seems someone has been putting things in the pens for the birds to pick up. They choke easily, you know. And there's the bits of wire that have been put in the fence so the birds can hurt themselves. But the worst"—she shuddered—"took place this morning. Someone . . . put a severed ostrich head in my cabinet."

"Oh, my," Gillian whispered, grasping the teapot handle.

"My Lord," Carolyn gasped. "How awful!"

"Franz was there, and he helped me. Otherwise I don't know what I would have done. The most frightening thing is, how did someone get the head inside my house without me hearing him?"

"I'll bet it's that horrible Lewis Tanner," Hildy said. "He wants you off that land. He's telling everyone who'll listen, he plans to get rid of those birds, one way of the other."

"But do you think even he would do such a horrible thing?" Beth asked.

"Beth, we're talking about Lewis Tanner," Carolyn reminded. "He'd do *anything* to get his way. You know that!"

They did know. Everyone in the room knew, that's what bothered Vonnie.

"Or P. K." Vonnie voiced her suspicion before she thought.

A pall fell across the small parlor.

"Adam's father?" Beth asked.

"Vonnie," Carolyn said, hushed. "Surely you don't think P. K. Baldwin is doing this to you?"

Vonnie realized she'd spoken out of place.

"Not really. I suppose at this point everyone is a suspect in my mind."

Although the awkward moment passed, the allegation had put a strain on the visit.

Vonnie left shortly after, promising to get started on Beth's dress the following Monday.

Chapter 15

"Beth, dammit, slow down. What are you saying?"

Adam stopped dead in his tracks and stared at Beth in shock. He was stacking hay in the barn when he recognized the sound of his fiancée's carriage whipping down the road. He'd waited for her, then listened in mounting fury as she told him about Vonnie's experience with the ostrich's severed head that morning.

Beth smoothed her skirt and ruffled petticoats, which had been crushed from the harried buggy ride to Cabeza Del Lobo.

"Adam! It isn't necessary to swear. I said Vonnie found a—"

"I know what you said."

"Then why did you ask—"

"How did someone get into the house to plant the head in the cabinet?"

"Vonnie hasn't a clue, the poor dear. She said she locked up the night before, as usual. My goodness, I don't know what I would have done," she said, adjusting a windblown lock of hair. "I mean, to have a . . . a head fall out of the cabinet and hit you . . . and get its blood all over you . . . and on the floor! It . . . it must have been . . . perfectly awful." She shivered. "But," she continued, "Vonnie is going to make my wedding dress! That's what I wanted to tell you!"

"Was it an adult bird?"

"She didn't say. Oh, Adam," she grimaced. "How perfectly awful, to have one of your . . . pets . . . die like that. Who could do such a horrible thing?"

"The birds aren't pets, Beth. They're stock—like cattle—Vonnie's livelihood."

"Adam, she's a *seamstress*, not a cattleman. Honestly, the way you jump to her defense you'd think you had some sort of personal interest in her welfare. The birds are a nuisance, and she should get rid of them before something perfectly wretched occurs. And, by the way, she thinks your father might have something to do with all the trouble she's been having lately. He wouldn't do something that awful, would he?"

Reaching for his saddle, he threw it across his horse. His features were tight as he cinched the belt. "You'll have to excuse me, Beth, I was on my way into town."

Beth blinked in surprise. "But, Adam, I just got here."

"I'm sorry, but I have—"

"—Business, I know. Well, I thought I'd just stop by to talk about lace, now that Vonnie's agreed to make my dress. But, we can decide what kind later. I personally prefer the *peau de soie*, but if you favor the Chinese Venice, I saw this perfectly gorgeous selection in *Vogue* magazine. The technique is the same as that of the Venetian type, but the thread and designs tend to be inferior unless good thread and well-drawn patterns are used. *Then* the Chinese Venice lace is excellent!

"Isn't that wonderful? Of course, it's entirely up to you—you have only to say Chinese Venice, and Chinese Venice it is. Maybe you could come for dinner this evening?"

"I'll try," he said, distracted.

"Wonderful!"

She clapped her hands together, stood on tiptoe, and kissed him. "I'll warn mother not to serve lamb," she confided, smiling up at him. "But whatever she decides, it will be special, you can be certain of that. No lamb. I promise."

Adam smiled wanly. Something "special" meant the best dishes, silver, and another long evening with Gillian fawning over him. Sometimes he felt claustrophobic in the Baylor house. When he and Beth married, this suffocation would stop. They'd be in their own house, and Gillian would be there by invitation only.

One Sunday a month—by request only.

It was early afternoon when Adam rode into Nogales. The dusty street was nearly empty. Tossing the reins over the hitching rail, he glanced through the open door of the sheriff's office.

"Tanner."

The sheriff shifted his bulk in the wooden chair behind the desk and looked up as Adam walked in.

"You want something, Baldwin?"

Resting both palms on the desk, Adam leaned toward the sheriff.

"Get off the Taylor girl's back."

"You her keeper now?" Tanner leaned backward, resting beefy hands across his belly.

"What do you know about what's going on at the Taylor ranch?"

The sheriff got up, using the excuse of filling his coffee cup from the smoke-blackened pot on the woodstove.

"Heard the little gal's been having trouble with her birds." He chuckled. "What a shame—been meaning to get out there. Just haven't had time—"

"Stay away from the Flying Feather. Far away." The tone left no doubt of Adam's intent if the sheriff didn't obey.

Shrugging, the sheriff sipped at his mug of coffee.

"Do I make myself clear?"

The sheriff set his cup on the edge of the desk and hooked his thumbs into his belt.

"You don't run this town, Baldwin."

Adam straightened, meeting the sheriff's hostile stare.

"When you start picking on women, killing their stock, and leaving detached heads in cabinets, you're stepping over the line."

A muscle jumped in the sheriff's jaw, and his hand moved to the gun on his hip.

"Get out of here, Baldwin, before I throw you out."

Stepping closer, Adam planted his forefinger in the center of Tanner's chest.

"And if I can ever prove that you've had anything to do with what's been going on, you'll answer to me, personally."

Tanner managed a derisive snort that wasn't entirely convincing.

"If one more bird is found dead out there, I'm coming after you. *Comprende?*"

"Go to hell, Baldwin."

"Mark my words, Lewis."

Tanner's voice turned belligerent. "I've had nothing to do with what's going on at the Taylors'. All I've done is offer to buy her out."

"Remember what I said."

Adam turned and walked out.

The incidents had gone past pranks. Now they were dangerous threats.

Adam's first inclination was to go to Vonnie and convince her P. K. had nothing to do with the strange happenings at the Flying Feather, but two things stopped him. Number one, it made him mad as hell to think that *she* would think a Baldwin would stoop to terrorizing a woman. Number two, he didn't have a right to approach her about anything.

It was after four o'clock when Adam left Joey and Pat to finish doctoring cattle in the new pasture and return to the house.

Bathing quickly, he dressed and rode to Beth's, his mind still on Vonnie's problems. Who, other than Tanner, had a motive? No one. Tanner wanted to sell his land, and Vonnie's birds stood in the way of it.

From what Adam had learned by asking around, the sheriff was overextended, having taken out several loans to finance the purchase of a large tract of land near Bisbee. If he didn't sell the fifty acres next to the Flying Feather soon, he could be in deep financial trouble.

He'd also checked around and found that there was a legitimate buyer for both Tanner's land and Vonnie's. Admittedly, he was surprised to learn there was such a person. An easterner. An easterner not fond of exotic birds.

"Hello, darling!" Beth greeted Adam at the porch

steps of the Baylor house. Dismounting, he brushed a kiss across her mouth. As they stepped upon the porch, she hooked her arm through his.

"I trust all went well today?"

"Today?"

"Your business—when you went into town."

"Oh, yes. It went well."

"P. K. depends on you so much," Beth praised. "Well, as you've said, when we're married, Pat and Joey will have to take on more of the responsibility." She tucked her hand in the crook of his arm as they walked into the house. "So we can have more time together. Oh, it will be so grand, won't it? In our own home, entertaining our friends, Mother and Daddy over every Sunday for dinner! I can hardly wait."

"Adam." Leighton came to the door to greet him. "There you go, Bethie, talking the man's head off. Let him get in the house before you start bending his ear."

Adam shook hands with Leighton.

"Leighton, don't you men go pouring yourselves a drink," Gillian trilled. "Supper is nearly ready. Cordy Lou's taking the roast out of the oven right now."

"Yes, dear." With a telling glance at Adam, Leighton escorted Beth into the dining room.

The table was again set with Gillian's finest—the gold-rimmed china and see-through cups. Adam glanced at the chandelier. Was he supposed to compliment Gillian on that or the tablecloth? Better be the chandelier; the cloth this time was lace with huge doily-type napkins.

"Beautiful chandelier. Nice accent for your decor."

"Why, thank you, Adam." Gillian fairly glowed with the praise.

Adam knew Leighton was a wealthy man who indulged his wife's every whim simply because he could. Not a pretentious man, but one who enjoyed his considerable financial successes, Leighton was an entrepreneur of sorts. Always studying the eastern papers for new inventions as well as investment possibilities, Leighton was, if nothing else, an interesting man to know.

"Well, now," Gillian began, smoothing her napkin over her lap, "has Beth told you about the china pattern she's chosen?"

"No, she hasn't."

"It's a lovely pale-green vine pattern that graces the edge of the plate. The others we considered simply didn't—"

"—Work. And Mother found the most divine linen pattern to match. It was such luck," Beth said. "An Irish linen with the same pale-green pattern embroidered at the edge. And—" She laughed, clapping her hands. "—the glassware has just the faintest hint of green. Can you believe it?"

Actually he could. If one bought glassware with a hint of green, one generally got glassware with a hint of green.

"Adam, you're not eating. Isn't the roast to your liking? Cordy Lou!" Gillian called to the cook, who appeared instantly. "There's something wrong with Adam's roast—"

"No, Gillian, the roast is fine. I'm just not hungry tonight," Adam assured the cook. "The roast is delicious, Cordy Lou."

Beth interceded. "Are you sure, Adam? If you're not, Cordy Lou won't mind taking it back, will you, Cordy Lou—?"

"Wouldn't be no trouble, Mr. Baldwin. Cordy can

bring you more—no bother at all. You just say, and I'll have it here in a wink."

Dammit, the roast was fine!

"The roast is fine!" he said, louder than he intended.

A stunned silence fell over the room. Shrinking back in her chair, Beth frowned, her eyes level under drawn brows. Picking up her napkin, she cleared her throat. "The roast is just fine, Cordy Lou. You may serve the vegetables now."

"Yes, um." Cordy Lou escaped to the kitchen.

The occupants at the table ate in silence. Adam realized his outburst was uncalled for and rude. He was sorry for the show of bad manners.

"Is something wrong, dear?" Beth finally asked, her smooth forehead creased in concern. "Something hasn't happened at the ranch—"

"No, nothing's happened. I'm sorry—I'm a little tired tonight. We have some cattle down sick."

"Oh, dear, that's what it is. Adam is just overworked. That's all that's wrong," Gillian said brightly. "Here, dear, try the potatoes. They're Cordy's specialty. Actually, they're just potatoes sliced, with cream and spices, baked in the oven. They're quite tasty."

"Thank you, but it's—"

"Not a man's dish," Leighton said, pouring himself another glass of wine. "I understand, son, understand completely. More wine?"

"Leighton, you're being silly," his wife chided gently. "Of course he doesn't want more wine, he hasn't tried the potatoes yet. You must try the potatoes, dear, you simply—"

"—Must. And the salad," Beth prompted. "It's another forte of Cordy's. A lovely, lovely taste."

Adam couldn't breathe.

"Well," Beth was saying, "perhaps we could take a ride after dinner, then have dessert later?"

"Yes, I suppose—" he murmured.

"Wonderful! It's such a lovely night for a—"

"—Ride! A ride is a delightful idea, dear," Gillian enthused. "Leighton and I will wait here while you young folks"—she smiled conspiratorially at her husband—"go for a ride. We used to go for some 'long rides,' didn't we, Leighton?" She patted her husband's cheek. "Oh, Leighton, why don't you let Beth show Adam your—"

"—Surprise? Oh, yes." Beth clapped her hands. "Please, Daddy? Please?"

"Well . . . hurummpt . . . you'll take care?" Leighton cautioned.

"Of course we'll be careful, you goose!" Looping her arm through his, Beth led her father from the dining room. "Come along, Adam. You'll never believe what Daddy has bought!"

The small entourage crossed the yard toward a newly built shed. Letting go of Leighton's hand, Beth flung open the double doors as if revealing a grand surprise, then laughed in delight, as Adam's mouth dropped open.

"It's a motor car! Daddy bought it!"

"A motor car?" Adam took a step forward, peering at the strange vehicle. He'd heard such a thing existed, but he had never personally seen one.

"Aren't you surprised?" Beth enthused. "Daddy read about it in a New York newspaper. Two of Daddy's college associates, the Duryea brothers—"

"Franklin and Charles," Leighton supplied.

"—have created the first American automobile," Beth gushed. "When Daddy read about it, he wrote his friends and ordered one. And, when one was available, he had it shipped here. Isn't it fabulous? They'll soon be all the rage!"

"An automobile?" Adam repeated, still stunned. "Steam or gas powered?"

"Gasoline powered, son. Gasoline powered."

Beth smiled. "No more horses to hitch. It runs on the same kind of gasoline that Franz uses in his streetlights. Isn't it wonderful?"

"Unbelievable," Adam murmured, studying the strange-looking contraption. "Leighton, I'm surprised you—"

"—Bought it?" Leighton guessed.

"You know how Daddy adores new things, and he's always interested in investments, so he had it shipped here so he could see how it ran. He's been teaching me how to drive it. As a surprise for you. Come, I'll show you how well I've mastered it."

"Drive? You're going to drive this thing?" Adam's eyes focused warily on the hood containing the "engine."

"Fine piece of machinery, son." Leighton patted the car affectionately. "Internal combustion engine—ever hear of one?"

"No—"

"Didn't think so. Not many have, but they're out there, son, they're out there."

"Get in, Adam!" Beth ran around to the front of the car.

"Beth, I don't think—"

"—You should? Of course, you should, silly. You'll love it! Driving is much easier than riding a horse. Come on. Climb up in the seat and sit here beside me."

It seemed nothing would do but for Beth to show off

her recently acquired driving skills. With him by her side. In a mechanical device with an internal combustion engine.

Stepping into the vehicle, Adam seated himself as Beth cranked a handle at the front. Coming to his feet, he peered over to see what she was doing when he heard a spark and a small explosion.

Dropping back to the seat, he gripped the side of the open-air car.

Scrambling into the seat beside him, Beth looked over, grinning. "Hold tight, dear!"

"Beth, now you be careful, you hear?" Gillian shouted. "Oh, dear, Leighton, I'm not at all sure this is safe."

"Don't floorboard it, girl—Bethie! Let her out easy!" Leighton shouted above the roar of the engine. "Let her out eassssssy!"

The motor car shimmied, belched, then started rolling.

"Beth," Adam leaned over to make himself heard. "Are you sure you know—"

"I know how to drive it," she assured him above the racket.

Beth engaged the gears, and Adam grabbed the door as she shot out of the shed at a teeth-rattling clip.

"Beth—"

She couldn't hear him over the sound of the engine. He gripped the dashboard as Beth guided the automobile along the rough ground and wheeled it down the lane at a reckless acceleration. It soon became apparent she couldn't drive an automobile any better than she could a buggy.

"It goes ten miles an hour!" she shouted. "In England there's one that goes *fifteen* miles an hour, and one that can carry as many as fourteen people! Can you imagine?"

Adam would have answered, but at the moment Beth was negotiating the turn at the end of the drive and hit a rut, nearly tipping them over.

He grabbed the seat with both hands.

Suddenly they were whipping down the open road. Beth's cheeks were flushed, her hair falling down her back, tongue between her teeth, as they bounced along. Grasping the steering handle with both hands, she drove like the wind. The rough surface caused the vehicle to lurch and tip at precarious angles as she attempted, with only minimal success, to keep the car somewhat in the middle of the road.

A rider approached on a horse, but before Adam could caution Beth, the animal had taken off across the nearest field at a frantic speed, nearly unseating its rider.

Adam winced as fragments of words unfit for a lady's ear floated back to them, the animal and rider disappearing over a rise.

"Beth—" he tried again, then shut his eyes as the vehicle suddenly veered sharply to the left.

"Rats, rats, rats."

Adam held on. "What's wrong?"

"Trees bother me," Beth muttered. "I always think they're going to run out in front of me. Isn't that silly?" She laughed.

Adam recovered from that jolt as another came. Stomping on a pedal on the floor, she sent the vehicle lurching forward at top speed again.

The car shot across the intersection in a boil of dust.

Slamming on the brakes, she threw one arm over the seat, looking behind, and backed up full tilt.

Lurching into forward, she pointed the vehicle in the other direction and floorboarded it.

"Missed my turn," she explained.

The sun was sinking behind the large juniper in the backyard. The Flying Feather was settling down for the evening. It was that special time of night that Vonnie liked best. The day was finished, work done, the animals fed and quiet. Even the ostriches were settled early.

Stepping off the porch, Vonnie wandered toward the pens. What was she going to do with her birds? Sell, like the sheriff wanted? Or stand up to him and try to raise and sell them herself?

Linking her fingers in the fence, she leaned her face against the wire and studied the birds.

What would Teague have done? That wasn't a fair question. Teague always stood up for what he believed, even if it meant a fight.

But what did she believe was right? Staying on the ranch? Was that the right thing to do? Was it the right thing for her mother?

Cammy wasn't improving. That was clear. A letter had come today from her aunt in San Francisco, but even when she read it to Cammy, it was as if her mother didn't recognize who had written it.

Both of Cammy's older sisters lived in San Francisco, in a house that she'd once described as "princely." Teague himself had admitted that the family had money and hadn't been happy when Cammy married him. Not long after the wedding, the two sisters moved to San Francisco, expressing the hope that Cammy would soon grow weary of the "quaint" life in Nogales and join them. But she never did. She loved Teague too much. Of course, all that changed when Teague won the birds. Cammy had as many assets as her sisters.

But Teague was gone. If Vonnie sold the ostriches and the ranch, there'd be nothing to keep them here. And it was certain that she didn't want to stay in Nogales once Adam and Beth were married.

She continued to hang on the fence, staring at the birds without really seeing them.

Suddenly she had the feeling she was no longer alone. A finger of fear trickled up her spine as her gaze searched the lengthening shadows.

When Andrew stepped out of the darkness, both relief and a touch of anger washed over her.

"Andrew? Is that you?"

He stepped nearer, the rough ground exaggerating his limp.

"Sorry . . . I heard what happened this morning—" He shrugged, as if embarrassed he'd startled her.

"You shouldn't leave your cellar door open," Andrew said, catching hold of the fence.

"Oh?" She glanced over her shoulder. "I didn't realize it was open."

Strange. She clearly remembered closing it that morning after Franz finished storing the last of the canned goods.

"Keep it closed. Anything can wander in there."

"Thank you, I'll remember," she said, turning toward the house. "I was about to take a walk around the barnyard," she said. "Join me?"

It was a lovely night. The air smelled crisp and clean. They walked for awhile, talking. At times it almost seemed that Adam was walking beside her. And yet,

Andrew wasn't Adam, no matter how comfortable she felt with him.

"Tell me about the trouble this morning," Andrew said.

She told him about the severed head and its frightening implications.

"Was the rest of the animal's body found?"

"No, we could find nothing."

"That's too bad. At least that would indicate someone here at the the Flying Feather is responsible."

"I thought of that."

"How did the culprit get into the house?"

"I don't know, Andrew. The doors are locked at night."

"No one heard anything strange that morning? The animal's scream?"

"Nothing," Vonnie conceded.

"Did Tanner ask about any of this?"

"No, and I found that strange. He didn't seem concerned about details."

The hour grew late as he walked her back to the house. Andrew offered a few suggestions, but no answers.

Blue eyes, so much like Adam's, assessed her affectionately. "Be careful, Vonnie. I'd hate to think of anything happening to you."

"Thank you, Andrew."

Leaning forward, he brushed her lips. "If you feel you can leave Cammy for awhile, we'll take a carriage ride Saturday night."

"I'd like that."

He kissed her lightly again before turning away.

A few minutes later she heard the sound of hoofbeats fading away.

At times like this, it was impossible for her to believe that any Baldwin could mean her harm.

Even P. K.

CHAPTER 17

Chapter 16

"Momma, I'm going for a ride. Eugenia's here with you."

Vonnie knew that it didn't matter to Cammy whether anyone was there or not, but she didn't want her mother to come downstairs, find her gone, and not know where she went.

"You take as long as you need," Eugenia told her. "Just as long as I'm home by dinnertime. My cat gets fussy if his meals aren't on time."

"Thank you. I won't be gone long."

Saddling her mare, Vonnie rode slowly until the house faded from sight. If only she could leave her problems behind as easily.

Kicking the mare into a gallop, she let the wind blow freely through her hair. It was early, but already the heat was shimmering off the desert floor; she could see it in the distance and feel it in the relentless beat of the sun on her head and shoulders.

She rode toward the mountains, thinking it would be

cooler there, and she might find peace. How long had it been since she'd felt carefree? Months, but it seemed like years. Since her father died? Or before? Since she and Adam had married?

Suddenly the sound of hammer against wood penetrated her consciousness. Her gaze followed the sound, and she saw Adam's big bay standing stock still, a rope wrapped around the saddle horn with the other end attached to wire, stretching it taut so Adam could nail it to a post.

Had she ridden this direction without realizing it, looking for him? How shameless could she get?

Adam straightened, hooked the hammer in his back pocket, and signaled his horse to keep stretching the wire as he moved to the next post.

She'd thought he was handsome when he was seventeen, but the years had added character to his face and substance to his body. Muscles that had been lean were now heavier and mature. Where he'd once been a charming boy, now he was a charismatic man.

How could she even consider staying in Nogales once he and Beth were married? It would be impossible. Moving to San Francisco with her mother was the only answer. Her seamstress business was growing; she was known back east. With a little word-of-mouth advertising and lots of hard work, she could build an even larger clientele in California.

Adam glanced up and spotted her. Straightening, he wiped the sweat off his brow with his forearm. Planting his hands on his hips, he studied her as she rode toward him.

He'd shed his shirt, and his denims rode low on his hips. Sweat glistened on chest and arms that were molded by muscle, with rivulets running down a stomach ridged washboard lean. Light-brown hair swirled across his chest, trailing down his stomach to disappear beneath the band of his trousers.

Her mouth was suddenly as dry as the desert dust. It was unusually quiet; not even a breeze disturbed the thread of tension between them.

She wished he would say something. Anything, but just stare at her. She would say something, but she couldn't think of anything to say. His face was shadowed by the brim of his hat, and she would have liked to see his eyes.

"I, uh, was just riding."

"Yeah," he said, pushing his hat to the back of his head. "Nice day for it."

She glanced around. "Where are Pat and Joey?"

"I was riding fence alone and found a section down. Decided to put it back myself. What are you doing out here? Lost more birds?"

"No."

She started to dismount, and he stepped forward to give her a hand. His fingers were like hot brands on her skin, his touch lingering even after he'd moved back. She let the reins trail, knowing the mare would stand all day unattended.

Her knees suddenly felt like applesauce, and she blamed the condition on not riding for several days. It was a very lame excuse, she knew. It wasn't a lack of exercise causing the problem; it was Adam affecting her this way.

"Just riding?" he asked.

"Yes, I needed some time alone."

"Your mother okay?"

"The same."

They walked side by side to the shade of a small birch.

"Any more 'accidents'?"

"No. Andrew gave me a start last night, though."

He frowned. "Andrew?"

"I was out at the pens last night and he stopped by to visit."

"Again? Why?"

"I don't know . . . I think he was trying to be helpful. He said he'd heard about the trouble yesterday morning."

"The severed head?"

"Yes." She glanced sideways in surprise. "How did you know about it?"

"Beth told me." His expression was taut and derisive. "Andrew's very obliging lately."

"I appreciate his strength," she admitted.

"You're flirting with him."

"Flirting with him?" She was offended by his implication. "I've never flirted with Andrew!"

"You've been doing more than your fair share of flirting with him lately."

"I have not—Why, you're jealous!"

"Ha!" He laughed hollowly. "Jealous of you and Andrew?"

"You have no reason to be."

His eyes raked boldly over her. "You were with him the other night, weren't you?"

"Yes—not that it's any business of yours."

When the silence stretched between them, she felt compelled to say something.

"What should I do about Tanner?"

"Shoot the bastard." Turning away, he picked up his

canteen and took a long drink. Wiping off the rim, he extended it to her.

For a moment, she looked at it, acutely aware of where his mouth had just been. His eyes lazily followed her movements.

"What do you mean, what should you do about him?"

A smile curved her lips. "I'd like nothing better than to shoot him, but I'm afraid there's a law against that. Do you think I should sell to him? Or should I stay?"

He took another long drink, letting the cool water splash on his heated chest. She found her eyes drifting back to the thick cloud of moist silk covering his chest.

Running the back of his hand across his mouth, he looked at her. "What you do is your decision."

Did her future mean so little to him? Of course it did. She had no right to expect otherwise.

"I'm sorry, of course it's my problem. I'm just worried. Tanner might not be behind all the trouble; but he hates the ostriches. But if he wants to buy my land, why would he try to scare me off it? Then again, who knows? Maybe I'm on the wrong trail. It may not be Tanner causing the trouble at all. Why not Roel or Genaro, even Franz, for that matter?"

"Or P. K.?"

Looking away, she realized Beth had been gossiping again. "I shouldn't have said that."

"You shouldn't have thought it."

"Do you know for certain your father isn't doing this?"

"Now you are talking crazy."

Nearby, a small stream struggled to survive the hot weather. Now reduced to a trickle, it left a bed of gray stones worn smooth by the water flow over the years.

On a whim, Vonnie sat on the bank and let her feet dangle. In the spring, the fast-flowing stream, swollen from mountain snow runoff, would cut through the desert, causing flowers to bloom where there was now only baked earth.

How whimsical nature is, she thought, realizing her own life was much the same. Her life had been a desert for seven years.

It was time for a change, and one way that change could come was by selling the ranch and moving to California. She needed to begin life anew.

Dried grass cracked beneath Adam's step. She didn't look at him when he sat on the bank beside her, but she couldn't ignore the feel of him, the smell of him. They were only inches apart, but it might as well have been miles.

She glanced at him, intending to share her plan to move, but her breath caught. He'd taken off his hat, and his sweat-dampened hair, grown long over the summer, curled at the nape of his neck and across his forehead. He'd put on his shirt, but it hung open, reminiscent of happier times, hours when she had been free to explore the mat of light-brown hair . . . to touch her tongue to his damp skin . . .

"Thanksgiving's a week away."

"Yes—I suppose Alma will cook a large dinner?"

"She always does."

It would be the first Thanksgiving without Teague. Then, the first Christmas.

Silence stretched between them.

"There's a pond just around the bend."

The statement hung heavy between them. She knew the pond.

"Probably dried up by now," she whispered.

"No, I took a cooler in it day before yesterday." Removing his hat, he assessed the faultless sky. "Another swim wouldn't feel bad right now."

She grinned. "Do you need to cool off?"

Peeling off his boots, he pulled off his socks and shed his shirt. Following his lead, Vonnie quickly dispensed with boots and socks, then, with a guarded glance back across the mesa, unbuttoned her blouse.

Adam had already disappeared around the bend, and she could hear splashes as he went into the water.

She wasn't thinking, wouldn't think, about what she was doing. Just once more she was going to throw caution to the wind and do something completely irrational, simply because she wanted to.

Adam was already in the pond, his trousers on the bank. His hair was slicked back, gleaming in the sunlight, his smile mocking.

"Turn around," she challenged.

"Why?"

"Adam—"

With a laugh, he turned his back to her. She slid out of her riding skirt and moved slowly into the water until it reached her hips, then sank up to her chin.

"Oh, this is heavenly." She surprised herself. She never thought of herself as wanton.

"Nothing feels as good as a swim after a day in the hot sun." He treaded water a few feet away, but it was as if his gaze was a touch, and her heart danced with excitement. She remembered another time, another pond, and an hour when they had not been so careful not to touch one another.

Quite the opposite. They hadn't been able to touch each other enough in that other time and other place.

As if he read her mind, Adam purposely broke the moment by splashing water at her.

A water fight broke out that left them both laughing and breathless.

Andrew watched their actions from behind a low bush.

Jealousy pierced like a spear, and his hands clenched tightly at his side.

Just as he suspected. Something existed between Adam and Vonnie.

P. K. had sent him to look for Adam, and he'd spotted the two horses standing together, the fence mending abandoned.

Recognizing Vonnie's mare, he'd left his horse a distance away and approached the pond quietly, half sure of what he would find, knowing how it would make him feel, but with a need to face the truth.

Vonnie was in love with Adam. She always had been.

And Adam was in love with her. Any fool could see it in their eyes.

Haven't you known that all along? Yes, there really was no surprise.

Yet, the blinding revelation was agonizing.

Adam had it all: Vonnie, Beth, P. K.'s favor.

Bitterness lodged in his throat as he watched the couple frolicking in the water.

Yes, as usual, Adam had it all.

"Oh, you beast!" Vonnie splashed Adam a final time before heading for the bank. "I have work to do, even if you haven't."

"Coward," he called, following her.

"Shut your eyes," she demanded.

He laughed as if sincerely amused, but he obeyed, though it was clear that he felt it a foolish request. He had, she knew, after all, seen her in less than a wet camisole and pantaloons. Much less.

Pulling on the riding skirt, she sat down on the bank to let the sun dry her clothes.

Averting her eyes as Adam left the pool, a rosy blush colored her cheeks as she waited for him to pull on his trousers.

He knew he was being watched.

"You never used to blush when you watched me get dressed. As I recall, you enjoyed it."

She gazed at the sky, finding it impossible not to return his disarming smile. "That was a long time ago."

"Not that long." He ran both hands over his hair to press out the water, letting it trail down his body. His bronzed shoulders glistened with dampness, and his trousers were molded to his wet skin, flooding her with memories she thought she'd buried years ago.

Adam was a man who was comfortable in his skin; a man who was all man and enjoyed being a man. The kind of man that appealed to women. To her . . . and to Beth, she reminded herself.

"Don't worry about Tanner."

She glanced up. "Why not?"

"We talked, and I don't think he'll be bothering you again." He picked up his shirt with one hand.

"You talked to him?"

"He claims he isn't the one causing the trouble."

"Do you believe him?"

"No, but then there's not much I believe unless I see it for myself."

When did he become so cynical? she wondered.

"Then you do think he would have killed the bird to scare me?"

"He's capable of it." He turned to her, his face serious now. "You be careful, Vonnie. I—"

He stopped; she knew that whatever he'd planned to say was about them—and he would never complete it. He was engaged to Beth, and he would not betray her.

"Just be careful," he finished, his gaze lightly caressing her face.

Warmth flooded her, followed by the usual wave of sadness that always followed when she thought of him. He had been hers once, if only for a short time. But that short time had been enough to alter her life forever. She would never look at a man in the same way as she did him; no man would ever touch her in the same way, or as deeply.

Chapter 17

Is this the way friends treat friends? Though nothing improper had happened at the pond, Vonnie felt guilty about Beth.

She and Adam had only talked, hadn't they? Aside from the fact that they stripped nearly to the buff and swam in the pond like innocent children, nothing had happened.

But neither one had been an innocent child for quite some time.

Taking a deep breath, she closed her eyes, as if that would erase the past two hours. It didn't. When she opened them again, the ugly truth was still there: friends did not go swimming in ponds on warm afternoons with other friends' fiancés.

She still loved Adam Baldwin as surely as the sun came up each morning. Loved him more than the day they'd run off to get married. She'd tried to deny it, told herself Adam wasn't worth the pain he caused, but the love did not diminish, it only grew.

She tried to believe he was simply a part of her past. For years she'd pushed her feelings out of her mind. What brought them back so strongly now? The fact that he'd become engaged to Beth. He was going on with his life. And she should move on with her own.

After unsaddling her mare in the barn, she went to the house.

"Oh, there you are," Eugenia said, laying her crocheting aside. The house smelled of fresh-baked cherry pie. For a moment Vonnie was overcome by a feeling of déjà vu. The house seemed almost normal.

"Hildy, Mora, and Carolyn were just here. I told them I didn't know when you'd be back."

"Thank you," Vonnie murmured. Leaning over, she patted Suki.

"I put a pie in the oven. Thought Cammy might enjoy a piece later."

"Smells heavenly. Did Mother come down?"

"No." Eugenia glanced at the empty stairway. "I'm afraid not. She's resting right now."

Gathering her sewing materials, Eugenia eased into her slippers. "I'll take the pie out as I leave."

After Eugenia left, Vonnie climbed the stairs, peeked in on Cammy, then retreated to her sewing room and closed the door. Just being in her room was comforting, but it didn't take away the weight of the day.

She was thankful she'd missed the girls' visit. Hildy, Mora, and Carolyn were Beth's best friends, as well as her own. What if she had a slip of tongue with them and mentioned she'd seen Adam? They'd surely tell Beth, and everyone would be upset over nothing.

Picking up the dress she was hemming, she tried to concentrate. After a few minutes of ripping out more than she saved, the gown lay pooled in her lap, the needle exactly where she'd abandoned it.

She wasn't sure how long she sat there before she heard a wagon drive into the yard. When she went to the window to investigate, she saw that it was Franz.

He laboriously climbed down from the seat, pumped water for his team, then went into the barn. She supposed he was planning to finish sorting out a harness that hadn't been touched in years. He'd told her he could repair and oil it, and then she could sell it, get it out of the way and into the hands of someone who could use it. Besides, it would give her a few extra dollars, too, he'd said.

Lord knew she was far from destitute, but it would be a while before the estate was settled, and it never hurt to be cautious.

Besides, she wanted to pay Franz something for all he was doing for her. She planned for the proceeds from the harness to go to him. It was the least she could do, in view of all he'd done to help, and the money would be needed for Audrey's medical expenses.

Restless, she tossed the dress aside and ventured downstairs. As she entered the barn, she heard Franz softly whistling a German Christmas carol.

Letting her eyes adjust to the dim light, she saw he was polishing a harness. He had it stretched over the side of a stall, whistling as he worked.

"Hello, Franz. How are you today?"

"Ah, Vonnie," he said, glancing over his shoulder. "It is a fine day, indeed."

She wasn't sure why she'd come to the barn. Just needing someone to talk to, she supposed, and Franz was like a second father. If anyone understood love, he did.

"Audrey feeling stronger today?"

His hand momentarily rested on the harness. "My Audrey is very tired."

Sinking onto a bale of straw, Vonnie sat quietly for a moment, watching him work.

Glancing up, Franz saw the tension etched around her eyes. "Something bothering you, little one?"

"I'm sorry. Your problems make mine small in comparison."

"You have problems? A pretty little thing like you? You should be married, you know. With a house full of children."

Looking at her hands, she said softly, "That's just the problem, Franz. I love someone I can't have."

Franz rubbed the harness to a dull shine with an oily rag. "This is a sad thing, to love someone who already has a wife—"

"Oh, he's not married," she corrected him, "yet." At least not to someone else.

He looked up. "Then I do not understand your problem."

"He's not married, but he is engaged," she confessed, which admittedly was nearly as bad as being married.

Nodding, Franz went on working. "I see. Adam Baldwin."

She wondered if she were that transparent, or if he was just unusually perceptive.

"Yes, Adam Baldwin. I've loved him forever." Leaning back, she stared at the rafters piled high with hay. "Once I thought he loved me, but he doesn't anymore." Sighing, she stuck a piece of straw into her mouth.

"I was so naïve. I thought we'd love each other forever, that P. K. and my father would solve their differences, whatever they were. P. K. would accept the fact that Adam and I were in love, and Teague would give us his blessing. But now Daddy's gone, and Adam is going to marry Beth Baylor on the 31 of December." She drew a deep breath, blinking against the tears suddenly burning her eyes.

"Love is a difficult thing," Franz consoled.

"Lewis Tanner wants to buy the ranch. I can sell the ostriches, and my immediate problems will be over. Mother's sisters want her to come to San Francisco to live with them, and maybe that's what she should do. I just don't know—"

"Making a decision too quickly can be a bad thing," Franz cautioned. "Too many times we live to regret it."

She loved Franz's quiet way, his precise way of speaking in that heavy German accent that had not softened over the years.

"What would you do, Franz?"

His voice was kind. "Ah, *Liebchen*, I cannot tell you what to do. I, too, have a great many worries."

"I know. Audrey's illness has been terribly hard on you." She felt small for bending his ear on her trivial problems.

"Sadly, there is nothing we can do for Audrey. You have been good friends to her." He let the harness hang while he added more oil to the cloth. "But perhaps there is something I can do for you. Advice, for whatever it is worth."

"I always value your advice. What would you do?"

"They are only my thoughts—"

"Please, Franz."

"Your father worked hard to build this ranch. I would not sell it. And I would not sell the birds. That, too, was your father's dream. He was a good man."

"Yes, he was," she said thoughtfully.

"But perhaps a change would be good for your mother. This is a place that . . . has many memories for her. Perhaps too many memories."

"Yes, maybe I am being selfish—Judge Henderson thinks the move might be good for her. I only thought staying here would be more comfortable for her."

"For some it would be this way. But for Cammy, perhaps a new place, without the memories, would be better for her. For a time."

"Then you think I should accept Aunt Josie's invitation to live with them in San Francisco?"

"At least for a very long visit," he said. "Cammy would be near to those who love her. I know my Audrey would like that, if she had family left. Perhaps the wound could then begin to heal."

"I think you're right," Vonnie murmured. "But there's the ranch to see about, and Momma can't make that trip by herself."

"I will stay here at the ranch, see that the ostriches are cared for until she is settled."

"I could be gone for some time," she said.

"I will bring Audrey with me, if that is all right with you. The change might do her good, like your mother."

"That's a lot of work for you, Franz. I couldn't expect—"

"I am an old man, but not helpless," he reminded her gently. "Besides, Roel and Genaro are here to help."

Vonnie's face became sober. "I know. I just didn't want to impose on your goodness, Franz. You've done so much for me already."

"Then you will allow me to help you?"

"I—Let me think about it, Franz. I'll talk to Mother and see how she feels about visiting Aunt Josie and Aunt Judith."

"And if she will go?"

"Then, perhaps I'll take her there."

Franz returned to cleaning the harness, and Vonnie stared out at the ostrich pens, her mind no more settled as to what she should do than before. What Franz said made sense. If she stayed, more than likely there was nothing but heartache ahead.

The birds were strutting around the pens, occasionally pecking at the ground. They were drumming now, males and females trying to attract one another in preparation for egg-laying season. Her father had enjoyed the process of choosing the best birds, pairing them, planning for the laying, and then the hatch.

They'd been through numerous hatchings and care of the new babies, and while it had been a tedious process—making sure newborn legs didn't bow, carefully measuring their feed—Teague had reveled in it. She smiled, remembering his joy at having 50 percent of the little hatchlings survive. A very good percentage, he'd boasted, especially for a first hatch.

"My father loved this ranch," she said, half to herself. "I feel like I'd betray him by selling."

"You will decide what is best."

"My father was a fighter, wasn't he?"

"That he was," Franz agreed.

"He would stay and fight."

Franz continued cleaning the harness, softly humming as he worked the oil into the dry leather.

"But if I lost Momma, too—"

Suddenly the answer was crystal clear to her. If the move would restore her mother to her former self, that would be Teague's wish.

"Thank you, Franz."

"You have decided what you will do?"

"Not entirely. But with Daddy gone, Momma not herself, Adam getting married, what is here for me?"

"Then you will sell?"

"I think it's my only choice." She patted the old man's arm. "Thank you, again. Give Audrey my love."

Judge Henderson settled himself more deeply into his favorite chair and sipped his drink, watching Adam stare out the window at the deepening twilight.

"What did you find out?"

The judge stared into his glass. "Lewis Tanner has a serious buyer. Spoke to him about it just this morning. He had a question on the title, so it was easy to find out who the prospective buyer is. A speculator from back east. Money. Plans to move out here for the health of a daughter with breathing problems. People are doing that more and more lately."

"So, Tanner was telling the truth."

"And it seems he told the truth about wanting Vonnie's ranch, too. His buyer is willing to pay her whatever it takes to get the land."

"But it wouldn't be beyond Lewis to threaten her, to frighten her into selling out to him?"

"Ordinarily, I'd say no, but in this instance, I can't be sure. From what Tanner tells me, he won't be making a penny on Vonnie's land. It's just a bonus for his buyer. His land is sold, providing the buyer comes to terms with the ostriches being there. And, from what I hear, they're not a lot of trouble."

Adam snorted. "Not trouble? I suppose that's a matter of opinion. They've been out enough lately."

"How did they get out?"

"Someone sabotaged the pens."

"Then, if someone stopped harassing Vonnie, there'd be no problem."

"I don't know." Stepping away from the window, Adam poured a glass of brandy. "Something is always going wrong over there. Frankly, I'm puzzled by what's happening."

"I heard about the latest incident," the judge said. "The severed head falling out of the cabinet. What a cruel, hateful thing for someone to do."

"I can't imagine how it was accomplished. Killing the bird without creating a disturbance, then getting into the house. Who, other than Tanner, wants to see Vonnie gone? And why? If Tanner has a buyer for his land and Vonnie's, or for his alone, then he has no motive."

"Teague had no enemies?"

"I'm sure he did—doesn't every man?"

"He and your father didn't get along," the judge suggested.

"P. K.'s a thorny old goat, but he wouldn't sink to this low, even if he had a motive, which he doesn't."

P. K.'s earlier conversation about the war came back to him. His father hated Teague enough to hurt him, but he would never seek bitterness and revenge on Teague's daughter.

"P. K. and Teague didn't care for each other and that's the bottom line. P. K. wouldn't go out of his way to create trouble for Teague, he just wouldn't go to any effort to help him out. Teague's gone. Past forgotten."

"Well, you don't have to remind me what P. K.'s like," the judge grunted. "Don't know how you've put up with him all these years."

"I know him better than anyone," Adam said. "Hard, unyielding, unforgiving, but evenhanded and fair. He's never dealt under the table, you know that."

"Then who is doing this to Vonnie?"

"I don't know," Adam said, going back to stand at the window. The thought was keeping him up nights. "I don't know. But I mean to find out."

Chapter 18

Vonnie cut the thread and pushed the needle into a pincushion before shaking out the dress she'd just finished hemming.

"One more completed," she said aloud, her elation only slightly diminished by the knowledge she had one more to go.

A knock at the front door set her gaze to the clock on the wall.

"Three o'clock already?" she murmured.

Time had gotten away from her again. Quickly hanging up the finished gown, she ran quickly downstairs to answer the door.

"Beth." Vonnie smiled. "I'm sorry, I lost all track of time—"

"That's all right," Beth said, stepping inside. "I'm a little early, by at least two minutes, and besides, I know you've got loads of work and I so appreciate your making time to fuss with me."

"I have the basic dress basted together," Vonnie said,

leading Beth into her sewing room. "I'll show you how I see it coming along. Of course, at this stage, Nell, Susan, and I can make any changes you'd like—"

"I'm sure I'll not want to change a thing," Beth chirped. "I can hardly wait to see it!"

Vonnie spread three versions of the same design across her drawing table.

"You see how this neckline goes here? I've seen you wear it before and it's very attractive. Of course, the lace here creates a very lovely line, softer, very feminine. And, with that, I thought the sleeve with a point over the wrist with the lace trim just peeking over the edge. The same lace will cover the front of the skirt and—"

"I love it," Beth exclaimed. "It's . . . beautiful." She clapped her hands together in delight. "It's perfect. Adam will love it, too." She picked up the drawing. "He's very involved in all the decisions, you know—china designs, napkins, even the lace. I think he prefers Chinese Venice, but we'll try and sneak the *peau de soie* past him—but, oh—he can't see this, can he? Before the wedding?"

"I think tradition says no," Vonnie said, wishing again that she didn't have to sew this particular wedding dress.

Her gaze avoided the small diamond engagement ring on the third finger of Beth's left hand. Adam's token symbol of a contract undertaken for life.

"Mother's leaning toward attendants' dresses in the same design as mine. Would that work? Could we get lace to match rose? Of course, we've got time to order it from back east—but not much."

"Ummh, yes, I know. December 31 isn't that far away."

Beth glanced up. "Did I tell you the date?"

Realizing the slip, Vonnie smiled. "You must have. That is the date, isn't it?"

"Yes ... I just don't remember telling you. Perhaps Adam mentioned it. Oh well, it doesn't matter. It is the 31 of December, and Mother and I decided the men's suits would be dark rose, with boiled white shirts. Father had a fit, and Adam simply refused to go along with the choice of color, saying the suits would be dark gray. How drab."

"I want Mama to see the drawing for my dress, but we're so busy there's hardly been time to even have Adam for supper. Wedding parties, you know? So fun, but *so* many." She laughed. "There's Thanksgiving coming up, then the Carltons' party, then the Bakers' the first of the month—oh, dear, I'm going to be exhausted by the time the big day arrives. But December is the *perfect* month to wed. You know the old saying, 'When December's snow's fall fast, marry and true love will last.'

"And Carolyn is having a tea for me, girls only, of course, a week from Saturday. You'll be there?"

Vonnie put the sketches away in a drawer, wasting as much time as possible to avoid facing Beth.

"I don't know," she began.

"Oh?" Beth's mouth formed a pout. "I know you're busy, but surely you can make time for my party. We'll have *such* fun."

"I haven't mentioned it, but I may be selling the ranch and moving Mother to San Francisco. Her sisters live there and would like to have her come be with them. I think the change will do her good."

"Moving," Beth protested. "When?"

"I don't know—soon, I think."

"But you'll miss the wedding. I don't know what I'll do without my very best friends there to be happy with me. Tell me you'll be there," she pleaded. Catching her hand, she held it. "Please?"

"I don't know, Beth—I'll try. Sheriff Tanner has a buyer for the ranch. I suppose it will depend on how soon they want possession."

"Ooooh, I'm disappointed, but I understand," Beth said, cooperative as always.

She lay a hand on Vonnie's arm, giving her a comforting squeeze. "We'll miss you so much. Life here won't be the same without my four best friends."

"I'll miss you, too," Vonnie said, and sincerely meant it. Beth, Hildy, Mora, and Carolyn had been her friends as long as she could remember.

She'd miss everything here. Her friends, the town, her comfortable life. Starting a new life and a new business wouldn't be easy. But it would be easier than staying here and seeing Beth and Adam together. Watching them move into a home, start a family. Her heart ached for the dreams she'd cherished that would never come true now. She wanted to crawl into a corner and hide.

Beth was still gushing about her dress and the wedding, and Vonnie felt she owed it to her to at least listen. After thirty minutes, Beth finally changed the subject.

"Did I tell you Daddy bought an automobile?"

"Really?" Vonnie asked.

"I took Adam for a ride the other night. My, how he enjoyed himself—I think we'll probably be buying an automobile, once we're married."

"That's nice." Vonnie had never seen an automobile, but she did see a picture of one in a magazine once.

It seemed forever before the visit was over. As Beth's

buggy finally rattled out of the yard, Vonnie went to the kitchen to have a cup of tea, hoping it would help relieve the headache that started at the nape of her neck and seemed to be getting more intense by the moment.

She took a steaming cup to Cammy, tried to persuade her mother to come downstairs for a while, then gave up. Cammy was content to stay in her room with the photograph album, believing that Teague would be coming home any moment now.

Sometimes it seemed Cammy thought Teague was still at war. Other times she seemed to know that the war was over and Teague had survived, but believed that he was in town, or on an errand, and would be home shortly. Sitting down at the kitchen table, Vonnie kneaded her temples, wishing things were different. Shoving her half-empty teacup aside, she got up. Things weren't different. She had to move on with her life.

Hoping fresh air would help her headache, Vonnie decided to take the carriage into town. She asked Roel to keep an ear out for Cammy since he was doing repair work on the front porch.

"I'm sure she will sleep the rest of the afternoon, but if she should call for me, please look in on her."

"*Sí, señorita*. Do not worry. I'll be right here until it gets too dark to work."

Vonnie planned to look at some new threads and buttons; anything to take her mind off Adam and Beth.

The streets of Nogales were busy. Just seeing people going about their everyday lives made her feel better.

Guiding the horses to the hitching rail in front of the mercantile, Vonnie climbed down and wrapped the holding rein around the post.

Shaking the wrinkles out of her skirt, she stepped

onto the sidewalk, only to come hard up against someone.

"Oh, I'm sorry," she said automatically. Her eyes
raised when strong hands steadied her.

"Where's the fire?"

"Adam? Buttons," she stammered. "Ran out an hour
ago."

"Had to come into town for feed," he said at the
same time.

He was still holding her arms; her hand still rested on
his chest. She noticed there was a button missing on his
shirt and almost mentioned it, stopping herself just in
time. Beth would be sewing his buttons, not her.

"I . . . must be going," she managed.

"Yeah . . . me too."

His hands left her arms, and she suddenly felt a
shiver move over her, like a cold breeze on her skin.

Tipping his hat, he said quietly. "It'll be dark soon.
Ladies shouldn't be out after dark."

She made herself turn away and go inside the
mercantile.

"Hello there, Miss Vonnie. Haven't seen you in several days," Mr. Beasley called out from the rear of the
store. "Something you need?"

"I just want to look around a bit," she said, longing
to lose herself in the bolts of cloth and ribbons.

"Take your time. I'll just finish filling Adam's order.
If you need anything, just sing out."

"Thank you." Adam's order. Was she hexed?

She walked among the ready-made dresses, forcing
interest in material and design, knowing those in the
catalogs she got from back east were much more recent
than Mr. Beasley's.

"Garrett?"

Adam's voice coming from the front door caught her by surprise.

"Yes?"

She peeked out at him from behind the tables stacked with bolts of calico and cottons.

"The wheel on Vonnie's buggy is loose. You got a bolt about four inches long?"

"I may have," the storekeeper said. "Let me see what's back here."

"Oh, dear," she murmured, realizing that it was too late for the livery to repair it for her.

"Can you fix it?" Vonnie called, keeping a safe distance.

"Well enough for you to get home. Then Genaro or Roel will have to take it off and fix it right. The axle may need to be replaced."

"Here," Mr. Beasley called out. "Will this work?"

Adam examined the bolt the storekeeper handed him.

"That should do it. Do you have a piece of heavy wire? About two feet long?"

"I have that."

"Vonnie, it'll take about fifteen minutes," Adam called.

"Can I help?"

"No," he said, closing the door.

She browsed a few moments longer before wandering outside. Adam was shedding his shirt, laying it over the hitching rail.

As he bent to look closely at the tilting wheel, she picked up the shirt and automatically examined it. Two buttons were missing.

"Will this do?"

Mr. Beasley came out of the store and handed Adam a length of heavy wire.

"That will work," he said, then thanked him.

The storekeeper turned to Vonnie.

"Did you see anything you wanted?"

"Yes, I did," she said, taking Adam's shirt inside the store with her.

Ten minutes later she'd purchased and sewn two buttons on his shirt and tightened the others. When she returned outside, Adam was finishing resetting the wheel, sliding in the temporary bolt and wiring it into place.

"That should do it," he told her. He stood back to survey the wheel. "It will hold until you get home, if you don't drive like a crazy woman."

"When have I ever driven like a crazy woman?" she asked.

"Sorry, Beth drives like one, so I guess I think all women do."

Vonnie laughed in spite of herself. She had ridden with Beth; she could put gray hair on one's head.

"You've taken a ride in Leighton's new automobile?"

He looked up, and she quickly looked the other way. The blue of his eyes always caught her by surprise.

"How did you guess?"

He leaned on the hitching post, smiling.

"I've seen her drive. I wouldn't put my life in her hands in a buggy, let alone an automobile."

"I couldn't get out of it," he admitted.

"Well." She realized she was taking up too much of his time. "Thank you for noticing the wheel was loose."

"Have one of the men check all of them."

"I will, I will." He was beginning to sound like Beth.

She felt his hand on her waist as he helped her aboard.

"By the way, I fixed your shirt," she said.

A soft smile curved his lips. "I appreciate that."

"I thought you would." Smiling, she picked up the reins. A woman liked to do things for her man—or so she'd heard.

"Alma noticed the missing buttons this morning, but she was busy and I was in a hurry."

"I don't mind. Besides, I had nothing better to do." She added, "Maybe Alma could use some help." Keeping up with three men took time and effort.

"You know P. K. wouldn't have anyone new in the house."

She wanted to ask—oh, she wanted to ask, but she didn't dare. After all, it wasn't any of her business. Still—

"How does he feel about Beth?"

Adam picked up his newly mended shirt and slipped it on. He buttoned it slowly, taking his time before answering.

"He likes her."

"Beth is a special girl," Vonnie admitted.

"Yes, she is," he said, his gaze never leaving hers.

"Well, I'd better be on my way. Ladies shouldn't be out after dark."

"Evening, Miss Vonnie, Adam."

Adam and Vonnie looked up to see Franz setting his stool beneath one of the lampposts. Without them realizing it, evening had approached, and Franz had begun his rounds.

"I didn't realize it *was* so late," Vonnie said.

"I started my rounds early," Franz said, picking up his stool again. "Audrey is worse today, and I wanted to be home with her this evening."

"I'm so sorry—can we help in some way?" Vonnie asked.

"No. I wish you could," he said sadly.

Moving on to the next lamp, Franz slowly worked his way down the street in the twilight.

"I'd better go," she said.

"I'll see you around."

"Yeah, see you around."

Vonnie slapped the reins against the horses, and the buggy rolled off.

Chapter 19

Thanksgiving came and went. There was no pretense of celebration in the Taylor household. Vonnie fixed a solitary dinner and ate alone in the big kitchen that once housed so much love and laughter.

By the first week of December, she was dreading the approaching holidays, for more reasons than one.

"Have another butter cookie," Carolyn said, pushing the china plate toward Hildy.

"I shouldn't," Hildy said, "but I will."

Beth, Mora, and Vonnie laughed, knowing Hildy's weakness for lemon butter cookies.

Vonnie had seen no way to refuse the invitation to have lunch at Carolyn's. If she sold the ranch, there wouldn't be that many more opportunities for the five girls to be together.

"So," Hildy said, "the wedding plans are moving along?"

"I think so," Beth said, "though I haven't made a

final decision on the flowers. Too much white on the altar will make it look like a funeral bier—"

It might as well be, Vonnie thought. *Mine.*

"But you don't want *too* many colors," Carolyn said. "That works for a spring wedding, but not for a winter one. I think it's so romantic to have a wedding on the last day of the year. Starting a new year together, a new life—"

Taking her teacup with her, Vonnie stood and wandered about. This room was her personal favorite. She and her parents had spent many a pleasant evening together with the Hendersons before the fire. She loved the paintings the judge collected, the rich colors in the wallpaper and matching draperies. She stopped at the Steinway and rubbed her hand against the mellow grain of the polished wood.

"What are you doing, Vonnie?" Carolyn asked. "You don't have an urge to learn to play the piano, do you?"

"No," she said, smiling. "But you know what I'd do if I were rich?"

"Oh," Hildy laughed, "a new game. What would I do if I were rich? What would you do, Carolyn?"

"I'd go on a cruise to Europe and stay for a year."

"You've never done anything for that long," Hildy teased, picking up the newest edition of *Cosmopolitan.* They all knew how often Carolyn changed her mind about hobbies and especially about men.

"How about you, Beth? If you had a million dollars, what would you do?"

"I'd build a house on a hill on the Baldwin land and fill it with all kinds of furniture and fine things."

"Oh, you're no fun," Hildy chided. "That's what you're going to do anyway. What about you, Vonnie? What *would* you do?"

"I'd buy this piano for Audrey and give it back to her."

This silenced the group.

"Oh, look here," Hildy cried, pointing to a picture in the magazine. "Just look at this. Isn't he the most handsome man? Wouldn't I love to go on a cruise with him!"

The other four laughed.

"A new game!" Beth said. "Who would you most like to be stranded with on a deserted island?"

"I'd choose . . . Henry Walters," Carolyn said immediately. "He could pay for any cruise I wanted."

"Who's Henry Walters?" Beth asked. "He doesn't live around here, does he?"

"You goose, you've not looked at anybody but Adam this whole year. Henry Walters is a wealthy Baltimore-born railroad magnate. His father, William Thompson Walters, is an old friend of Daddy's. He made a fortune in railroads. In fact, it was Henry who got Daddy interested in buying art. Henry first became interested in art, Daddy said, when he lived in Paris with his father."

"Paris," the others echoed.

"Uh huh. He returned to America eons ago and graduated from Georgetown, holds a bachelor of science degree from the Lawrence Scientific School of Harvard University," Carolyn related.

"Then he's got to be practically decrepit," Hildy pointed out.

"He *is* scandalously older than us," Carolyn said, "but he's well on his way to becoming one of the richest men in the South. He makes buying trips to Europe where he acquires paintings, prints, sculpture, jewelry, textiles, watches. Well, look at this." She pointed to the gold lapel watch she wore. "Henry sent it to me for Christmas last year. He also buys illuminated manuscripts—"

"What's that?" Beth asked.

"Illustrations of the gospels and other religious books. Things from the fifth century. I recently read that he's just acquired an exquisite set produced by Irish and Northumbrian monasteries. And," she emphasized, "he's creating a very large art library. Wouldn't he be the most interesting man to be alone with on a deserted island? The things he's seen and done—"

"How on earth would *you* carry on a conversation with him?" Hildy asked incredulously, and the others laughed.

"Hildy, who would you choose to be lost with on a deserted island?"

"Well," Hildy said, setting aside her teacup. "My first choice is . . . Joey Baldwin."

"Joey? What would you have to talk about?" Carolyn demanded. "All he knows about is cows!"

"Who said we'd be talking?" Hildy winked.

Drawing her legs up beneath her, Mora sighed. "Andrew would be the Baldwin I'd choose. Good-looking, intelligent . . . the serious type."

"What about his . . . you know . . . ?"

"Limp?"

"Well, I don't mean to sound cruel, he just seems so aware of it all the time. Would he ever let anyone forget about it?"

"Andrew's limp doesn't bother me in the least. He has too many other attractive qualities to worry about a slight limp."

"Adam knows about more things than cows," Beth defended.

Vonnie had to agree, though silently. If Andrew were

anything like Adam, he would be an excellent choice to share a deserted island with.

"Choose somebody else. Somebody we don't already know you've got a crush on," Carolyn demanded.

"Well, then, John L. Sullivan!"

"John L. Sullivan! The fighter?"

"Heavyweight boxing champion of the world at one time," Hildy amended.

"He's a brawler!"

"I thought he lost that title several years ago."

"Nobody's perfect, Mora."

"He beat Paddy Ryan in a fair fight, a *bare*-knuckle match, to take the title."

"But he *fights* for a living!" Carolyn exclaimed.

"Not that much anymore," Hildy defended. "He's a popular hero. He's mingled with dignitaries in America and Europe. He'd be fun to be with, and he could protect me."

"Why, he must be at least forty by now!"

"So? I find older men interesting."

"A man's age doesn't make any difference if he's stimulating," Vonnie said, defending Hildy's choice. "Who would you choose, Beth?"

They all knew who she'd choose, and they weren't mistaken.

"Adam, of course. He's handsome, intelligent, very protective, loyal, and good, and he'd fight to the death for me."

"Well," Carolyn said, "that about covers it. How about you, Vonnie?"

Vonnie would have chosen Adam, for all the same reasons Beth named. But of course she could never admit it.

But she said instead, "A writer. Rudyard Kipling."

"I've heard of him," Beth said. "How old is he? What's he written?"

"He's barely thirty—"

"Young enough," Hildy reminded Carolyn.

"He's British—"

"Cultured," Carolyn reminded Hildy.

"And he's written a book called *Plain Tales from the Hills* that I enjoyed very much."

"Intelligent, young, and cultured," Carolyn added. "An admirable combination. Is he good-looking?"

"I think so."

"John L. Sullivan's good-looking," Hildy inserted. "Heavily muscled, and an impressive mustache."

"Oh, Hildy, if he had the brains of an ant you'd be impressed as long as he *looked* good. I have seen pictures of him."

"And he's handsome."

"So-so."

"Well," Hildy defended, "you do have to look at the man you spend time with, don't you?"

"And you have to talk with them sporadically," Carolyn argued back.

"It's hard to find a good-looking man with brains," Hildy commented, sipping her freshened cup of tea. "But if I had to choose, it'd be looks every time."

If she chose Adam, Vonnie thought, *there'd be no compromise to make.* As Beth had said, handsome, intelligent, protective, and loyal to a fault.

Adam sat lost in thought in front of the fireplace, staring at the flickering flames. What had he gotten himself into? Marriage? To Beth Baylor? Could he actually go through with it?

Beth was a pretty girl, but he didn't love her. He'd

tried to tell himself he was over Vonnie, but that was a lie. He realized that now. What a fool he'd been.

Ever since Vonnie happened on him Thursday morning, he'd known that he couldn't marry Beth. She'd drive him crazy in less than a month. He dreaded even the few hours they were together each week.

Beth and Gillian were so much alike. The whole damned family was alike. They never let anyone finish a sentence.

And that crazy automobile. Beth could drive him nuts, slamming to a stop at every tree, jolting around corners, lurching into ruts. She would probably want one of those contraptions after they got married. Well, she could just want; he wasn't buying one.

She fussed over him. Fussed until he thought he'd go mad. Did he want this, did he want that, was everything all right? Did the woman never have an opinion of her own?

He'd never catch Vonnie without her own opinion, and she wasn't afraid to voice it. At every opportunity.

Vonnie. Being with her was like drinking from a cool well on a hot day. She was bullheaded, but so was he. Merely thinking about the arguments they'd had and the making up that followed aroused him.

He kicked a log and sent sparks spiraling up the chimney.

And then there was Andrew. What was going on there? Was Vonnie attracted to Andrew? What if Vonnie and Andrew were drawn to each other? What if they happened to marry? How would he live with that? Vonnie as his sister-in-law while he was married to a woman he didn't love? Family dinners. Holidays. Hell.

Sinking deeper into his chair, he stared morosely at the fire.

* * *

He was in the barn shoeing a horse when Andrew found him the next morning.

"I noticed your black was favoring his left front foot yesterday. Have you checked the shoe lately?" Adam said, pumping the bellows and holding the iron shoe he was shaping in the coals.

"No," Andrew said. "But I will, if you're in the mood to replace it."

"Bring him over and we'll see if that's what he needs. Could be he has a stone bruise."

"Could be a bruise," Andrew said. "I was out in the north section the other morning, by the stream that cuts through the west corner." Aloofness showed on his face.

Recognizing the location as the pond he and Vonnie swam in, Adam stilled, his expression turning serious.

"Were you, now?"

"Saw you and Vonnie there." Andrew's gaze met Adam's and held.

Straightening, Adam let the tongs hang loosely in his hand as he waited for Andrew to go on.

"Thought you were engaged to Beth."

"I am."

Adam hated saying it, wished suddenly that it wasn't so. Andrew took a step toward him, his hands balled in fists at his side.

"You two-timing, womanizing, cheat—"

Before he could finish, Andrew threw himself at Adam's middle. The breath exploded from him, and he staggered back against the side of the barn, cracking his head.

Reflex brought both arms up to break Andrew's hold on him. Andrew fell back, caught himself on a post in the middle of the blacksmith shed, and came up swinging, catching Adam squarely on the cheekbone beneath his left eye.

Lunging at him, Andrew swung, but Adam dodged the blow. When Andrew swung again, Adam gave up trying to avoid a fight and countered with a hard right, connecting solidly with Andrew's jaw.

In the next instant, they were both rolling around on the floor, straw flying in all directions, some blows connecting, others meeting only air. When they both finally came to their senses, they each had bloodied noses and Andrew's shirt was half torn off.

They stood, breathing hard, glaring at one another, knowing the physical blows were finished but still raging inside.

"What the hell's the matter with you?" Adam demanded.

"You have no right to be with Vonnie when you're engaged to Beth!" Andrew shouted.

"What's between Vonnie and me, or between Beth and me, is none of your damned business!"

"You don't care about Vonnie. You're just going to hurt her."

"It's none of your business," Adam repeated.

"Beth deserves to know what kind of man you are."

Adam studied his brother, filled with angry humiliation. "You thinking of taking care of that?"

"I might."

Adam knew better than to create any kind of challenge situation with Andrew. The last thing he needed was for his brother to tell Beth that he'd been with Vonnie. They hadn't done anything. Andrew knew the truth if he'd really spied on them. But it wouldn't make any difference to Beth. She'd be hurt and feel betrayed by both her friend and her fiancé.

Picking up his jacket, Adam headed for the house, his work forgotten. Washing off at the pump, he dried with his shirt before going into the house. Bathing in his room later, he examined his face in the mirror over the washstand. There was a deep cut on his cheek, a lump on the point of his chin, and by morning he'd have a glorious shiner.

"Women," he muttered.

"Boys, dinner is ready," Alma called up the stairs.

Finishing his wash, Adam changed into clean trousers and shirt, then went down to face P. K.

Andrew looked even worse than he did, Adam decided. His lip was split, his cheek was bruised, and his eye was already beginning to darken.

P. K. shook out his napkin as Alma bustled around setting dishes on the table.

"What did you boys do today?" she asked.

"Looks like they met up with a wildcat," Pat said, laughing at his brothers.

"Yeah," Joey said. "Must have been a big one. Cat step on your toe?"

"Pass the tortillas," Adam ordered.

"Well, what was it about?" Pat pressed.

"Looks to me like someone I know forgot they were grown men," Alma sniffed.

"I stepped on a rake," Andrew murmured.

"And you?" she nudged Adam.

"Broke through a rotten board in the hay loft."

"Uh huh," Alma said. "Fell through on your face? I was not born yesterday, Adam Baldwin. Your mother would be ashamed, the way you lie. It is no matter if you two want to act like fools. Some people have better sense. Vonnie Taylor for one."

"Vonnie Taylor?" Pat asked, reaching for another tortilla to scoop up his refried beans.

"I hear she is selling the ranch and moving to San Francisco. Her mother has sisters there, you know."

"She's selling the Flying Feather?" Joey asked.

"*Sí,* to Sheriff Tanner. He has an offer for his ranch and, I am told, he will buy Vonnie's place also."

"Is she seriously considering it?"

Adam noticed that P. K. was ignoring the whole conversation, concentrating on his plate.

"It is rumored she is," Alma said, pouring fresh coffee for all the men. "If you want to know what I think—"

"That's enough," P. K. said quietly.

Recognizing P. K.'s tone as meaning business, Alma sniffed in irritation and waddled her way back into the kitchen.

Chapter 20

Adam was in a bad mood by the time he reached Beth's that evening. To top everything else off, his eye throbbed like hell.

"Oh, my goodness!" Beth exclaimed when she opened the door and saw him. "What happened to you?"

"A little accident."

"A little accident! Goodness me, it's more than that. Mother, come see what's happened to Adam!"

"It's nothing," he assured her.

"Adam!" Gillian exclaimed. "You poor thing! Come sit down, and I'll get a piece of steak to put on it. Corrrdy Loouuu, bring a piece of steak for Adam's eye!"

"It's nothing," Adam repeated. "You don't need to fuss."

Beth tried to lead him inside. "You poor dear, would you like something to drink? Of course you do. Corrrdy

269

Loouuu, bring Adam a cool drink when you bring the beef!"

"No, I just—"

"—Want me to stop fussing over you. But your poor eye—and Cordy Lou has made some delicious lemonade."

"Fine." Adam said. "Bring me the damned lemonade."

Gillian discreetly left the two lovebirds alone as they settled into the porch swing. The sun had gone down, bathing the air with a purple haze.

"Really, Adam, what happened to your eye? It looks as though you've been in a common brawl."

"I fell through a loose board in the loft."

"Fell!" Her hands flew up to cover her mouth, and he found himself hoping it was permanent.

"I wasn't hurt."

"Thank goodness. I saw my dress today," Beth said, turning toward him. "It's going to be simply beautiful."

He started to reply but didn't. It didn't matter. Beth went on.

"And I think we've decided to make the attendants' dresses a simpler version of mine—Vonnie really does such beautiful work—except they won't be ecru white, mind you, I don't want you to get your hopes up and be disappointed. They'll be rose, of course, but they'll look nice."

Adam nodded, his gaze pinned on the horizon. He'd be moving cattle tomorrow, and his ribs were going to hurt like hell. It didn't matter. He wouldn't be able to see out of one eye.

"—and the men's suits will all match. Adam, you're not paying the least bit of attention to me."

"I'm listening," he said automatically, not remembering a single thing she said.

"Well, I forgive you," Beth said, taking his arm. "Let's take a carriage ride. I'll drive."

"I don't think so, Beth. I'm tired tonight."

"Oh, let's do. It'll be so pleasant. You can relax—"

"Beth, I do not relax while you're driving."

She pouted prettily. "Are you saying I'm a bad driver?"

He got to his feet suddenly, leaving her swinging crazily in the swing. She blinked in surprise.

"I'm saying you drive like a maniac!"

"You're shouting at me." She sniffed.

"Beth—"

"You're moody and irritable, Adam Baldwin! And you've never shouted at me before. You've never said you didn't like my driving, not ever! Not even when I hit Aaron Mister's flock of silly guineas last Sunday afternoon. Feathers and birds going everywhere, and the squawking—why I do declare, it sounded like Gabriel blowing his horn at the Second Coming. You didn't say anything then." She flounced her skirts and tucked in her chin like a pouting child. "I don't understand you."

"Beth—"

"Andrew doesn't shout at me like this."

"Andrew?"

"He's kind and generous. He didn't mind when I made a few, tiny mistakes driving my carriage . . . and the automobile." She slanted a look up at him. "Why, when I took him riding in the automobile, he thought it was quite the grandest thing."

"You took Andrew riding?"

"And Joey. They quite enjoyed the adventure—they didn't accuse me of driving like a maniac."

Adam relented, realizing that he had been short with her lately. "Beth, I'm sorry I yelled at you. I apologize for raising my voice. It's been a long day, and I'm not in the mood for a carriage ride."

"The automobile?"

"No."

"Well, all right," she said. "I forgive you *if* you promise not to do it again. Come, sit down. We'll talk about something else."

Adam sat down in the swing beside her.

"What shall we talk about? I know, did you know Vonnie's moving to San Francisco with her mother? How I shall miss her!"

"She hasn't made a decision about that yet."

"Yes, she has."

He looked at her. "No, she hasn't."

"Yes, she has."

"When?"

"I don't know—recently, I guess."

"That's crazy—what does she think she'll do in San Francisco?"

"Why, the same thing she does here, except she won't be ranching, of course. She said she planned to start a bridal-gown business, expand, and grow. She sounded happy about the move, of course, she'll have to call her shop something other than 'bridal-gown business.' That sounds so ordinary, and Vonnie is anything but ordinary or dull. She's extremely bright, but she'll think of something—I'm surprised she isn't married herself by now, a smart, pretty girl like her—she's a wonderful homemaker, any man would be proud to get her, but with her mother so ill I guess she won't marry for a long time now, if she ever does at all—hummmm—she would have chosen maybe a light dusty rose for her bridesmaid gowns instead of the deeper rose, like me, but I rather like the darker, more vivid colors, don't you?"

He nodded. "I don't think—"

"—She'll like the city? Of course she will." Beth frowned. "Why wouldn't she? There's shopping, and fine restaurants, theater, fine art museums, hats, different sorts of ice cream . . ."

Slumping low in the swing, he listened as the list went on.

"Besides, why are you so concerned about how Vonnie will like San Francisco, anyway? I know it will be different, but she'll have her aunts there."

"It won't be the same," Adam said. "Vonnie will be homesick before the week is out. What do her aunts know about bridal gowns?"

"I don't know." Beth frowned. "I suppose Vonnie doesn't need their advice."

"She's doing this for her mother."

"Darling, I really don't think it's something you need to worry about. Vonnie's going to be perfectly fine, always was the independent type. And talent, she has talent, the gown is absolutely divine, you'll love it, but don't ask to see it ahead of time. Like I said, Vonnie says that's a no-no. It will be your grand surprise to finish up the year. Won't that be a perfect ending for a perfect year, and of course a perfect beginning for . . . Adam, are you listening?"

Adam knew he was making far too big an issue about Vonnie—a matter that was none of his business.

"Beth, I'm sorry to cut the evening short, but I think I'll head back to the ranch."

"Oh, pooh. I wanted to talk about the wedding."

"I'm sorry—another time will be better."

"Well, you have been in a particularly bad mood." She brightened. "Adam, I've been thinking, you know, it isn't a pleasant subject, but when we die—I mean if I go first, I want you to marry again, no matter how old you are, because a man needs a woman, and if I'm not around to care for you I want to know someone will be—"

"Beth, I'll go first."

"Well, now, not necessarily so, darling. Many men outlive their spouses, although admittedly the odds are on the woman's side, but I could go first—"

Setting his hat on his head, he smiled, "I'll go first, Beth. I promise you."

"Oh, it's your eye making you so pessimistic, isn't it? It looks terrible. *Corrrrdy Looouuu!* Where is that *beef!*"

"Momma, won't you come down to breakfast? It's a lovely day outside."

"I think I'll just rest a while."

Raising the shade, Vonnie let a little light into the bedroom. "Nelly and Susan will be here soon. We should have Beth's dress finished by next week."

"That's nice, dear."

"You have another letter from Josie and Judith. Shall I read it to you?"

"From Josie and Judith? Yes, please."

Vonnie read the chatty letter aloud to Cammy, all about the sights of San Francisco, the lovely bay, the tea they'd hostessed earlier in the month.

" 'We do so hope you are considering our invitation,' " Vonnie read. " 'It has been so long since we've been together, and the days grow short. We look daily for your letter of agreement. Your loving sisters, Josie and Judith.'

"Wasn't that nice?" Vonnie said, refolding the pale-pink sheets of stationery that held Josie's spidery script.

"Yes, it was," Cammy agreed, her hand caressing the photo album that had become her constant companion.

"What do you think about going to San Francisco?"

"Oh, I don't know."

"Wouldn't it be nice to see your sisters again?"

"Teague is so busy—"

"Think about it, will you, Momma?"

"I'll think about it," Cammy said vaguely, her attention already wandering to the photo album in her lap.

"I'll fix your tea."

Returning to the kitchen, she prepared Cammy's favorite blackberry tea and set it on a tray to carry upstairs. As she passed from the kitchen to the stairs, she noticed that the door to her sewing room was ajar. Frowning, she thought back, certain she'd closed it the night before, as she always did.

Her heart started pounding as she remembered the severed head incident. Setting the tray aside, she cringed as she heard Cammy's fragile cup strike the floor and shatter.

Climbing the stairs, she slowly pushed the door open.

"No!" she cried. "No!"

She couldn't believe her eyes.

Beth's wedding gown, which had been so near completion, now hung in ragged ribbons on the dress form. Someone had slashed the fine silk from waist to hem. The delicate *peau de soie* lace was shredded, and the tiny exquisite seed pearls were scattered across the floor.

Stunned, Vonnie backed slowly from the room.

"Vonnie?"

Spinning around, her heart in her throat, Vonnie nearly fainted in relief when she saw Eugenia standing in the open doorway.

"Child! You're white as a sheet. What's wrong?"

"So-someone—Look," Vonnie stammered, pointing to the destruction in her sewing room.

"Oh, my land's sakes alive," Eugenia whispered, her eyes wide with fright. "Who on earth could have done such a thing?"

"I d-don't know. The dress was perfect when I stopped sewing last night. I—I just don't—"

"We've got to get the sheriff out here!"

"Yes," Vonnie responded vaguely, her mind a fog of confusion and fear. "Yes, I'll go after him. . . ."

"I'll send Genaro. He was at the barn when I came in."

Her knees suddenly too weak to hold her, Vonnie sank into a chair while Eugenia sent Genaro for Sheriff Tanner. Suki seemed to understand that something bad had happened, jumping into Vonnie's lap to lick her face. Who could have done such an awful thing? And how could they have gotten inside to do the damage?

The idea that someone had come into the house during the night, while they were sleeping, was as frightening as the incident with the ostrich's head.

She had no idea how long she sat there before Eugenia again interrupted her thoughts.

"Vonnie? Sheriff Tanner's here."

Suki jumped up and, standing out of kicking range, barked at the sheriff as he approached.

Vonnie looked up. "Sheriff?"

Lewis Tanner loomed over her. "Hear there's been another incident."

"In there," she said. "Someone's destroyed ... Beth Baylor's wedding dress. Sometime in the night—"

"Someone got in here during the night?" Tanner stepped to the door of the sewing room and took in the devastation. "What was that damned dog doing then, sleeping? Did you leave a door open again?"

"No. I'm sure I didn't. I always make sure all the doors are locked before retiring. And you're right, it is strange that Suki wasn't disturbed either time someone came into the house."

The sheriff went into the sewing room and looked around.

"Nothing here. The window's locked." Leaning over, he picked up a pair of Vonnie's sewing shears from the floor and held them for a moment before putting them on her cutting table, where they were the night before.

"They must have used those."

"I'll look around outside, see if any of the hands heard or saw anything, but if it's like the last time ... well, I'll ask around."

He started toward the front door, then paused.

"It's none of my business, but this is a sure sign someone is out to get you. If you're smart, you'll take my offer and leave here before someone gets hurt."

Vonnie stared at him a long moment.

"Is that what this is all about? My selling my ranch to you?"

Tanner frowned. "You sayin' you think I did this?"

"Did you?"

His face flushed with anger. "I have a legitimate buyer, made you a good offer. I don't need to play games to get what I want."

Laying her head in her hands, she whispered, "I don't know anything."

"I'll go talk to your men now."

Wonderful, she thought, after the sheriff slammed the front door behind him. If he didn't have anything against her before, he would now.

Not wanting to deal with the devastated workroom, Vonnie went upstairs to see if the commotion had disturbed Cammy.

"Momma?"

Cammy stood in the middle of the room, holding her dress as if she'd forgotten what she was about to do.

"What was that noise? Did you drop a plate?"

"Yes—a teacup—sit down, Momma. We need to talk."

"Oh, you broke a piece of the good china, didn't you? Naughty girl."

Vonnie could have cried. Cammy had regressed to when Vonnie was a child, and a sense of hopelessness washed over her.

"It wasn't the good china. Remember when we talked about going to see your sisters?"

"Josie and Judith? They were always such bossy things."

"It's been a long time since you've seen them and . . . maybe it's time we took that trip to California."

"I don't know," Cammy started, twisting the dress in her hands.

"I think we need a change of scenery. You start thinking about what dresses you'd like to take, and I'll arrange our transportation. Eugenia is here. She'll be happy to help you pack."

"Josie and Judith." Cammy nodded vaguely, as if she were just now realizing who the two were. "It might be nice—"

"I've forgotten your tea," Vonnie said. "I'll ask Eugenia to bring it up with her."

She returned downstairs to find Eugenia cleaning up the shattered china.

"I thought I'd clear this away—"

"Thank you. I appreciate that. I'll make a new pot for Momma." Vonnie hesitated. "I've made a decision."

"What's that, dear?"

"Momma's sisters have been wanting her to come stay with them ever since Daddy died. I thought a visit might be good, and if everything goes well, perhaps we'll stay."

"Oh, child," the older woman said, reaching out to her, "I do hate to see you leave this place, but it might be a good thing for Cammy. A new place, seeing family again."

"Yes ... well, I'll fix that tea. Maybe you can help Momma sort through her dresses? I would really like to leave by the end of the week. And while we're gone, maybe you can start taking some of Daddy's things out of the closet. I know Momma will never be able to do it, nor will she let me."

"Anything I can do to help," Eugenia said, patting Vonnie's arm comfortingly. "I know how difficult this must be for you. I hope the change helps. You go fix that tea and I'll see to Cammy."

Eugenia set to work straightening the sewing room while Vonnie took a tea tray up to Cammy.

"This green is very nice," Eugenia was saying as she spread a dress across the bed for Cammy's approval.

Vonnie could see that Cammy wasn't paying any attention to her. Once again her mind was absorbed by the photo album. Eugenia gave a little shrug that told

Vonnie she'd made little progress with Cammy this morning.

"I'll take these tea things down," Eugenia said later, "and finish cleaning up that other . . . thing."

"Thank you."

Vonnie glanced at the trunk that Eugenia had dragged in from the spare room and had begun to fill with Cammy's dresses.

"I think we should take the green dress, don't you? It would be perfect for afternoon tea," Vonnie said, carefully folding the pale-green batiste. "I'll have to get some extra hat boxes—"

"Vonnie, come look at this picture."

"Momma, no. Put the album away."

"No, come see this. See how handsome your father is."

"Momma—"

"Please dear. It will only take a moment."

Vonnie surrendered, going to kneel beside Cammy to look at the pictures that fascinated Cammy and seemed to give her some sense of comfort.

"See how handsome he is in his uniform?"

Cammy pointed to a photo that showed five men standing together, each in uniform with their rifles beside them.

"How young they look," she commented. "That's Daddy, and P. K."

Vonnie frowned, peering more closely at the picture at which Cammy pointed. A face that looked vaguely familiar caught her attention for the first time—the square face, thick hair, and something about his eyes.

"Is that Franz?"

Suddenly Cammy snatched the photo album to her chest.

"Mother?" Vonnie frowned. "What's wrong?"

Cammy's eyes were wide with fear and her lips trembled.

"I don't want to go to the cellar! Don't make me go to the cellar! Teague said I never had to go there. Not ever!"

"It's all right, Momma," Vonnie soothed, alarmed at her mother's reaction.

"I hate it down there," Cammy snapped.

"You don't ever have to go down there," Vonnie assured her.

"I don't want to go—I don't want to go . . ."

It took some time to calm Cammy, but Vonnie was finally able to pry the photo album from her mother's hands and persuade her to lie down for a while.

Eugenia was able to stay with Cammy most of the day, managing to sort through her wardrobe, while Vonnie made purchases they would need for the trip and briefly visited with Judge Henderson.

That evening, exhausted after the stressful day, Vonnie moved through the house turning out the lamps.

As the wick died away in the front parlor, the window glass shattered, sending shards of the pane across the rug.

Smothering a frightened scream, Vonnie watched horrified as a rock bounced across the room and came to rest at her feet.

Heart pounding, she ran to the window to look out.

A shadow with a distinctive limp separated itself from the woodshed and made its way quickly back across the open space to the barn.

Andrew?

Letting the drape fall back to cover the window, she

picked up the rock and unwound the piece of paper wrapped around it.

Holding the paper in trembling fingers, she read the cryptic message—

SELL OUT WHILE YOU CAN, it warned.

"Andrew," she whispered. "Is it you who has been doing this to me?"

Chapter 21

The closest newspaper office was in nearby Tuboc, where Adam had ridden earlier that morning. Staring at the thirty-three-year-old newspaper, he studied the article and the accompanying picture.

"Find what you're looking for?"

"I think so," he said, closing the huge drawers that contained the dusty back issues in the back room of *The Arizonian* offices. "Thanks. I may be back."

"Any time," the editor said, closing the door and locking it.

Emerging from the newspaper office, Adam paused on the sidewalk, then mounted his horse and rode back to Nogales.

Later that morning he dismounted in front of Franz Schuyler's house. Dr. McDonald answered his knock.

"Sorry to disturb you, Doctor. I wanted to speak to Franz."

"Audrey's not doing well, Adam. Perhaps—another time?"

"I'm sorry—I'll come back later—is there anything I can do?"

"I wish there were. But no. There's nothing."

Adam returned to his horse and rode further outside of town to a small hacienda that sat alone, with only an aging barn and corral for company.

El Johnson had lived on his ranch for as long as Adam could remember. Though he ran a few cattle, he wasn't a rancher. Many wondered how he made a living, but no one asked. El was the town's hermit, and few ever went near him.

Rapping on the worn door, Adam looked across the open desert. *What a desolate place this is*, he thought. *A man could die of loneliness out here.*

The door opened a crack, revealing a pair of faded blue eyes. "Yeah?"

Johnson's greeting was less than friendly, but at least the hermit didn't shoot him on sight.

"El, I'm Adam Baldwin."

"I know who ya are. What d'ya want?"

"I'd like to talk to you."

"Can't think of anything we'd need to talk about."

"Could we go inside?"

El looked like he wasn't going to cooperate, but finally he stepped back and motioned for Adam to come inside.

The main room of the hacienda was large, joining a small kitchen area and dining and living space. It was obvious, from the dust that coated every surface and the stack of unwashed dishes, that El didn't have a woman.

"Sit if it suits you," he said, pulling a shabby wooden chair forward.

Adam sat.

"You said you knew who I was," he said. "You know my father?"

El nodded. "I knew him."

"But you don't know him now."

"No."

"Would you tell me why?"

"No. It's none of your business."

"What's between you and my father is none of my business, unless it affects me."

Johnson studiously avoided Adam's gaze. His eyes burned with such intensity that Adam wondered if the man was entirely sane.

"Whatever happened between the two of you has cost me the woman I love."

El sat, staring reflectively at the soiled tablecloth. "Your papa ever tell you about the war?"

"No," Adam admitted. "He doesn't speak of it."

"Didn't think so," El said, digging at a dried egg splatter with a broken fingernail.

"A lot of men don't like talking about the war."

"Yeah . . . some don't."

"You and my father, Teague Taylor, and Franz Schuyler were friends at one time, right?"

Johnson's eyes shifted warily. "Could be."

"You served in the same company."

"We did," El confirmed slowly.

"And you all came back here. To Nogales to live after the war."

There was no immediate answer, and Adam took that to be a positive sign.

"Then why was it that only Teague and Franz remained friends all these years since? Why did my father hate Teague so bitterly, and why did you choose to hide out here?"

El's hackles rose. "Not hidin'."

"But you keep your distance from my father, and the others. Why?"

"Things change."

Adam studied the man for a moment, wondering what kind of man, what kind of soldier, he'd been. Lean, tall as P. K., a firm jaw that was scruffy with a week-old beard, El Johnson was the oldest of the group.

"What things changed?" Adam asked.

"Just things."

"It's important for me to know, Johnson. What changed and caused the four of you to become bitter enemies?"

"Why do ya want to know? I came out here to be left alone—you got no right to come out here nosing around."

"Someone I love is in danger. I don't know why, but I think it may have something to do with what happened among you four men."

Lifting his eyes, El looked at him. "A woman?"

There was a long, brittle silence. "Vonnie Taylor. Teague's daughter."

"Teague's baby girl?"

"She's not little anymore," Adam said.

"Yeah . . . heard she's been having some trouble."

"You know Teague is dead."

"I know. He was a good man."

When El didn't continue, Adam pressed harder. "If he was such a good man, why didn't you remain friends?"

"Old memories. Painful memories," the old man said softly. "Things best forgotten."

"The four of you went through the war together. As a rule that strengthens friendships. The four of you came here, built lives, had families, sat in the same church every Sunday morning, and yet you never acknowledged one another. My father refuses to hear Teague's name." Adam's handsome face changed and became hard.

"I want to know what happened."

The old man squinted his eyes, momentarily lost in his own reverie.

"El, help me. Tell me what happened to cause the hate and animosity."

"Nothing we're proud of," he said. "We was comin' home," the hermit began, so softly Adam had to strain to hear. "Just young bucks, full of havin' survived. Sick of war." He rubbed his hand down his face; his beard against the calloused hand sounded like sandpaper against wood. "We . . . come upon the farmer . . . his wife, and kids."

Tears filled his eyes as the story unfolded. It was the same story P. K. told. Hurt, remorse, shame colored his voice.

"Teague wouldn't have no part of it. Said them jewels wasn't ours to take. Said we was thieves, but I was young . . . foolish . . . without a brain in my head. I shoved part of the loot in Teague's hands and told him to take it and shut up.

"He had a young wife waiting for him when he got back. I knew the money would keep them going until they could get a new start. No one knew I left him holding the valuables and rode away. I thought he'd realize later that he might as well have it, as leave for the next drifter who came along."

He hitched himself up straighter in the chair. "Teague was hardheaded. Heard he hid his part of the pillage and wouldn't touch it, even when he needed it. Said he'd sooner starve."

"Then my father thought Teague took those jewels, but he didn't?"

"He took them, but not because he wanted to. I left him holding them."

Adam's mind raced, fitting the clues together like a puzzle and not liking the picture that was starting to emerge.

"Thank you, El. I respect your honesty."

"How's your pa?" Real interest showed in the old man's face and voice.

"Slowing down. He's got a knee that gives him trouble. A horse fell on him a few years back."

"One fell on him during the war. His right leg as I remember."

Adam nodded. "It's the right knee he favors."

Johnson nodded slightly.

Adam rose, extending his hand. El got up slowly, warmly clasping Adam's hand.

"Thank you."

"I hope it helps," he said. "It's been a terrible load to bear. If I could live that day over . . ." His eyes misted over. "Well, things would have been different for all of us."

It occurred to Adam that all four men had paid a heavy price for the transgression. The atrocity had eaten Teague alive; P. K. had become a bitter old man; the knowledge of his sin was so intense for El that he had withdrawn from life and became a hermit; Franz was the only one untouched by that day.

El stood on the hacienda porch, watching as Adam rode away.

The last Adam saw of him was a broken man, thin as a shadow, still standing on that porch.

Vonnie stopped at the mercantile to order glass for the parlor window and was heading to the post office to get the week's mail when she ran into the pastor's wife.

"Oh, Vonnie, I was just on my way out to the ranch."

Noting Pearl's red-rimmed eyes, Vonnie guessed it was bad news. "What's happened?"

"It's Audrey—"

"Oh, no."

"She's gone to be with the Lord."

"When?" Vonnie whispered.

"About an hour ago. I knew you would want to know right away."

Vonnie was saddened and dismayed that she hadn't been to see Audrey in several days.

"I'll go to Franz immediately."

"The poor man is beside himself with grief. Pastor is with him, but he could use your support."

Vonnie hurried to her buggy, forgetting the mail.

She arrived at the Schuylers' thirty minutes later. Hurrying up the walk, she was surprised when the door opened before she reached it. Adele Wilson and Shirlene Majors, both deacons' wives, visibly upset, lace handkerchiefs to their noses, came toward her.

"Oh, Vonnie, thank you for coming so quickly. Poor Franz. I don't know if he can handle this. Go on in."

The front door was ajar. Pushing it open, she stepped inside the foyer. She found Franz in the kitchen, sitting at the kitchen table with his face buried in his hands, sobbing.

At the sound of her footsteps, he looked up with glazed eyes.

"Franz . . . I'm so sorry."

Shaking his head, his face crumbled. "She's gone . . . Audrey is gone."

Coming to kneel by his chair, Vonnie tried to comfort him. "I know the hurt you're feeling. It's so hard to give up one you love so dearly."

Her own wounds were still very tender.

Looking up, Franz's eyes suddenly hardened. "It's your fault."

Vonnie's eyes turned puzzled. "Franz . . ."

"You killed her. If Audrey had her piano, she would have stayed with me longer." He suddenly looked wild. "If I'd only had a little more time, I could have found the jewels, bought the Steinway back."

He was rambling, Vonnie realized. His grief was so new that he wasn't thinking coherently.

"She would have played, like before, lost herself in her music. I would have had more time—"

"Time wouldn't have helped, Franz," Vonnie comforted.

Tears rolled down his weathered cheeks. "My Audrey loved to play, the music flowed from her . . . you saw it, you saw how she made the keyboard come alive."

Vonnie reached out to him, but he moved away. She understood the rejection. He had loved Audrey so deeply it was impossible to imagine her gone.

"You did everything you could, Franz. Audrey loved you deeply."

"She didn't know," he said. "No one knew where he hid them. Just me. Now it's too late. Too late to help her."

The despair in his voice was heart-wrenching for Vonnie. If only she had the words to lighten his grief.

Later, he would realize that he'd done everything that could be done.

People started arriving, the women of the church to help lay out Audrey's body, the Women's Missionary Circle with food, neighbors, close friends. The small house filled, and Vonnie, knowing her immediate help wasn't needed, went home to break the news to Cammy and Eugenia.

When Eugenia heard the news she was distraught.

"Oh, the poor, poor soul. 'Tis a far better place she is now."

"Franz is upset. He feels he's not done enough for her."

"We all feel that way at times like this, but there's so little anyone can do."

"He kept saying he wished he could have gotten her piano back for her. That if she could have played her piano she'd have lived longer. How odd he would think that would have made the difference."

"Grief does strange things to a body. Why, I remember when John passed on, I kept thinking of things I could have done, should have done. Silly things. Like, I didn't ask if he wanted a second cup of coffee that morning. And I'd thought to fix his favorite dinner the night before, but I hadn't because I'd been at a church meeting that afternoon and didn't want to take the time to catch a chicken, and clean and fry it. If only I'd done that, I thought, then he'd have known how much he meant to me." Eugenia dabbed her eyes again. "As if a scrawny chicken could have made any difference."

"Franz has always regretted selling that piano. Audrey didn't feel half as bad about it as Franz did," Vonnie mused.

"Time will lessen his pain, child. Just as time will allow your mother to pull herself together."

"I hope so, Eugenia." Vonnie sighed. "I'm hoping this trip to San Francisco will help."

"I hate to see you go," Eugenia said, gathering up her things. "But you must do what you think is right. Now, if you don't need me anymore, I'll go see what can be done at the Schuyler house."

"You go along. I'll go up and tell Mother."

"Oh, I let that foolish dog of yours in the house. Nearly chewed off the back door wanting in."

Vonnie smiled at Eugenia's description of Suki. She was a dear little dog in spite of her excess amount of energy.

"I was going to take Beth's dress off the form, but I didn't know what you wanted to do with it. Not much left for you to work with."

Beth! What was she going to do about Beth's ruined dress? She, Nelly, and Susan had worked endless hours trying to complete the gown on time. There wasn't time to start over. Beth would be reduced to ordering her gown by mail and praying that it arrived in time.

"It's a shame. A cryin' shame that somebody has to be that jealous—"

"You think that's what it was? Someone jealous of Beth?"

"Why, of course. Don't you think? I mean, why would someone do such an awful thing if it wasn't jealousy? She is marrying one of the most sought-after men in the county."

"I'd never considered that." Pressing her fingertip to her mouth, Vonnie thought about the implication. She had assumed it had something to do with the birds, but maybe not. "But who would be jealous of Beth and Adam?"

Who, except her?

"I'm sure I don't know, but you have to admit, it's a drastic thing to do. Well, I'm off. You're sure you'll be all right here?"

"I'll be fine. I've got Suki, remember?"

"That fool dog." Eugenia chuckled, waddling to the door. "You be careful, child. What with dead birds, ruined dresses, rocks through the windows," she muttered, half to herself. "What will be next?"

Vonnie closed and locked the door behind her, and went upstairs to tell Cammy about Audrey.

Chapter 22

It was nearing dark when Adam rode into the Taylor farmyard. Handing the reins to Genaro, he proceeded to the house.

Vonnie answered the door.

"Hi."

"Guess you know about Audrey?"

"Yes, I'm on my way to pay my respects." Adam looked past her shoulder. "How did your mother take the news?"

"I don't know . . . hard, though five minutes later she was saying she didn't know how to tell Daddy."

His features sobered. "Is it true what I hear?"

"I don't know, what do you hear?"

"You've decided to sell to Tanner."

Leaning against the door, she wiped her hands on her apron. "Mother and I are going to San Francisco."

"Permanently?" His eyes locked on hers.

Vonnie tried to keep her heart cold and still. "Permanently."

"Why?" His voice rose and a telltale jaw muscle worked as he waited for her answer.

"Why not?"

"Is this about you and me, or about your mother?"

"All three."

"What about your business?"

"I'll start a new one out there."

His voice dropped, but his eyes never left hers. "Are you aware that Franz served in the war with P. K. and Teague?"

Her eyebrows quirked. "That's strange."

"You didn't know?"

"I did, because Momma used to tell me about her friendship with Audrey while the men were away. I had forgotten about it though, until this morning when I saw a picture of Franz and Daddy taken right after the war. Why do you want to know about that?"

"I'm not sure I have a reason—I just wondered if you knew that Teague, P. K., Franz, and El Johnson were once close friends."

"Daddy never talked about the war."

"P. K. either. Did your father ever mention jewels— some he might have acquired during the war?"

"Jewels?" She frowned. "Daddy didn't have any jewels."

"You're sure?"

"Of course I'm sure. Anyway, I don't think so. Why? Do you know something I don't?"

"Vonnie, I'd like to talk to you later—after you've paid your respects to Franz."

"Will you be seeing Beth tonight?"

She had to break the news to her about the gown. She could tell Adam, but she'd rather let Beth know first.

"I'll be seeing her, why?"

"Will you tell her I'll be coming to see her first thing tomorrow morning?"

"Yes . . . is something wrong?"

"Just relay the message, please. I need to talk with her."

"Are you going to the Schuylers' later?"

"Yes, I have a cake in the oven. I'll bring it over . . . Momma will want to see Audrey."

Their eyes met again.

"Don't go to San Francisco." The startling request hung heavy between them.

"Don't marry Beth."

"Vonnie, damn it, I'm trapped." It was as close as he'd ever come to saying he didn't love Beth. But it wasn't enough. Not nearly enough.

"Frankly, I'm feeling a little restrained myself lately, Adam."

"We need to talk about that, too."

"Will talking change anything?"

"No, but it will get a hell of a lot off my conscience."

"You want me to purge your soul?" She laughed.

"I'm sorry. If things were different . . ."

"They are different."

"Yes, but it isn't just us any longer." His voice softened. "What do I do about Beth?"

What did he do about Beth? She wished she knew.

"You don't love her?"

"I'm finding out that there's a far greater hell than a man's pride."

"I took your rejection that morning to mean you had second thoughts, that you didn't love me. I was young too, Vonnie." His eyes met hers and she saw the old Adam. "I wouldn't let you go that easily today."

She had been too young and easily intimidated, afraid to tell the truth, not wanting to see the look of betrayal in Teague's face.

His eyes searched hers for an answer.

"How dare you?" she blurted, suddenly angry that he was putting her in this position. Everything was settled. She was going to San Francisco, and he was marrying Beth.

"I *dare* because I love you. Don't leave me, Vonnie. If you go to San Francisco it will be over."

Tears suddenly burned her eyes. "Excuse me, I smell my cake burning."

"Vonnie."

Closing the door, she left him standing on the porch.

There was only so much she could deal with in one day, and she'd reached her limit.

Clearing the table later, she carried the empty frosting bowl to the sink. A fresh chocolate-fudge nut cake sat waiting to be delivered to the Schuylers'. Cammy was upstairs dressing. Vonnie could hear Suki barking enthusiastically as Cammy moved around her room.

She wasn't sure if Cammy understood the significance of the visit they were preparing to make. It was hard to tell these days what she retained and what was lost in her confused state.

As she turned from the sink, a movement in the doorway caught her eye.

"Franz? Wha— My goodness—"

Franz stood there, viewing her paternally. "Why, Puddin', *why* didn't you just leave?"

Tears trickled down his cheeks. "You were always here—always coming down to see how I was doing, al-

ways checking on me . . . If you'd just left me alone . . .
I could have found them. Then, I could have bought
Audrey's piano back and everything would have been
good again."

"I don't understand," Vonnie said. A cold chill ran
through her. When he confronted her earlier, she had
supposed grief was causing Franz to be so distraught.
Now, it seemed to be even more serious. She suddenly
wanted him to leave.

"The jewels. I never did find them." His eyes glinted
with madness. "All I needed was a little more time.
They're here someplace. But Audrey left me, and now
you'll sell the ranch. Oh, yes, I know that's what you're
going to do. And then it'll be too late—I'll never find
them. . . . I have to find them, don't you understand—"

His head bowed. "It's already too late. Audrey's
gone."

"Jewels? There are no jewels here, Franz." Adam's
earlier puzzling inquiry raced through her brain.

"They're here. I know they are," Franz shouted.
"Teague hid them. He vowed to never touch them himself. But I needed that money."

He took a step forward, and Vonnie backed against
the table.

"P. K. never forgave Teague. He was angry with me,
too . . . thought I was in on it, but I wasn't. It was El
and Teague—" He paused, confused.

"No . . . P. K. thought Teague took the jewels, but he
didn't. I saw what happened—El shoved the pouch at
Teague and told him he had a family to think about—
Teague didn't want them—called it blood money . . ."

He was ranting now. "Buried the jewels somewhere
around here—" He looked up plaintively. "You

understand—Teague didn't want the money, despised it—I could have used it—not for myself, it was for Audrey." Tears poured from his eyes. "I wanted her to have her piano back—that's all I wanted. I didn't want to hurt you, Puddin', but you wouldn't let me find those jewels—"

Grief had driven him out of his mind, Vonnie realized, just as it had her mother. She searched her brain for a way to distract him and go for help.

"Franz, you're not thinking straight. There are no jewels—"

"No—no. It's true! I know it is. Teague knew where the jewels were, but he wouldn't tell me. So righteous, he was, that day it happened. Those dead people couldn't use them anymore. Why shouldn't we have them?"

What was he talking about? His ramblings didn't make sense, but she had the awful feeling that his words were somehow connected with the strange things that had happened at the ranch recently.

"It was so long ago that no one would know—and Audrey can play again—she can play again. . . ."

"Know what?" Vonnie prodded gently.

"Why . . . about the jewels."

"How did you know about the jewels?"

Franz frowned as if trying to remember.

"So young. So young. War makes men do strange things. Things they wouldn't ordinarily do—

"But Teague—Teague said it wasn't right. Said we had no right to them. But we did—we did! They couldn't keep them," he reasoned. "They were dead."

"Wh—who was dead?"

"The farmer and his wife—they had the jewels." He

leaned forward slightly, as if confiding a secret. "It was El. El took them. I—I didn't approve of what he was doing, but I didn't speak up—just kept quiet all these years, that's why I thought it wouldn't hurt if I used the jewels—I could have told, but I didn't, even when I knew P. K. hated Teague after that. It's too late now, too late to make it right." He grew angry again. "But you wouldn't let me find them."

He changed his thoughts in a breath, and Vonnie knew his mental state was becoming even more unstable.

"Audrey needs her piano. If she has her music, she'll get better—you'll see. She'll be her old self again. I *need* that piano. I must find the jewels."

Lunging forward, he caught Vonnie's arm. Her cry was smothered by his free hand as he twisted her arm behind her back and propelled her out of the kitchen, toward the attic stairs. He was much stronger than Vonnie had imagined.

Forcing her up the stairway, he jerked her when she stumbled and pushed her past the second-floor bedrooms toward the attic workroom.

"Franz, no, let me go. You're not thinking straight . . . you don't know what you're doing!"

"I have no time—Audrey's waiting for me."

Pushing open the attic door, he shoved Vonnie inside. She stumbled to her knees, catching her hand on the edge of the sewing machine.

"Franz—"

"Hush," he hissed. "I must look for the jewels."

"Please," she tried again. "You don't know what you're doing. Please—"

Softening, he reached out, touching her hair. "My

lovely baby girl. I would never, never hurt you. You'll be safe here; Franz will let no one hurt you."

He whirled and disappeared through the door before Vonnie could get to her feet. Reaching the door just as it slammed shut, she heard the ominous thunk of the heavy wooden bar dropping into place on the other side.

"Oh, please!" she whispered, resting her face against the rough wood. "Don't do this. . . ."

Only one window in a dormer across the east wall allowed light in, and with the fast-approaching twilight it would be dark. She shivered with apprehension as to what Franz intended to do. What if Cammy wandered downstairs? Would Franz hurt her?

Jewels. Were they a figment of Franz's imagination? Or were there really gems hidden somewhere in the house? Had Adam known? Why didn't he tell her?

If the jewels existed, had the four men really killed someone for them? She could hardly believe her beloved father could be a part of that.

If what Franz said was true, then the trouble between P. K. and Teague was a terrible misunderstanding. Adam's father believed Teague had stolen the jewels, and he didn't. Why were the two men so stubborn they didn't bother to find out the truth?

Knowing she had to keep a clear head if she was going to get out of this, Vonnie pulled herself to her feet and began to search for a way out.

"Got to search—" Franz was mumbling as he made his way back down the stairs. "Clive will sell the piano—I must hurry . . . I'm hurrying, Audrey . . . don't leave me . . ."

The dog's bark startled him as he neared the bottom of the stairs.

"Go away—I have to look—"

Suki leaped up, greeting him enthusiastically. Franz lost his footing and slipped on the step, his feet flying out from beneath him.

Throwing out his arms to catch himself, he hit the burning oil lamp on the hall table, sending it crashing to the floor. Oil splashed out on the carpet and onto the drapes at the parlor window.

Suki obediently ran over to lick his face in apology.

There was a crackling sound as flames reached the drapes, the tongues of fire licking up the patterned material and inching their way across the flowered wallpaper.

Alarmed, Franz struggled to his feet. Confused, he turned in a circle. "Cammy!" he cried softly. "Vonnie—? Puddin'—? Audrey . . . Audrey . . ."

The parlor, fully consumed by flames now, poured smoke into the foyer. Fire licked at the edge of the Aubusson carpet and at the foyer wall as Franz crawled toward the stairs.

Ignoring the roar of flames and the sound of breaking glass, he inched up the stairs.

"Cammy!" he cried out, coughing black, oily smoke from his lungs. He reached the top stair and felt his way down the hallway.

Kicking the bedroom doors open one by one, his eyes streamed from the thick smoke as he searched for the wife of his old friend. He had to find her and save her. Teague was his friend . . . Audrey, *where* was Audrey?

Adam was returning from paying his respects at the Schuylers'. As he passed the entrance to the Flying Feather, he glanced toward the house.

The yapping of a dog caught his attention, and he pulled his horse to a standstill when he saw Suki running toward him. It was unusual for the dog to be so far from the house. She was clearly agitated, barking with high-pitched yips.

"What's wrong, girl?"

The little dog danced up and down excitedly, barking all the while.

"Suki," he greeted, getting off the horse.

The little dog ran to him, yapping, then reversed his direction and ran back toward home a few paces, then back to Adam again.

"What is it?" he asked, peering into the distance. A thick cloud of black smoke rolled across the desert sky.

Remounting, he rode hard toward the ranch. The east side of the house was already engulfed, and the farmhands had formed a bucket line to fight the fire.

"Where's Vonnie?" Adam shouted.

"Not here!" Roel shouted back.

"Where is she?"

Confusion drowned out the reply.

Spotting Franz's carriage, Adam ran to check on the nervous horses tied to a post near the barn. "Where's Franz?" he yelled. No one had seen him.

"Is anyone in there?" Adam asked, rushing frantically from one to another. Neighbors had begun to arrive and were passing buckets of water down the line. "Where's Cammy?"

No one seemed to know.

Turning, Adam ran back to Roel. "Are you sure there's no one in the house? Did anyone go in?"

"We do not know, *Señor* Baldwin. We only saw the smoke a few *momentos* ago. We are trying to put out the fire."

Dashing toward the house, Adam reached the porch and kicked in the front door.

"*Señor* Baldwin!" Roel shouted.

Shielding his face from the heat, Adam dropped to his knees and felt his way through the dense smoke.

"Vonnie! Cammy!"

He tied a handkerchief across his nose and mouth, and bending low, he fought his way toward the stairs. At the top of the first landing, he crawled over Franz's sprawled body.

Holding his fingers to the old man's neck, he frowned. There was no pulse.

Adam made his way to Vonnie's bedroom and kicked open the door. Finding it empty, he went on to the end of the hall, where he knew Teague and Cammy had shared a room. There, he found a confused Cammy huddled at the side of the bed.

"Teague, I'm glad you're here. The smoke scares me," she whimpered.

"I'm going to carry you out," Adam said gently.

When she hesitated, he swung her into his arms and headed back to the stairs.

Upright now, smoke burned his eyes and his lungs nearly burst from lack of oxygen. He nearly fell down the stairs and out onto the porch with Cammy in his arms.

More neighbors, having seen the smoke, were arriving in buggies to join the bucket brigade.

"Son!" P. K. yelled, as Joey took Cammy from Adam's arms and Pat helped him off the porch.

P. K. came over to him, his expression tight. "Have you lost your mind?"

"Franz—" Adam choked. "Franz is in there."

"Franz?" P. K. started into the burning house.

Gripping his father by the shoulder, Adam said. "He's dead, Dad. Leave him be. Cammy's out now."

Stunned, P. K. turned to look at him. A great sadness touched his eyes.

"There was nothing I could do. It must have been the smoke—or maybe even a heart attack from shock."

Squeezing, P. K.'s shoulder, he headed to where several women were hovering over Cammy in the yard.

"Adam," Beth cried, coming up to him. "You could have died in there—"

"Beth, what are you doing here?"

"We heard the Taylor house was on fire. Naturally, Daddy wanted to help—"

Adam turned back to Cammy. "Where's Vonnie?" he demanded. "Was she in the house?"

"Why, I don't know. Maybe she went to Beth's."

"No, she didn't. Think, Cammy, where was she when you last saw her? She was getting ready to take you to Franz Schuyler's. Was she downstairs?"

Suki nipped at Adam's boot, jumping up and down, up and down. It was unnatural, even for her, to be so hyperactive.

Darting toward the burning house, she darted back again, yipping her high-pitched bark.

"Get back, Suki!" Pat shouted.

"Suki!" Joey yelled as the dog tangled in his feet, nearly tripping him. Again, she darted back toward the burning house.

"The dog's nuts!"

"No, she's not." Adam's eyes suddenly glimpsed movement at the attic window. He realized what the dog was trying to tell him.

"Vonnie's in there."

Those close by turned at his words, and before he could be stopped, he charged back into the house.

The flames were high, and the heat too intense now to enter the front. He raced around the house and broke in the back door. Fire had not reached the kitchen or back hall. Pulling the handkerchief back across his face, he squinted against the gray, choking smoke and crept on all fours until he reached the stairs.

Leaping quickly, he grabbed the railing and pulled himself up and over it, swinging onto the second-floor landing.

He stumbled up the attic stairs and threw his shoulder against the door.

"Vonnie!" he shouted. The roar of the fire engulfed his words.

Repeatedly kicking the door, he fought to gain entrance. He groped the bar and finally dislodged the barrier. The door gave way.

"Vonnie!" he thundered. The room was a roaring inferno. Rolls of tulle, yards of colorful ribbon, bolts of elegant lace, spools of delicate thread blazed out of control.

In the far corner, a sewing form draped with pieces of fabric, the pattern still pinned in place, hoisted hot flames to the low ceiling.

Above the flaming holocaust he heard a weak cry.

"Vonnie!"

"I'm here," a faint voice answered.

Dropping to his stomach, Adam crawled across the floor, groping for her. His hand finally latched onto hers. Grasping her tightly, he held onto the hand that he had taken a vow to "love until death do us part."

"Adam," she choked, wrapping her arms around his neck.

Lifting her into his arms, he carried her toward the door but was forced back by orange flames licking halfway up the steps.

"I'm going to try the window," he yelled.

Her arms tightened possessively.

Backing into the workroom, he fought his way along the wall back through the billowing smoke.

When he used a chair to break the window, the flames multiplied, turning the room into a fiery cave.

He pushed her through to the eaves and shouted for her to hold on as he crawled out beside her.

A roar went up from the crowd that was gathered below to watch and wait, anxiety written on every face.

Pulling Vonnie into his arms, he held her. Burying his hands in her hair, he gazed down into her smoke-smudged face, now showing the paths of tears across her cheeks. As she looked back at him, he whispered in a husky, choked voice.

"Damn, you make me nervous."

Laying her hand gently across his cheek, she coughed. "It seems I'll do anything to get your attention."

"Momma," Beth gasped, when she saw the affectionate exchange.

"Oh, my, Adam's a hero," Gillian cried, clasping her hands together. "Aren't you proud—"

"Momma," Beth repeated.

"What is it, dear?"

"He's—he's embracing her!"

"They've just escaped death," Gillian reasoned.

"No," Beth said, staring at the couple as they clung to each other tightly. "He's *never* held me that way."

"He hasn't?" Gillian frowned. "Oh, dear."

Chapter 23

Friends and neighbors gathered close as Adam carried Vonnie to the large juniper in the backyard. He lay her on the ground and knelt beside her until she was able to push herself up to a sitting position.

"I . . . I'm all right," she said. "Momma—?"

"She's safe. Neighbors are looking after her."

"Franz?"

Adam shook his head.

"Adam, it was Franz . . . Franz is behind all the things that have been happening," she whispered. "Apparently Audrey's illness was slowly driving him insane. He thinks Daddy hid some sort of jewels in the cellar. In his troubled mind, he thought that if he could find the jewels they would enable him to buy Audrey's piano back. That's why he's been over here so much; why he was constantly down in the cellar. She gazed up at Adam. "Is it true about Franz and Daddy and P. K.?"

"Yes, I planned to tell you about it tonight." Adam admitted. "El Johnson took those jewels and pawned them off on your father. Apparently P. K. witnessed the exchange and thought Teague was capable of taking blood money. That's been the source of their feud all these years."

"But how did you know to go to El?"

"I was suspicious when I realized the four men had been close friends during the war. I wanted to know what happened. I thought it was strange that though the four of them were in the same company, none of them had associated since coming home.

"El turned hermit, P. K. and Teague never spoke. Franz was the only one that kept in contact with any of them, and that was only through your father."

"Only because of Cammy and Audrey's friendship."

"I tried to talk to Franz earlier today, but he was with Audrey. Dr. McDonald suggested I wait until another time. So, I went out to El's place instead."

"And he told you about Daddy and P. K."

A low rumble turned all heads toward the flames. A great roar suddenly went up, bringing a stunned cry from the spectators.

The house collapsed in a shower of sparks. Smoke billowed and debris shot upward, then dropped. Neighbors scurried to stomp tiny wildfires leaving small black circles dotting the yard.

"The birds!" she cried suddenly.

"They're taken care of," Adam reassured her. "Genaro and Roel moved them to safety."

Defeated, Vonnie lay her face in her hands. "It doesn't matter anyway. I'm selling them.

"Oh, Adam," she sobbed. "I saw Andrew throw a rock through my window."

"Andrew? You saw him?"

Andrew stepped closer and bent toward her to speak.

"She's right, I did do that. I can explain." He glanced at Adam, then back at Vonnie's questioning eyes.

"I saw you and Adam at the pond the other day, and it seemed he was leading you on, playing you for a fool. I knew about the strange things happening here, and I didn't want you to get hurt. I was afraid you wouldn't leave the ranch."

"So you broke my window?"

"Yes, I threw that rock through the window to scare you into leaving. I thought it would be best for everyone if you started a new life somewhere away from here . . . away from Adam."

"Andrew." She reached for his hand.

"I'm sorry. It wasn't the best way, I see that now." His eyes went to Adam. "I guess I've been wrong about a lot of things."

He stopped when they saw P. K. approaching.

Sparing Vonnie a concerned glance, P. K. inquired gruffly. "Are you all right?"

"Shaken, but greatly indebted to Adam," she said, hesitantly. It was the first time in her life P. K. Baldwin had ever addressed her personally. It was as if God had spoken to her.

Glancing up at his father, Adam said quietly, "Don't you think it's time she knew the whole story?"

Clearing his throat, P. K. looked away. "Tell her if you want."

"No." Adam stood up, facing his father. "You tell her, Dad."

"Feel like standing?"

"Yes," she said, letting Adam help her to her feet. Listening to the story of how Teague and P. K. had come to sword's point left her numb. All those years of hatred over a simple misunderstanding.

P. K. took the news grimly. When told that the dispute had been born of miscommunication, he simply walked off to be by himself.

How easy it would have been for Teague to come to P. K. and set the story straight; or for P. K. to have gone to Teague and demand an explanation. It would have been their right; the two had loved each other like brothers.

But instead, pride governed, and for thirty-three years, they carried a bitter grudge that affected not only them, but those they loved the most. Teague took his grudge to the grave.

But then, Vonnie forced herself to admit, it was not always easy to speak up, and misunderstandings had a way of getting worse as the years passed. She could attest to that.

Drawing Vonnie to his side, Adam said quietly, "You're coming home with me."

"Adam, I can't." Her gaze followed P. K., walking away from them, old and beaten.

"Don't argue." Taking her arm, Adam led her over to Beth, who was standing beside Andrew. "Andrew, will you see that Cammy is taken to the house immediately?"

"I will." Andrew limped away.

"You're welcome to stay with us." Beth hugged her tightly. "Oh, Vonnie, I was so afraid that something had happened to you."

"Beth, your beautiful dress." Vonnie realized now that Franz, poor, grief-demented Franz, had slashed the dress in yet another effort to drive her away so that he could resume his search for the hidden jewels.

"Don't worry about the dress. I can always *buy* a dress, but I could never replace you." Beth hugged her tightly again.

Vonnie saw no reason to tell Beth it was not the fire that destroyed the gown. Franz was gone, the gown was gone, and no purpose would be served in telling the awful truth.

"I'll help you select the gown and personally order it for you," Vonnie told her. "It will be here in time for the wedding, I promise. And it will be the *peau de soie*."

"Well," Beth hedged. "I've been thinking . . . maybe I'll switch to Brussels lace—in cream—no white—no oatmeal—oh, I don't know, what do you think, Vonnie?"

"Whatever, Beth."

Adam turned to Beth. "Vonnie and her mother will be staying at Cabeza Del Lobo until other arrangements can be made. Would you like to come with us now?"

"Is there anything I can do to help?"

"No, Alma will see to their needs."

"Then I'll wait and come tomorrow morning. I know this has been a terrible ordeal for Vonnie and Cammy. Oh, wait, it may be day after tomorrow before I can be there. Momma and I must meet with the pastor in the morning to decide—candles or lanterns? Which do you think, Vonnie?"

"I don't—"

"Well, I don't either. Adam?"

Adam pretended he wasn't paying attention to the conversation.

"Well, no matter. We must make so many decisions. Then tomorrow night is the church quilting bee. You must come, Vonnie. With your talent . . ."

Vonnie embraced her friend. "Don't expect me unless you see me. I must be sure Cammy—"

"—Is taken care of. Of course, you must. Well, you know you're always welcome."

Vonnie nodded and turned away as Adam brushed a benign kiss across Beth's cheek before she hurried away.

Andrew brought the carriage from the barn, controlling the nervous horses, while Adam gave Roel and Geraro instructions about clearing the remains of the house when the embers cooled.

Then, after loading Cammy into the carriage, the four drove immediately to Cabeza Del Lobo.

Alma fussed over the two women, ordering bathwater heated immediately, providing warm gowns for Cammy and Vonnie to wear to bed, and supplying a light supper for all of them. She was a whirlwind of activity, accepting nothing but complete compliance with her mothering.

Soon Cammy was settled in a room and tucked in by the clucking housekeeper. Vonnie had a room next door.

Later, Vonnie stood at the window and stared out at the darkness. How strange it felt to be under the Baldwins' roof. It seemed it had been her due all along. The lamplight reflected her silhouette, and she smiled. The voluminous gown Alma loaned her was so large it fell off her shoulders.

She was working a tangle out of her freshly washed hair when Adam knocked and then entered.

"Has Alma taken good care of you?"

"She has been the proverbial mother hen."

His hair was still wet from his bath. He was wearing a blue shirt and matching trousers. Alma had insisted on putting salve on burns inflicted on him during the fire. A large white bandage covered the back of one hand.

Vonnie was acutely aware, when he came to stand behind her, of the smell of soap clinging pleasantly to his skin.

"What about you?" he asked softly. "Are you all right?" His warm breath fanned her ear.

"I'm wondering why your father allowed us to be here, in view of his feelings toward all Taylors."

Removing the comb from her fingers, he drew it gently through the tangles in her hair. She closed her eyes, drinking in the sensual moment.

"Perhaps he saw the truth today. What happened between four young boys more than thirty years ago is no longer relevant. It was a tragic mistake, but it should not have stood between them. P. K. realizes that now."

He pulled the comb through her hair, fashioning an ebony curtain down her back.

"What about the jewels?"

"I hope they're never found. If they were in the house, it's doubtful anyone will ever find them."

"Perhaps that's for the best. They ruined four men's lives."

"Franz is gone, your father is gone, El has had no life because of them."

"And your father?"

"We know what the incident did to him."

He lay the comb aside, smoothing the hair from her face with gentle hands. Weariness overtook her, and she leaned against him.

"Tired?"

"Uh huh."

Adam suddenly turned her into his arms, holding her close.

"I was scared . . . so damned scared when I saw that house on fire," he whispered into her hair. "I thought—" There was incredible sadness in his eyes.

Aware of his impropriety, he stepped back, his gaze searching hers. Then he slowly dipped his head, his mouth inches from hers.

"Forgive me . . . I've wanted to do this for so long. . . ."

His mouth captured hers hungrily.

His hands cupped her face gently as she responded, kissing him with long-denied desire. Years fell away, and the passion that had once consumed them did so again.

Without a word, he abruptly broke the embrace, turned, and left the room, closing the door gently behind him.

Sinking onto the bed, Vonnie touched her fingertips to her lips, where his taste remained. She would have cried but she was too empty to cry anymore.

Chapter 24

Hildy and Carolyn arrived midmorning, bringing clothes and bursting with curiosity.

"I'm so sorry," Hildy said, giving Vonnie a quick hug. "What a terrible ordeal for you."

"It seems I've been a lot of trouble to everyone lately."

"Nonsense, we're just relieved you weren't hurt. Does anyone know how the fire started?"

"No, we suspect Suki may have knocked over an oil lamp." The truth about that night would never be known. The thought that Franz might have purposely set the fire was too terrible to consider.

"It's a miracle you survived. You were trapped in the attic?"

"Yes," Vonnie said. "The bolt must have fallen into place accidentally."

"How odd," Carolyn said, "and how ironic that Audrey and Franz died the same day."

"Yes, and sad," Vonnie said. "Thank you so much for bringing the dresses. I only had Alma's nightgown to wear."

Both Hildy and Carolyn giggled, imagining how the gown of the portly housekeeper must have swallowed Vonnie's slim figure.

"I heard that Adam went back into the burning house to find you. How brave!"

"Very brave," Vonnie said, toying with her teacup. "He could have lost his own life. I'm so grateful to him, and to his father for letting us stay here."

"I guess ol' P. K. has a heart after all," Carolyn whispered, casting an anxious glance toward the parlor door.

Vonnie just smiled. She hadn't seen P. K. since the fire, and she wasn't sure what she would say to him when they met again.

"We asked Beth to come with us," Hildy said, "but she had things to do, and she didn't feel up to visiting. Realizing that her wedding dress burned in the fire . . . well, it's very upsetting to her, although she's happy you weren't hurt."

"Beth will have her gown."

"How awful it is, all your things gone—clothes, furniture, pictures, all your sewing things. I just can't imagine," Carolyn said. "And your poor mother."

"I received a telegram this morning. An interested buyer has contacted me about purchasing the ostriches. Several dealers knew I was thinking about selling."

"Will he buy all of them?"

"It seems so. He arrives tomorrow morning. Mother and I already have plans to go to San Francisco. I'll telegram Josie and Judith this afternoon and tell them we're leaving on Thursday."

"Oh," Hildy said, "I feel so bad about your leaving. I don't know what we'll do without you. The five of us have been friends for so long, it just won't be the same around here."

Vonnie was reluctant to go, too, but not for the same reasons. It would be hard to leave everything she'd ever known, those who'd been friends since she was born. Just the thought of never seeing Adam again was unbearable.

The fire was the catalyst to move on a decision already made.

"Oh," Hildy exclaimed, as if the thought just occurred to her, "you won't be here for the wedding—unless you bring Beth's dress back yourself. Won't you think about it? It would be so wonderful, and I know it would make Beth's day even more special."

Smiling, Vonnie nodded. "I'll think about it, Hildy."

"Well, we shouldn't keep you," the two girls chorused, picking up their bags. "We just wanted to check on you and bring you something to wear."

"I appreciate that. Will you be at the station when I leave?"

Carolyn hugged her tight. "You know we will be. We'll make such a scene you'll be embarrassed."

"I don't doubt it." She laughed, wishing she could feel more excited about the new direction her life was taking.

Standing on the verandah, she waved good-bye as Hildy and Carolyn drove away.

After dressing in one of Hildy's day dresses, she went to her mother's room and knocked.

"Momma?"

Cammy was seated in front of the window, looking

out. Her eyes brimmed with tears. "Momma, what's wrong?"

"The house is gone, isn't it?"

"Yes, I'm afraid it is."

Wiping her eyes, Cammy said quietly. "Franz was there. Why?"

"He was confused, Momma," Vonnie said softly.

Her mother's mouth worked as if she tried to hold back tears.

"My photo album. It's . . . gone, too, isn't it?"

"Yes, Momma, it is."

"Where are we?"

"Cabeza Del Lobo."

Her eyes met Vonnie's. "The Baldwin ranch? Oh, dear. Teague wouldn't like that. He and P. K.—"

"Momma, Daddy's gone." Vonnie's voice was harsher than intended, but Cammy had to get a grip on reality for her own sake. "He's gone, Momma, and he's not coming back."

Her mother's fingertips trembled against her thin lips. "Yes, he's gone. I know that," she said softly. "I know that." Tears spilled over onto her cheeks. "The house doesn't matter now. It was only lumber and nails without Teague. He was the one who filled it, you know."

Vonnie felt her own tears. "Yes, I know."

"It will be good to see Josie and Judith again."

"Yes, Momma, it will be good for both of us," Vonnie said, beginning to see a light at the end of a long, dark tunnel. "I'm going into town to make arrangements for our trip. Will you be all right here?"

"Yes, Alma invited me to the kitchen to have tea with her this afternoon. I think I'd like that."

Vonnie hugged her mother hard, confident things were going to be all right. Going downstairs to tell Alma she was leaving, she paused on the bottom step and looked at the room for the first time.

The hacienda-style house, with adobe walls the color of the desert and tile floors that gleamed with Alma's care, was a man's home. The furniture was large, substantial, covered in Indian-style throws in burnt orange, red, rust. Mexican pottery sat in corners holding desert sage, and pinecones were heaped in a flat pot on the long dining table. Native woven cloth hung at the tall windows and matched the rugs that covered the floor beneath the dining table.

All in all, it was a comfortable house, a warm home, reflecting the wealth of its owner as well as Alma's devotion.

"You look mighty pretty this morning."

Vonnie turned to see Adam watching her from the foyer.

"Good morning."

His eyes skimmed her lightly. "Going somewhere?"

"Into town to do a little shopping."

"Oh?"

"I want to purchase a few things, and I'm supposed to meet the man who may be buying the ostriches. He said he would arrive around noon."

"Do you want me to drive you in?"

"No. You and your father have been more than gracious. I'll take my buggy, if you'll have someone hitch up the team."

She waited as Adam harnessed the team. When he finished, he gave the horses a pat on the rump.

"Nice pair."

"They were Daddy's favorite."

"Are you sure you don't want me to go with you? I'm good at carrying packages."

She smiled. "I think I can buy a couple of dresses by myself."

"Of course. Be careful." His eyes were compelling, magnetic.

"I will."

He assisted her into the carriage and, with a last glance at him, Vonnie slapped the reins against the horses' rumps and left him standing in the stable doorway.

After a stop at the mercantile, where she accepted sympathy from at least a dozen people, and at the telegraph office, where she sent a telegram to San Francisco and spoke with a half-dozen more friends, she drove out to the Flying Feather to check on the ostriches.

Roel and Genaro were hard at work clearing smoldering remains that were once her home.

"*Buenos días, Señorita* Taylor—*cómo está usted y Señora* Taylor this morning?"

"We're both fine this morning, *gracias.*"

"*De nada, de nada*, we are *lo siento*, sorry, we could not save the house."

"You did all you could. I had already decided to accept Sheriff Tanner's offer to sell the ranch."

"*Sí,*" Roel said. "Perhaps the new owners will need two good hands, *sí?*"

She smiled. "I'll make certain they do."

Genaro tipped his hat. "*Gracias.*"

The ostriches seemed none the worse, having settled down well after the excitement of the day before. A few had huddled against the fence in fear, but the wire held and the few scratches and bruises would heal.

"I have a potential buyer who will be here to look at the birds this afternoon. Please make certain they look their best, and the pens are clean."

"Sí, gracias."

As the hands went back to work, Vonnie walked slowly around the charred rubble. Half of the remains had fallen into the cellar so that any hope of searching there for hidden jewels didn't exist.

Sadness washed over her; sadness for her father's death, the destruction of the house, sadness for her mother's loss, and for her own.

She'd always thought that one day she would marry for good, spend Christmas and Thanksgiving in this house with her parents, show off her children to doting grandparents. That wasn't going to happen.

By the time she purchased a few necessities for her mother and herself, met Perry Logan—the potential buyer and affluent California entrepreneur—and seen him settled comfortably into the hotel, her head ached.

Alma was sweeping off the front verandah when her buggy wheeled into the yard.

"Buenas tardes!"

"Good afternoon," Vonnie returned. "Did Mother join you for tea?"

"Sí. We made cinnamon buns. The kind with lots of cinnamon and pecans. Adam's favorite. And now she is upstairs resting." She glanced at the packages in Vonnie's arms. "It looks like you've been busy."

Alma set aside the broom and took some of the packages.

"Yes, I think I have enough to last us until we get to San Francisco."

"You will be leaving us soon?" Alma sounded almost disappointed.

"Yes, we're leaving on the four o'clock train tomorrow."

"Tomorrow? Ah, so soon?"

"Aunt Josie and Judith are expecting us." Vonnie climbed the stairs ahead of her. "With the house gone, there's no use delaying any longer."

After depositing the packages in her room, Vonnie checked on her mother. She showed Cammy the three dresses she'd bought for her—a yellow, a blue, and a green sprigged—along with a gown and wrapper she'd been able to find. Fortunately, the mercantile had just received a shipment of ready-mades.

"Mother," she said, packing the clothes away in one of the new valises. "I think I've sold the birds." She braced herself, waiting for the recriminations. She didn't know if Cammy had been listening when she'd mentioned selling the birds.

Walking to the window, Cammy looked out.

"Did you hear what I said, Mother? I met with Mr. Logan this afternoon, and he assures me he plans to purchase the ostriches if they live up to his expectations."

"There's nothing wrong with the birds."

"I know, they're excellent stock."

"Then sell them," Cammy said softly. "It's what your father would want you to do."

"Momma," Vonnie came to stand behind her, "did you know that Daddy buried jewels in the cellar?"

For a moment it seemed Cammy was slipping away

again. Then, straightening her back, she said, "I knew about the jewels."

"Is that why you never wanted to go into the cellar— was it the jewels that you feared?"

"Yes," Cammy whispered. "Teague hated those jewels. They never brought anything but heartache and pain."

Vonnie recalled how upset Cammy got when she looked at the photograph album. Now she knew why. In her quest to keep Teague alive in her mind she was reminded daily of the atrocity Teague had tried so hard to forget. Franz, Teague, P. K., and El Johnson stared back at her every day.

"Did Franz know the jewels were buried in the cellar?"

Nodding, Cammy brought her handkerchief up to cover her mouth.

Poor Franz. The jewels, in the most ironic way, had destroyed his life, too.

Wrapping her arms around her mother's shoulders, she held her, gently rocking her back and forth.

"It's all right momma. Now we can start to heal."

That evening the dining table was set with beautiful blue crockery ware. Adam escorted Vonnie to the table, and P. K. graciously performed the honors for Cammy.

Andrew sat at his place, nodding as she appeared, Vonnie managed an affectionate smile for him.

Pat and Joey carried on a conversation about their day's perils. They had moved a large herd of cattle from the upper range down nearer the ranch headquarters for the winter.

". . . and about that time that ol' crooked-horned steer took a sharp turn to the left and the whole herd followed." Pat laughed. "You should have seen Joey's face!"

"Did you get them settled?" P. K. asked.

"Sure thing. And just in time. Looks like a storm brewing to the west."

"Just as long as it doesn't come from the north," P. K. said.

He glanced at Vonnie.

"You've made plans to move to San Francisco? A little sudden, isn't it?"

"No, we'd already decided to visit Mother's sisters before the house burned."

She wasn't sure how to feel about P. K's sudden softening of attitude toward her. Glancing at Adam, she saw he was concentrating on the meal.

"What about the ostriches?"

"Perry Logan arrived from California this afternoon. He'd expressed some interest a few months earlier. I found his letter among Daddy's records. I sent him a telegram a few days ago. I'm hoping he'll take them all."

"And Tanner wants the ranch?"

She nodded. "I talked with him today. His buyer has agreed to take both places. He isn't concerned that the house burned; he had plans to build a new one anyway."

"Vonnie has made certain that Roel and Genaro can keep their jobs," Cammy offered.

"I hear San Francisco is a beautiful city," Andrew said. "I've always wanted to visit there."

"Perhaps you'll come see us," Vonnie said, hoping he would.

She was silenced by Adam's angry expression. "Are you sure you've given this enough thought? You've lived here all your life—this is your home."

"I guess it's true what they say: home is where your heart is." Her eyes met his in silent challenge. "It seems the proper choice for us now."

Vonnie could not refrain from needling Adam. "I'm so sorry Beth couldn't be here. I know she had to be at the quilting bee."

Adam fixed her with a glare. "Do you plan to join them later?"

"I told Beth I probably wouldn't make it," she answered brightly. "What about you?"

"No."

P. K. cleared his throat, and Alma served the main course.

After dinner, Vonnie wandered out to the verandah, hoping some fresh air would help clear her mind. She found P. K, almost hidden in the shadows, smoking a cheroot.

"Sit down," he said, indicating a wicker chair.

"I don't want to disturb you—"

White teeth flashed in a rare smile.

"Sit down. You know me well enough to know I am never merely polite."

She sat down.

Drawing on the cheroot, P. K. stared at the distant mountains. Vonnie was struck by the strong resemblance between father and son. In another twenty years, Adam would look like this, still ruggedly handsome and in command.

"Your father was a good man."

"Yes, he was." She relaxed a little, leaning back in

the wicker chair to study the clouds drifting past the moon. "I'm sorry you both forgot that."

"Guess none of that matters now. Don't know what happened with Franz ... must have gone out of his mind after Audrey died."

"He only wanted to give her piano back."

"Do you love my boy?"

The question took her by surprise. Should she be coy and ask which one? No. He had no need to identify the son; they both knew which one.

"Very much."

"You ever stop to think about Beth?"

"Every moment of the day."

Drawing on the cigar, he blew smoke into the chilly night air. "Don't think I can't remember what it was like to be young and in love.

"Getting cold," he said. "You're going to catch a chill. Better get on in the house and have Alma fix you something warm to drink."

Rising, Vonnie did as he said. "Forgive yourself, P. K."

"Good night."

She left him sitting on the verandah, smoking, rubbing the right leg stretched out in front of him.

The next morning, Vonnie rose and dressed early, knowing that a new part of her life was about to unfold.

After a light breakfast with Cammy in the sunroom, she asked one of the hands to hitch up her carriage, and she drove to the Flying Feather. Perry Logan arrived promptly at nine.

After walking slowly around the pens, examining the

birds, asking questions that she, fortunately, could answer, he made an offer that she felt was more than acceptable.

"Thank you, Mr. Logan. You've just bought yourself some ostriches."

"Good," he said. "Do you use the bank in town?"

"Yes, I do. Shall I meet you there?"

He glanced at his pocket watch. He seemed anxious to conclude the sale and be on his way. "Around noon? I need to make arrangements to ship the birds."

Three hours later, they met at the bank and arranged for a transfer of funds. When the business was finished, Vonnie left the bank with a lighter heart. Only the sale of the ranch remained.

That afternoon, Franz and Audrey were laid to rest. Side by side, they shared eternity. The ceremony was difficult for Cammy. Vonnie sent her home with Andrew and P. K. directly after the burial.

After checking the post office for mail, she returned to the Baldwin ranch. When she entered the house, Adam was just coming out of the library.

"Finish your business?"

"The birds are sold, and Sheriff Tanner is at this moment sending his buyer a telegram informing him that I'm ready to complete the sale of the land."

He followed her down the hall.

"How long will that take?"

"A month, six weeks."

A strange look crossed his face.

"Is something wrong?"

"There is one other matter."

"The divorce?" She attempted a smile, while a chill

settled around her heart. "I haven't forgotten that, Adam. Do you have the papers?"

"They arrived about an hour ago. Make sure you sign them before you leave."

She whirled, slapping him hard.

Lifting his hand to his cheek, he looked at her. "I deserve that, but why now, Vonnie?"

Her voice caught. "For making me care."

He looked as miserable as she felt. Brushing past him, she walked into his study, readily locating the papers on his desk. Picking up the pen, she began to sign her name.

A hand suddenly covered hers.

"Don't do that."

Frowning, she stared at him. "What?"

"Don't sign those papers. I can't marry Beth."

"Adam—"

"Damn it! I can't marry Beth." The angry retort hardened his features.

"Adam, this is crazy. Listen to me, you've gone too far to back out now." She tried to pull her hand from his, but he held her firmly.

"No, *you* listen to me. I've known marrying Beth was a mistake from the beginning. I don't love her, I never have."

Trying to squirm away, she said, "You're mad."

"You're damned right I am, about you." He caught her other arm and drew her to him. "About you, Vonnie Baldwin, and I don't give a damn who knows it."

Vonnie Baldwin. He had never called her that, not once.

"You love me? And I'm supposed to forgive you for the misery you've put me through and forget that you asked another woman to be your wife?"

"That's what I'm hoping."

"Well, maybe I can't, Adam, maybe it's too late."

"Love is never too late, Vonnie. I should have stood up for us seven years ago. I should have never let you talk me out of telling our parents about our marriage."

He grasped her shoulders, and the smoldering flame in his eyes startled her.

"I have always loved you."

"Beth—?" she asked.

"I can't marry Beth. Even if you leave, I can't marry her. I've known it for some time now."

"Oh, Adam." Melting into his arms, she admitted she was tired of fighting. The war was over. She surrendered.

"You do still love me, don't you?"

"You know I do."

"Then start acting like it." He started to kiss her, but she stopped.

"Not until it's over between you and Beth, Adam."

"Do you know how much I want you at this moment?"

"Yes. I want you just as much."

"Then you know what I have to do," he murmured, holding her tightly.

Nodding, she closed her eyes. "I'll go with you."

"You don't have to. I'm old enough to handle it properly this time."

It wouldn't be easy going to Beth. There would be hurt, disbelief, recriminations, accusations, and tears. It would be hard. But there was no choice. She had to be told.

"We both care deeply about her, Adam. I'll go with you.

"Then we'll both tell P. K."

Chapter 25

"Hard" was putting it mildly. Onerous, exhausting, arduous were only some of the feelings experienced that long afternoon.

Gillian had answered the door. "Why, Adam, dear, we didn't expect you—and Vonnie—how nice to see you! I am so sorry about the fire. Oh, my, where are my manners? Come in, do come in."

"Gillian, I'd like to speak to Beth, please," Adam said.

"Why, yes, dear, I'll get her."

An uncertain look entered her eyes as she glanced from Adam to Vonnie.

"Beth," she called, going toward the rear of the house. "Beth, dear, Adam and Vonnie are here to see you."

In a few minutes, Beth came down the hall toward them.

"Adam? Vonnie? What a nice surprise." She looked at them questioningly. "I was just sorting quilt squares,

I've decided on the wedding-ring pattern—is something
. . . wrong?"

"Beth, may we speak to you in the parlor?"

Beth looked from one to the other.

"Has something happened—"

"Beth, please. In the parlor?"

Glancing at Vonnie, tears welled in Beth's eyes. She
knew. Vonnie could see she knew. "Of course. Mother,
will you excuse us?"

"I saw the way you looked at her at the fire," Beth
murmured softly when they told her. "You never looked
at me the way you looked at her. I knew then that things
weren't right between us. You never loved me, did you,
Adam?"

"No. I'm sorry," Adam apologized. "I hope you can
forgive me, Beth. I should never have allowed this to
happen."

Adam had been magnanimous, as Vonnie was learning he could be. When Gillian reappeared carrying a
tray of glasses and tea, she paused, seeing the tears glistening in Beth's eyes. "What's wrong?"

"Beth has decided to break the engagement," Adam
explained.

Sinking to the settee, Gillian was aghast.

"It's all right, Mother," Beth said, pulling herself up
straight in a show of strength that surprised Vonnie and
Adam. "It just isn't the right time." She smiled. "You
know how fickle I can be."

They rode in silence back to Cabeza Del Lobo, but
this time Vonnie's hand rested possessively on Adam's
thigh. She wasn't sure how Beth felt about her; betrayed, surely hurt, most definitely stunned. It would

take time for the wounds to heal, but she hoped some-day, with time and effort, to restore the friendship.

Though P. K. had softened toward her, she wasn't sure how he would react to learning that she had been married to Adam all this time . . . and planned to stay that way.

Darkness had fallen when they reached the ranch.

"I want to talk to P. K. alone," Adam said, helping Vonnie from the carriage.

"No, I want to be with you."

"Vonnie, I'd prefer to talk to him alone."

She knew this was important to him. She sighed. "I'll be nearby, if you want me."

Leaning over, he kissed her, hungrily and thoroughly for the first time in years. "Want you? Give me fifteen minutes to dispense with this matter, and I'll show you how much I want you."

"Exactly, how much?"

"It could take all night." His eyes caressed her.

"Can you make it ten minutes?" she whispered.

When they entered the hacienda, hand in hand, they saw that P. K. was in the library with his familiar glass of whiskey.

Giving Adam's hand a squeeze of support, she headed toward the kitchen while Adam went into the library, closing the door behind him.

Adam and P. K. still hadn't come out of the library when Alma began putting supper on the table. Vonnie cast anxious glances toward the closed door as she leafed nervously through a magazine. An explosion had yet to rock the library, so she felt encouraged. And scared. Terribly scared. She and Adam were so close to being together—so very close—

Vonnie looked up as Cammy came down the stairs. She looked more like her old self tonight, dressed in lavender, her hair combed and held back with pearl combs Teague had given her last Christmas.

Pat and Joey appeared, dressed for dinner.

"Supper is ready," Alma announced.

Vonnie glanced at the closed library door. "Aren't we going to wait for Adam and P. K.?"

"I've lived with the Baldwin men long enough to know their ways. When the door is closed, supper gets cold."

As they were about to sit down, the library door opened. Vonnie's mouth went dry as she searched Adam's face for a clue as to their fate. His expression was unreadable.

Taking the chair next to her, he sat down as P. K. assumed his place at the head of the table.

"It seems there is an announcement to make," he said.

Twisting the napkin into a knot in her lap, Vonnie waited. Reaching under the table, Adam took her hand, squeezing it as he solemnly winked at her.

"What's the announcement?" Pat asked, stealing a tortilla from the platter Alma was carrying.

P. K. cleared his throat. "Seems we have an addition to the Baldwin family."

Joey glanced up.

"A pretty one, if I do say so myself," P. K. added.

The guests seated at the table looked at each other.

Getting to his feet, Adam drew Vonnie to his side. "Family, I would like to introduce my wife, Vonnie Baldwin." Vonnie thought he looked for all the world like a cat that had just swallowed a canary.

Alma hurriedly made the sign of the cross as a soft gasp escaped Cammy.

Joey glanced at Pat. "What happened to Beth?"

"Oh, Momma, don't be mad," Vonnie said, letting go of Adam's hand and going round the table to kneel beside Cammy's chair. "Be happy for me. I love Adam so much. I always have."

Gently soothing back her daughter's hair, tears of joy filled Cammy's eyes. "I'm just surprised . . . not angry."

Gazing back at her mother, Vonnie said softly, "I wish Daddy could be here."

Lifting her eyes to P. K., Cammy said quietly, "Teague loved you like a brother, P. K. He was hurt, hurt to know you would think him capable of such an atrocity. Pride kept him from coming to you."

Moisture glinted in P. K.'s eyes. "I was hurt, too, Cammy. It pained me to think Teague *could* do such a thing. I'm sorry—it's too late to tell Teague, but you should know. I'm sorry, I loved Teague, too."

"When in the hell did you and Vonnie get married?" Pat asked, still puzzled by the announcement.

Adam's eyes searched Vonnie's. "Seven years ago, Pat. I just forgot to mention it."

Alma murmured, crossing herself again.

"It's my fault Adam and Vonnie haven't been together these past seven years," P. K. said.

"No P. K., it isn't fair for you to take the blame," Vonnie said. "Daddy shares it." Her eyes traveled to Adam. "Most assuredly I did my part. Adam wanted to come to you, to tell you we were married, and I begged him not to. In doing so, I lost him for a time."

Drawing her to him, Adam kissed her.

Pat softly gave them a hand.

Clearing his throat loudly, P. K. restored the table to

order. "Vonnie, I ask your forgiveness. I'd like to start over—if you have no objections. I'm an old man. I'm tired of fighting. If there's going to be Baldwin and Taylor blood running through my grandchildren's veins, then by God, I want to spoil them shamelessly."

"You're not that old." She took the hand he extended, then came around the table to give him a hug.

P. K. grunted. "I think I'm going to like having a daughter-in-law. What do you say, Cammy, my girl. Should we give these two whippersnappers our blessing?"

"Whatever you say, P. K.," Cammy agreed.

P. K. looked up. "What about you, Teague, you old coot." He pretended to listen. Nodding, he smiled. "He said, 'What the hell? Why not?' "

"Oh, *muchas gracias*," Alma exclaimed, clapping her hands together. "I have waited for the day the boys would marry and bring their wives to this houses. Now we will have *bambinos—mucho bambinos* in the house again!"

"Momma?" Vonnie said, kneeling again beside her mother's chair. "Thank you for understanding."

"You need not thank me," Cammy said, taking Vonnie's face between her hands. "I want only your happiness. Remain as in love with your husband as I did your father, and I'll wish for nothing more." She glanced at Adam, then back to Vonnie. "I can see that I have no worries. He looks at you the way your father looked at me."

"Thank you, Momma."

Vonnie hugged Cammy, then was immediately caught in a bear hug first from Pat, then Joey.

Andrew caught Vonnie to him warmly. "Congratulations, sister-in-law. I guess I knew all along you and Adam were destined to be together."

He then extended his hand to Adam, who took it. They clasped hands, their eyes no longer challenging.

"Take good care of her, brother. If you don't, you'll answer to me."

"Like that would keep me up nights?" Adam grinned. Leaning closer, he said quietly. "I'm willing to share her—up to a point."

Grinning, Andrew slapped him on the back good-naturedly. "I'll get my own woman, thank you."

Christmas Eve arrived on a brisk wind. Candles glowed in every window in Nogales as the citizens prepared to celebrate the holiday. Little children went reluctantly to bed, too excited to sleep with the prospect of gifts under the fragrant, decorated tree in the living room.

But at the First Freewill Baptist Church near the center of town, there was more than a Christmas Eve service planned.

Each pew was marked with a red ribbon. Fragrant sage and juniper in adobe pots graced the front of the church as it filled with happy people.

While the organ began to play, Adam took his place at the front of the auditorium, followed by Pat and Joey.

P. K. sat stiffly in the front seat, loosening his collar as Alma nudged him to sit still. He glanced over, sending a look of satisfaction toward Cammy, who sat on the other side, along with her sisters, Josie and Judith, who had journeyed from San Francisco for the happy occasion.

A hush fell over the congregation as Hildy, Mora,

then Carolyn came slowly down the aisle. Their holly-green dresses, trimmed with red velvet, glowed in the flickering candlelight.

As the wedding march began, everyone stood and turned expectantly toward the back of the church.

A hushed stillness fell over the chapel as Vonnie, on the arm of Andrew Baldwin, walked slowly down the aisle. Wearing a simple, straight, floor-length ivory silk gown and matching wide-brimmed hat, she carried a single red rose on top of her father's Bible.

As they reached the altar, Andrew took Vonnie's hand and placed it in Adam's, giving her a reassuring wink before he took a seat beside Beth Baylor. The pastor began the ceremony.

"Does this bother you?" Andrew asked, leaning to whisper to Beth. "Adam and Vonnie deciding to take their vows before the church?"

"No worse than cutting my heart out with a butter knife," she whispered back. "But they belong together. Even I can see that."

"Yes, I think they do. They look happy, don't they?"

"Deliriously . . . Andrew." Beth perked up.

"Yes?"

Looping her arm through his, she leaned closer so as not to disturb the service.

"Would you like to go for an automobile ride Sunday afternoon?"

Later, Adam carried his wife up the stairway. There were too many people in the house to reconsummate the marriage without appearing obvious. Out of respect for P. K. and Cammy, they had waited.

Now, the marriage bed called to them.

Closing the door with his boot, Adam set Vonnie

lightly on her feet. Their mouths came together ravenously, as eager hands reacquainted themselves with impatient bodies.

Alma had turned down the bed, leaving Vonnie's wedding rose on her pillow. Candlelight lit the room. A fire burned low in the grate.

A bottle of champagne and two glasses sat waiting by the bedside.

Twining her arms around Adam's neck, Vonnie snuggled closer to her husband.

When he made no move to immediately undress her, she took the initiative. Her fingers began to loosen the buttons on his shirt.

Grinning, he was touched by her enthusiasm. "Anxious?"

"Curious."

"About what?" They kissed.

"If anything's changed."

"Such as?"

"Well, you were seventeen, a young, randy buck. I was fifteen, naïve . . ."

"Nothing's changed," he said, kissing her again. "If anything, it's improved—I'm now an *old* randy buck and you're—"

He jumped, chuckling wickedly as her hand grew bolder.

"Shamefully forward," he observed.

"Uh huh. Terribly forward." His kiss urged her to take all the liberties she wanted.

"By the way," he murmured. "I have a wedding gift for you."

"You gave me the gift. A lovely strand of pearls and matching earrings."

"I have another one."

"And I have one for you." He had been so busy lavishing gifts on her, she hadn't had time to give him hers.

"May I give you mine first?"

"Adam."

"Please?"

"Very well." She felt momentarily bereaved as he left to collect a round cylindrical container from the small cherry writing desk.

"What is it?" she asked as he handed it to her, wondering at the odd packaging. Opening the end of the cylinder, she dumped a rolled sheet of paper onto the bed. As she unfolded it, she saw it was a drawing.

"What is it, Adam?"

"Our house."

"Our house?" Grinning, she glanced up. "We haven't even talked about a house."

"Look closer."

When she did, she realized it wasn't just a house, it was her house. The house Teague and his father and brothers had built fifty years ago.

"Oh, Adam," she whispered. "Where did you get this?"

"From P. K. Teague gave him the plans, long before he had you. P. K. thought he would build one like it someday, but of course, he didn't. When we return from our honeymoon, the construction will be under way. After a good, long visit with her sisters, Cammy can come home."

"But Sheriff Tanner—"

"I've informed the sheriff that the Flying Feather is no longer for sale. We may not raise ostriches—then again, we might. I figure we have plenty of time to decide on that."

Flying into his arms, she smothered his face with wild kisses.

"I love you, I love you, I love you!"

"Prove it," he challenged huskily.

"Ever so gladly . . ."

The clothes were dispensed with haste. Yards of creamy satin pooled to the floor. Delicate pantaloons and lacy chemise joined black trousers and a pristine white shirt. None of the shy fumbling they had experienced on their first wedding night encumbered them; hot, unchecked desire reigned.

They had been apart too long. Far too long, but the separation was finally over.

As he lay her gently on the bed, she gazed up at him, her eyes filled with undying love.

In a voice soft with need, he petitioned her as he had one morning seven long years ago.

"Promise me we'll stay together forever, Vonnie Taylor."

Meeting his worshipful eyes, she whispered, "I promise, Adam Baldwin. Forever."

Live the

romance of

Lori Copeland's

historic

America!

Lori Copeland

brings to life the adventure, passion, and
beauty of the Old West with the authentic
detail and charming characters sure to
captivate your imagination—and capture
your heart.

Published by Fawcett Books.
Available in your local bookstore.

Experience the hot
romance of untamed
hearts and blazing skies!

Wildsong

by *Catherine Creel*

Catherine Creel's romances of the
historic Southwest will set your pulse
racing and your heart fluttering like
the wings of a dove.

Look for her latest tale of love on the
windswept plains…

Wildsong

Published by Fawcett Books.
Coming this fall to bookstores everywhere!